Dreams Become My Life
by Megan Johnson

Published 2017 by The Light Network
Copyright © Megan Johnson

Printed in the United States

Interior layout by Christi Koehl

Edited by Keidi Keating

ISBN: 978-0-9987043-0-2

Dreams Become My Life

The Final Book in The Dreams Trilogy

By Megan Johnson

I would like to dedicate this book to my very supportive family and all my fans who have followed this series.

Acknowledgments

I would like to give a very special thank you to Keidi for editing this whole series and teaching me to become a better writer one book at a time.

I would like to thank Your Book Angel for publishing this book and the other two in the trilogy.

A very big thank you to all my fans for supporting this trilogy, and whom have waited anxiously for each book to come out. I couldn't do it without you all!

Chapter 1

MUSC Hospital; September 12
7:00 a.m.

I can't believe I am staring into the eyes of our handsome son. My eyes fill with tears. "Yes Michael, I'm going to be okay now." He puts his arms around my waist and rests his head on my stomach. I look up at Luke as the tears now fall from my eyes.

Luke puts his hand over mine and whispers, "It's all going to be okay now." *How can everything be okay when it seems like only yesterday I was holding Michael, who was only months old, in my arms? I need answers now!*

Luke buzzes for the nurse to come in and check my vitals. "I want details as to why I'm here and why I was in a coma for almost six years!" Many thoughts parade through my mind, such as May's wedding, missing Michael grow up, and then Luke…how could he stay faithful for six years? *Why did this happen to me?*

I shake my head as more tears fall from my eyes. *How does Michael even remember me?* Michael raises his head from my stomach and looks into my eyes. His large, blue, powerful eyes stare right back at me. "Mom, I'm glad you're better. I missed you. Dad told me everything about you. I love you." I smile back at him and bend over to kiss him on the forehead.

"I love you too, Michael and I can't wait to talk to you more. I'm so sorry I missed the last six years of you growing up. I can't imagine how hard that was without a mom around."

"Don't worry, Momma, Dad took great care of me. I understand that you were sick." I smile at both of my two boys. *He's so mature already; he's just like his father.*

After the nurse checks everything, she gets the doctor to come and talk to me. As we wait for the doctor to arrive we talk about

Michael. He's into soccer now. He is in first grade and he loves school. Hearing all this makes my heart ache.

"What about my parents? And May? I missed her wedding!"

Luke shakes his head. "They didn't get married."

I cock my head to the side. "What? Why?"

"They wanted to wait for you." My heart drops into my stomach and more tears fall.

"They waited six years to get married. I can't believe they did that."

"They did."

"I want to see them all now."

"Okay, I'll call them as soon as we hear from the doctor," Luke says as he rubs my head. Michael is sitting on the chair in the corner reading a book. Not playing on an iPad or a Gameboy, but reading a book.

"Wow, look at him! Luke, you've done a great job. I feel like I have no part in who he becomes as he gets older."

"Linda, don't say that. I took everything you taught me about being a better man and raised our son the way we'd both have raised him together. He's a lot like you."

"I can't wait to find out."

Dr. Hue walks in, his head as shiny as ever. His smile instantly brightens the room and my mood. "Well hello there, sleepy head."

"Hey doc," I don't sound as enthused as he does.

"I know you have a million questions."

"Yeah, you've got that right."

He pulls up a chair next to me and takes a seat. "Well, let's get started."

Luke sits on the other side of me and listens intently to what Dr. Hue is saying, holding my hand for comfort.

"You were in a coma for about six years and it took us a while to figure out why you were in there for so long." As he talks the images of Tom tying me up to the bed and seeing him get shot to the ground flash through my mind. *What happened to Tom? Is he dead for good?*

The doctor continues speaking and I try to stay focused but I feel exhausted. "We ran many tests to get answers but you were completely healthy. We did see some strange activity in the brain. Your brainwaves are different than any other I have seen. A human's brainwaves come in different stages; The Delta waves, which are slow and usually occur during sleep and meditation; The Theta waves, which occur during a dream sleep; The Alpha waves, which are normal thoughts; The Beta waves, which occur most often, and during daily routines; and then we have The Gamma waves, which are the fastest and the ones we see less often. How Gamma waves are generated is still a mystery to researchers. Most humans range from Delta, Theta, and Beta waves daily. This is because we sleep and then get up and do our daily activities. But Linda, your brainwaves only occur in two very rare stages that should never occur back and forth like they do."

I look at him with a concerned look and tighten my grip on Luke's hand. "Linda, your brainwaves jump from Theta stage straight to Gamma stage. I've never seen this occur with any other human. And these waves jump during sleep and also while you're awake."

My heart begins to race. This is why I have the talent to see the things I can see. "So what does this mean?" I say with a shaky voice.

"It means you have a very special gift. Luke told me everything. The reason why you were having flashes and blackouts before your coma was because your brainwaves were switching drastically from Gamma, the fastest brainwaves, to Theta, the dream waves. This was causing you to black out and enter a dream state."

"This is all making perfect sense. When I'm awake I feel like I'm always on an adrenalin rush. Do you think because my brain only acts on those two waves is why I can see the future with my dreams?"

"It definitely adds fuel to your gift, but Linda, you're truly something special. I remember seeing you on the news, and as a doctor I never believed such a thing until I saw those brainwaves for myself."

I take a deep gulp and breath. "Wow, this is a lot to handle. I'm feeling very tired."

"You need to get some rest. You'll be in the hospital for at least a few weeks. You need therapy to regain your strength and ability to eat. We also need to run some more tests to make sure nothing else is wrong. Your body is in shock and it will be for a while. You're going to have to get used to this hospital for a bit," he says with a nice smile.

"Seriously? Why can't I just go home and have a physical therapist come there?"

"Linda, just because you're special that doesn't mean things can always go your way," he says with a joking tone. "I still need to treat you like a normal patient."

"Well, what if I heal quicker because of my so-called brainwaves?" I say motioning with my hands. They all smile.

"You really are stubborn, aren't you?" Dr. Hue says as he lowers the bed so I am lying flat.

"Yes, she is, but that's why I love her," Luke says with a wink.

"It's time for you to get some rest, Linda. When you wake up we'll start the therapy process right away."

"Okay, wait. Will I wake up?"

"Yes, you don't have anything to worry about."

I nod my head and begin to close my eyes. "I'll call everyone and let them know you're okay. They'll be here when you wake up."

"Thanks Luke, I love you."

"I love you too."

From a distance I hear Michael yell, "I love you Momma." I smile and drift into sleep.

I am walking into a nice, clean, well-furnished house. I feel like I need to step on my tip-toes so I don't break anything. It's late at night and I don't hear a single sound. I search around the house wondering what I'm doing here. I walk into an open kitchen with an island in the middle. The tiles are marble and the tan/yellow color accents gives me a warm feeling as soon as I enter. I am taken aback by the strong smell of bleach. I put my arm to my nose to cover the stench. Someone recently cleaned this entire kitchen, but why? To cover up something that went wrong? There are no signs of struggle anywhere. This house is cleaner than any house I've ever seen.

I walk around the kitchen and pay close attention to as much detail as I can. On the kitchen counter near the stove I see a small glass tube. What is this? It's weird that this is the only thing lying on the kitchen counter, and I walk closer to get a better look. I turn on the lights to make sure I am seeing this correctly. A glass tube filled with red liquid. Is this what I think it is?

I grab a paper towel, pick up the vial, and turn it upside down. The thick red liquid moves in a slow motion. Holy shit, this is a vial of blood! What in the world happened here and what is going on? What sick-minded person would leave a vial of blood on the counter? Better yet, what kind of sick game does this person want to play?

I place the vial of blood back on the counter. I need to wake up and talk with Fredrick. I close my eyes and concentrate, breathing slowly and deeply. "Linda, wake up."

My eyes slowly begin to open. The sun is shining through the blinds making it harder for me to open my eyes. Luke immediately rushes to my side.

"Babe, how are you doing?"

"I'm okay. I had a weird dream that's going to take a lot of work to solve…I can already tell."

"Okay, do you want me to call Fredrick?"

"No, I'll do that. Can you hand me my phone please?"

"In a little while. There are people here who want to see you." A smile grows on my face when I realize I get to see my loving family. I take a breath and brace myself for a room full of emotions.

Mom walks in first with her curly hair and overdramatic dangly earrings. She still looks exactly the same after six years. Tears automatically drop from her tired eyes. "Oh honey," is all she can say as she grasps me in her arms.

I begin to bawl. And the two of us cry in each other's arms. "Mom, I can't believe this happened to me. Six years and it only feels like a short time for me. I missed so much. I hope everything is okay with you and Dad."

She pulls away with her hands on my face. "Linda, everything is perfectly fine. You shouldn't be worried about us after everything that happened to you. I'm so glad you're okay. We didn't know if-." She doesn't finish that statement, and instead she simply hugs me again. I open my eyes to see May, Charlie, and Dad standing there waiting with red faces and swollen eyes.

Mom moves away and Dad steps in. "My baby girl, oh how I missed you. You're one strong woman," he says as he embraces me in his hug. "You better and I mean better do what the doctor says, and rest and heal before you even think about going back to work."

I smile at his protective side. "Don't worry Dad, I promise I'll take my time this time around. I know Luke wouldn't allow me to do anything less." Dad and I both glance at Luke and smile.

"Good," he says as he kisses my forehead.

I can hear May sniffling in the background. "May, come over here," I say as I open my arms. I whisper in her ear as we hug,

"Why did you wait to get married? What if I never woke up?"

I feel her tears drop onto the back of my neck. "There was no way in hell I was going to get married without my big sister and my maid of honor. I knew and we all knew that you were going to wake up because of how strong you are."

"I'm so sorry you had to push your plans back this far."

"Don't worry, Charlie and I have been plenty busy. We'll pick a date as soon as you're out of here and back on your feet."

"Sounds like a plan," I say kissing her cheek.

"I'm so glad you're okay," Charlie says from the background.

"Thank you, Charlie." Then I stare at my family standing before me. I thank God for saving my life and bringing me back to them.

"How's the coffee shop?" I ask out loud for anyone to answer.

Mom responds quickly. "It's doing just fine. Sarah and Bobby are doing a good job running it. They hired two new employees because Sarah had a baby two years ago."

"What!? And I missed that?" I say shaking my head.

"Don't worry; they captured pictures of every moment. Even though it has been six years, everything is still the same," Mom says.

"It's going to be hard to think that. It'll take some getting used to."

"And all of us will be here for you every step of the way," Dad chimes in.

"Thank you, guys. I don't know what I'd do without you. I love you all so much."

We all exchange hugs and kisses one last time and then they leave so I can rest some more. My physical therapist will be here in an hour. Luke heads back to work as I start my treatment. It works out perfectly that he is only a building away.

"So how are you feeling today?" asks my therapist, Rich.

"Still shocked. My body feels heavy."

"That's normal and it's why I'm here. We're going to start with some basic exercises." His white smile is reassuring and positive. He sits up straight in his chair in front of me. He has a very good posture. His brown eyes are soothing; he has a kind face that makes me sure I'm in good hands. I do some arm movements as I sit up straight in bed and begin slowly moving my legs. He asks me questions about my life to see if my memory is intact, which it is. I remember everything. I remember working with Fredrick and Arnold and thinking about leaving my shop to become a full time detective. I remember seeing Tyler's dead body. I remember every frightening moment with Tom. I sigh deeply as relief floods through me now that he is finally dead.

I close my eyes as I remember Luke's soft, warm, gentle touch over my body. Each time we ever made love. The moment Michael was born, and the moment I saw him as a handsome grown young boy. Tears begin to flood my eyes, but I stop them from falling.

Then I remember the dream I just had about the vial of blood and the horrible feeling in my gut. Something big is coming and it is going to take everything the Charleston Police Department (CPD) and I have to solve it.

Soon after therapy I get ready to eat and sleep some more when a reporter comes in. *How in the hell did she get in here? I'm not ready for this. How does she remember who I am?*

The doctor comes in quickly after. "Please get out of here. She isn't ready for this."

"Mrs. Jackson, just one question please?" I see the desperate look on this woman's face. She is itching for some information.

"It's okay, Dr. Hue. It'll be quick." *What the hell? Why not answer a few questions?*

"Oh, thank you," the short, blonde-haired woman says with a cheesy grin. "The people are dying to know."

I give her a questioning look as I raise my eyebrow. "We'd like to know, are you doing okay? Do you think being in a coma will affect your ability?"

"I'm doing just fine, and no it won't affect my ability. After some therapy I'll be out of here and back to work."

"What kind of work are you talking about? Your coffee shop or CPD?"

I smile faintly. "I'll continue to work both. I have to keep saving lives as being I have no choice."

"We're glad to hear that and we all wish you the best recovery. Thank you for your time." She shakes my hand and her long red fingernails graze my wrists.

"Thank you and you're welcome." Then just like that she is out the door.

"I'm so sorry about that, Linda. She walked in and no one thought to stop her," says Dr. Hue.

"It's okay. It's just crazy that the word is out already that I'm awake. I didn't think it'd be such a big deal."

"Well, you were a big Charleston celebrity." Dr. Hue's smile is as bright as the light shining off of his head. "Barely, but thank you."

"Now it's time for you to really get some rest."

I yawn and stretch in agreement. I close my eyes wondering if I will dream about this vial of blood case. And then my mind fades into darkness.

Abandoned warehouse
Charleston SC, September 12
5:30 p.m.

"Ah, would you look at that? Mrs. Jackson is alive and kicking. It's about time. Thank you for giving me enough time to create my master plan; a few killings down and way more to go. Let's see if you can see me and my killings coming."

I turn up the volume on the TV and watch Linda sitting helpless in that hospital bed. My stomach is in knots thinking about what I have planned. The best part is she will never see it coming. I sit down at my desk and sharpen each one of my knives. I have to make sure all twenty of them are sharp and ready to use.

I look over at the couch and see pretty little fragile Maria tied with duct tape with no way out. Oh, what I have planned for her! I walk over to her with a needle and syringe. I've got to continue using my trademark. I draw her blood as she attempts to squirm on the couch. Her water-filled blue eyes staring into mine gets adrenalin pumping into my veins.

I pour her blood into a vial and close it. I grab my brown leather jacket and head for the door. It's time to make my next move.

Chapter 2

Jackson Household

I walk into our home and the aroma of vanilla and cinnamon fills my nostrils with joy. I smile and take in a big breath. "Wow, it feels so good to be home. Even though it doesn't feel like six years for me, the past six weeks in the hospital makes it feel like forever since I've been home.

"Well baby, you're here to stay forever this time. If you thought I was protective before, then you're in for a rude awaking," Luke says as he takes my bags and winks at me.

"Oh babe, you're over-reacting!"

He looks at me coldly. "Really?"

I don't respond as he walks up the stairs. I sit on the couch and Michael comes and sits next to me. It is such a strange feeling seeing him so grown up. I don't know if I'll ever get over the fact that I missed so many years of his life. I feel like he is a stranger and I'm sure he feels the same way about me. He sits there looking at the TV that is turned off. This is an awkward situation. I mean, how do I start a conversation?

"So Michael, it looks like we have a lot of catching up to do," I say with a smile.

He smiles briefly. "Um yeah. Well, Dad told me all about you, but you don't know much about me?" he says with a questioning tone.

"You're right. We're going to change that starting now." He finally sits back on the couch, brings up his legs, and faces me. A smile lights up his beautiful tanned face. I can't get over those bright blue eyes that shine when he speaks. We talk all about school, sports, and his favorite things. Luke is in the kitchen whipping up some dinner. He walks in handing me a glass of wine and he joins us on our large suede sectional couch.

"How's it going in here? I can hear a lot of chatter."

"Yes, Mom and I are finding out a lot about each other!" Michael says with grace and maturity.

"Well, I'm sure you've already found out that your mom is one amazing woman," he says with his heart-stopping grin.

"Yeah, she's pretty cool," he says. I glance over at Luke and smile.

"Dinner will be ready in about forty-five minutes. I decided to cook your favorite meal."

"What's your favorite meal, Mom?"

"Chicken parmesan with steamed broccoli."

His face lights up, "Really? That's my favorite too!"

"I guess we have a lot in common." We smile at each other and continue talking. Luke sits back and takes a sip of wine watching the two of us as we speak. The grin doesn't leave his face for one second. Gosh, it feels great to be home with my family.

After eating a delicious meal, we all relax on the couch and watch TV. Michael lays his head in my lap and after only a few hours with him I already feel we are much closer. He visited me often in the hospital in the last six weeks, but that wasn't enough. Now that we are in our home together it feels like I've never left. Luke flips through the channels and passes the local news channel. "Luke, stop here."

"No, I won't let you start now."

"Please," I say with desperation.

He sighs and turns back to the news. The red-haired news reporter who I remember from my outbreak is speaking. "Missing girl's body found mutilated in a garbage bag floating in Cooper River. The body had specific knife markings similar to another girls' body that was found two weeks ago. The CPD won't give many details because it is too violent and gruesome. They promise that they are working their hardest to catch the murderer. They have a few leads but continue to work day and night. They advise women between the ages of 18-40 not to go out alone. We will keep you updated as we find out more information. Jeremy, back to the weather."

I stare wide-eyed at the TV. *Shit, I need to help. I can't let this go.*

"Linda, please don't"

Michael stares at us. "Luke, I can't just sit here. I had a dream while I was in the hospital and I bet that has something to do with it. I have to help. It's my job, it's my calling, and it's my life now."

He shakes his head and sighs. "And the coffee shop?"

"Sarah and Bobby seem to be doing fine. They've hired new employees. I'll talk to them tomorrow."

"You really want to start working for the CPD full time even though you've only been home one day?"

"I've had weeks of therapy. I've been having this same nagging dream over and over. I need more details and I need to get to work."

"Okay, just please be careful."

"I will."

"Mommy," Michael interrupts.

"Yes honey." He has a confused look on his face, a new expression for me.

"Daddy says you have a special gift that no one else has?"

"Uh, yeah I do. It's very hard to explain."

"Well kids at my school say their parents talk about you. They say that you're psychic and you can see things before they happen?" *How can he even think about something like that and understand it?*

"Well, their parents are right. I can see things before they happen while I sleep. I use my dreams to help catch bad people."

"And protect and help people?"

"Yup, that's right."

"How did you become psychic?"

"I'm not sure, sweetie. It just came to me one day and since then I haven't been able to live without it. So it's a part of me forever."

He looks up at me with his eyebrows raised. "Well, what does it feel like when you have the dreams?"

"Like I'm not asleep. It feels real. I'm sure you've had dreams where you realize it's too crazy to be real; you know it's fake? Well mine are always real and it feels like I'm always awake." *I wonder what's going through his head right now. He's thinking hard.*

"Oh okay. I think it's cool that you're a hero. I want to be just like you when I grow up," he says as he hugs me. *Oh no you don't sweetie. I don't want you to have a life like mine.*

I put Michael to bed as Luke prepares the shower. I will call Fredrick first thing in the morning to make sure it's okay for me to come down to the station and continue discussing me becoming a full time detective – that's if they still want me after all this time.

I cover Michael in his blue comforter, which is decorated with images of sports equipment; a typical young boy's bed. He grabs my hand and places it over his heart. "Daddy and I always say a prayer before I go to bed." Tears form in my eyes. *Wow, I'm impressed with my son. He's definitely magical, and so grown up.*

"What prayer do you like to say?"

"I'll say it first, and then we can say it together." I hold his hand and listen intently as he says his prayer.

"Now I lay me down to sleep. I pray the lord my soul to keep. If I should die before I wake, I pray the lord my soul to take." Tears fall from my face. *Did Luke give him this prayer because he didn't think I was going to wake up? What a powerful thing to say, yet perfect for the situation.*

"Mommy, are you okay? Why are you crying?"

"I'm fine ,sweetie. I'm just happy to be home with you and Dad."

"Me too Mom. Are you ready to say it together now?"

I nod my head and together we say it in perfect sync. I kiss his forehead. He looks up at me. "Goodnight, Mom. I love you. Maybe someday we can dream together."

My heart immediately drops into my stomach. *Is that foreshadowing something? Is he trying to tell me something? Why would he say that? No, he doesn't mean anything by it…does he?*

Taken aback by his response, I kiss him again. "Goodnight Michael, sleep tight. I love you with all my heart." And his eyes drift into sleep.

I walk in a state of confusion, still thinking about what he said. I hear the shower running and instantly perk up. Luke is already in the shower. I take off my clothes quickly and stare through our glass shower of Luke's body outline. I can see the curvature of his muscles through the glass. The water is making them glisten. *Oh, how I've missed that body on mine.*

I walk in and Luke looks me up and down and smiles. "Oh baby, how I've missed you." *Six years, how could he stay faithful for six years? No sex, no kissing, no touching, no nothing. How?*

He wraps me in his arms and my body starts to tingle. He grabs my face and brings me to his lips. I kiss him softly. My heart beats quickly. But then tears start to fall. "Linda, baby what's wrong?"

"Luke, it's been years. I know how hard it was to stay faithful. But if you weren't faithful I'd try to understand. You didn't know if

I was going to wake up."

He puts his finger over my lips. "Shhh," he whispers, shaking his head. A rush of heat fills my body. "Linda," he says with a serious tone. "I knew you were going to wake up. I didn't care how long it was going to take. I wasn't going to give up on you. I would have waited my entire life for you to come back. You'll always be the only one for me."

Tears continue to fall and I hug him tight. The hot water falls on us while we are lost in our embrace. He kisses me again and puts shampoo in his hand. I smile when I see he got my favorite shampoo. He scrubs my head and it feels alluring. I moan softly as the shampoo drips down my breast. *I can't believe how sensitive I am. There's nothing I want more right now than to be completely lost with Luke in so many ways.*

He runs his hands softly and seductively all over my body. I kiss him hard and he gently pushes me up against the wall. We are both aching for it. I can't imagine how he feels right now, how badly he wants it. I want to fulfill the part of him he's been missing. I run my hand down his tight abs and feel his erection. Woah, he's ready already!

We can't wait anymore. He turns off the shower and opens the door. We don't bother getting a towel. He picks me up and carries me into the room. He lays me gently on the bed. Water drips from his forehead and my hands slide down his muscles smoothly.

"Oh baby, how I've missed your kiss, your touch, your love," he says as he kisses me hard.

"I want all of you, Luke. I want you to love me and consume every inch of me." He kisses my neck as his hand makes his way down. He slips a finger in me slowly to get me ready. I moan into his ear and thrust my hips towards him.

"Are you ready, baby?" he asks with a sexy grin.

"Born ready for you, babe." He enters me slowly. In and out, slow and deep; he keeps this rhythm and I am completely lost in him. He feels so good. I moan louder and we start to breathe heavy. It won't take long for me to reach my climax. I feel it building within seconds as he moves faster and deeper. He kisses me deeply and he lets out a moan.

"I'm almost there, baby," he says.

"Me too baby. You feel so good."

He's pounding deep, faster and faster. We both cry out with

pleasure. He holds himself inside me as I feel him release. My body is spent. He pulls out and I roll over on top of him. I feel my mind and body fading. "I love you and I'm so glad you're back in my arms," Luke whispers in my ear.

"I love you too, baby." I can barely get out the words. My eyes become heavy and darkness fills me.

I am walking down a dark road that is dimly lit by the yellow streetlights. I look around this familiar neighborhood when I spot a house I've seen before. A two-story brick house with a clean cut front yard. I pass by the big tree that holds a tire swing. I glance in the window and look around and notice I've dreamt about this house before. There are no signs of movement inside or outside the house. It is a quiet and dark evening that is glowing with the rays of the full moon. A cool breeze blows as I hear soothing wind chimes in the background.

I walk around the house to see if I can get a glimpse of something, when I notice a dark shadow move quickly through the kitchen. My heart jumps and adrenalin takes over. I step up on the back patio that is lined with padded furniture. I slide open the back door into the kitchen and on the counter I see the same vial of blood. But this time there is blood splattered all over the wooden floors. Then I spot a blood trail leading into the basement door.

I hear scuffling from downstairs and panting. I slowly and nervously creep down the stairs realizing I have no weapon to use. I stop when the stairs make a creaking noise and a shiver runs through my body. "Mommy, stop. Don't go any further."

I turn around quickly at the sound of the familiar voice. "Michael?" I whisper out loud. What the heck is he doing here? I turn around and begin to walk back up the stairs.

"Linda Jackson, what a nice surprise. I was wondering when you were going to visit me." My palms begin to sweat and my knees shake as I turn around. At the bottom of the stairs I see a tall, lanky, scrawny man standing with blood dripping from a long knife. I've never seen a knife that long before.

I get the courage to speak after taking a deep breath. "How do you know my name?"

"How can any killers in the Charleston area not know your name? You're the famous woman who can catch the bad people. I'm honored to be in your presence. I was hoping I'd see you sooner. I mean, I've been at work for a little while now."

I try to get a look at his face but it's not bright enough. All I can see is silhouette of an abnormally long nose. He begins to creep up the stairs with awkward movement. He tucks his head so he doesn't hit the ceiling. I begin to turn and run when he yells, "I can't wait to play this game with you. Let's see if your talent can catch me. I've been working on this for a while." Then he laughs; a high-pitched laugh that echoes through the house. It sounds like a clown's laugh from a scary movie.

I run out the front door and hide behind a bush. I close my eyes tight and concentrate on waking up.

I stare at the ceiling confused at why I heard Michael's voice. *How did he get there?* I carefully climb out of bed trying not to wake up Luke. I put on my slippers and walk into Michael's room. His eyes are wide open staring up at his glow-in-the-dark stars. I walk over and sit next to him rubbing his head.

He turns to me, sits up, and hugs me. "Mommy, I didn't want you to get hurt." Tears flood from my eyes. *No, no, this isn't happening.*

"Michael, what do you mean?"

"Well, I saw you going down those stairs and I saw the red stuff that I thought was blood. It was like I could watch you but not touch you."

I shake my head from side to side. The one thing I was worried about is happening. Michael has my gift.

I hug him tightly. "Oh Michael, I'm so sorry this is happening to you."

"It's okay Mommy, I want to help you. That's why I asked so many questions about what it feels like to dream like you do."

"But these dreams are so violent, and they should never be experienced by a six-year-old."

"It is scary but I get to be with you all the time now."

Tears fall down my cheeks. "No, no, there has to be something we can do."

"I can't help it though. I think of good things before I go to sleep but tonight I ended up with you." My thoughts immediately go back to when he was a baby and I woke up in the dreams at the bad parts as soon as he started crying. *Was that the first connection we had with dreams?*

"I'll figure something out," I whisper to him and kiss his forehead. "Was this the first dream you've had?"

He shakes his head no. "I saw you with that bottle of red stuff before."

Oh God.

"I didn't know what was happening. As I saw you again tonight I thought I'd try to talk to you and it worked."

What if the dreams become more intense and he'll be able to be in the moment with me? No! That can't happen.

"I'm going to take us to see someone special. I hope she can give us some answers." He looks me in the eyes and nods in response. He yawns and I tuck him back into bed.

"Sweet dreams this time, baby." I walk towards the door and before I walk out I turn around and look at Michael's sweet and innocent face. *What have I done?*

***

I wake up feeling refreshed on this gloomy Monday morning. It is time to get back to work. I eat breakfast prepared by my one and only and we talk about what the week has in store for us.

"I have a math test on Tuesday. I's on chapter 3," Michael says with a mundane tone.

"Do you feel you're ready for it?"

"Yeah, well sort of. It's hard stuff. We're already getting into making money with all the coins and dollar bills now."

"Do you want your dad and I to help you study this evening?"

A smile forms on his face. "Yes please."

We take more bites of our oatmeal and I sip on hazelnut coffee. The sweet, warm liquid feels good traveling down my throat. I need to get motivated for everything I need to do today.

"Do you have many cases today?" I ask Luke.

"I have four scheduled knee surgeries. But I'm sure some emergencies will come through today. I'll drop Michael off at school."

"Okay, I may have Grandma or Grandpa pick you up. I'm not sure how busy I'll be today."

A big smile forms on his face. "That's fine with me. Grandma always gives me freshly baked brownies."

I smile and shake my head. "Leave it up to Grandma to break your healthy eating habit."

"Oh honey, a couple brownies won't hurt him. He is a six-year-old growing boy."

"You're right, I know," I say with a smile. "My first stop will be at the shop. I need to talk with Sarah and Bobby about taking over. Then I'll head down to the station and speak with Fredrick about getting my job started!"

"Okay, if you need anything let me know."

I kiss Michael on the forehead as he walks out of the door. "Have a good day in school, here's your lunch."

"Thanks Mom. I love you."

Hearing him say that to me will never get old. "I love you, too."

I walk into the shop that I used to call home. I feel distant from it after everything that has happened. The infamous bell rings as I open the door and Sarah and Bobby turn to face me. The looks on their faces are of shock. They both stop what they are doing and come over to me.

"Oh my God Linda," Sarah says as tears fall from her face and she embraces me with a big hug. She looks into my eyes, "Are you…" She couldn't finish what she was saying because she starts to choke up.

"I'm doing great," I reassure her and Bobby with a smile.

Bobby then gives me a hug as well. "I'm glad to see you back in the shop."

I smile and look around breathing in the coffee smell. "It looks great. You haven't changed it much."

"We didn't want to change our legacy. This is how we started and we'll keep it that way." I half smile. I don't know how Sarah is going to take me giving up the shop.

"Take a seat and I'll get you some coffee."

"Are you sure? I don't want to keep you two from the business." It's booming right now and I hope it's like this all the time.

"Yes, it's fine. Eric and Lucy can take over for a little while." I eye them over at the counter and smile. They seem like nice people.

Sarah and Bobby both join me on the comfy couch and I take a sip of the coffee that I've missed so much.

"Wow, that tastes even better than I remember."

"Well it's your favorite recipe," Sarah says with her kind smile.

"I came to see you both today to show you I'm okay and to talk to you both."

"Uh oh, this doesn't sound too good," Sarah says with a blank look.

I take another sip of coffee and a deep breath to prepare for this talk. Images of the blood vial and the tall lanky man rush through my mind, but I stop it in time before it affects me. I know I need to get down to the station right away.

"Well, as you know things were getting serious and time consuming with the job at the CPD before I went into the coma." They both nod their head and listen.

"Well, I've talked with Fredrick, Arnold, and Luke and I've decided that the best thing is for me to work full time as a detective. This means I'd have to give up the shop." They don't take their eyes off me for a second as I speak. "Sarah, I know this was our dream and we promised to work here for as long as we could, but I can't handle both jobs mentally, especially co-owning a shop. The dreams I have are getting more intense and real than ever before. I have a case right now that's going to be tough and it's going to need all my attention. You don't understand how hard it is for me not to give full attention to these dreams because I can save lives. If I don't save a person in time, then I blame myself. It's really hard to explain, but I hope you and Bobby understand where I'm coming from. You've done a wonderful job taking care of this place that I know if it's in both of your hands full time, this place will survive. I want to give you my other half of the ownership, Sarah."

Her eyes become watery but no tears fall. She swallows hard. "I can understand where you're coming from, but we put so much into this shop. I can't imagine running this place without you, Linda."

My heart breaks and my stomach is in knots. I was hoping for a better reaction. "I know, but trust me, this isn't easy for me. Thinking about it makes my stomach turn. But I figured you can either take full ownership or give the other half to Bobby. You two make a great team."

They smile at each other. "Yeah, I guess we do. Do you want me to buy the other half from you?"

I am a little shocked by the question. "Absolutely not! I'm going to do the paperwork and you'll sign it, and that is that. I'd never want to sell my half to you. You've done too much for me to do something like that."

She smiles. "Okay, well I want you to sign it over to Bobby. Both of our names can be on the ownership."

"Oh good! I feel so much better knowing you two will take it over for good."

"Thanks Linda, but I'll miss working with you more than you know."

"I know, me too, Sarah. But we live so close so the four of us will hang out often. Plus, you know I'll be in here often to get coffee."

"Sounds great."

"By the way, congrats on the baby! I want to meet her."

"Of course! Let's plan on dinner this weekend at our place and you can bring Michael and Luke?"

"Sounds amazing."

"Good, I'll text you later with details."

"Perfect. Thanks for being so understanding."

"Linda, you're my best friend. How could I not?"

We give each other a hug and kiss on the cheek. And I am out the door. Alright, next step the station.

CPD
Monday October 3
10:00 a.m.

I pull into the station and an eerie feeling takes over immediately. The last time I was here I was kidnapped. To be on the safe side I decide to call Fredrick and tell him to meet me outside.

As I see him walk down the steps from the front of the building I get out of my car and rush over. He puts out a hand to shake.

"Linda, I'm so glad to see you healthy and well."

"It's good to see you and be back. Thank you for walking to get me."

"No problem, I understand. I know the crew will be happy to see you walk through those doors, especially Arnold." I smile because I can only imagine what crazy things will come out of his mouth.

"I'm as ready as ever!"

When I walk in all the cops and detectives turn to face me. They all stand and begin to clap. I'm overwhelmed with this greeting. I smile and I know my face turns red. I wave to everyone and say thank you.

"Linda!" Arnold screams from across the room as he prances over to see me. He gives me a hug, picks me up, and swirls me around.

"Alright, really Arnold? Don't you think that was a little unprofessional?" Fredrick asks as he rolls his eyes.

Arnold backs down and shakes his shaggy hair to the side. "Alright, you're right. Sorry Linda, but I'm excited to see you back here."

I laugh. "It's okay, Arnold and Fredrick, don't worry about it. I'm happy to be back."

We sit down and talk about how everyone is doing. The sound of telephones ringing and the talking in the background makes me smile. *This is my real home; this is where I belong.*

Captain Sanders and Sergeant Gordon walk over and Captain hands me a coffee. "I'm glad to see you back, Linda." He shakes my hand and gives me a badge. My eyes instantly moisten. The shiny shield with my name on it makes my heart race with adrenalin. "This badge has been in my desk for a while waiting for you."

"Captain, -" I couldn't finish my sentence without tears falling. "I feel so blessed. I can't thank you enough."

"No, Linda. Thank you for all you've done and will continue to do with this department and for the city of Charleston. We need you."

"We're glad to have you on board," Sergeant Gordon says.

I smile even bigger.

"As for the gun, I'm going to wait and give that to you after you start and finish the training program. This will begin tomorrow if you're up for it," says the Captain.

"Of course I am! I can't wait."

"Great, you'll get started with Fredrick tomorrow morning at eight sharp." I nod my head and he walks back into his office.

"Welcome to the team officially," Fredrick says with a smile. Arnold is beaming with excitement.

"Fredrick, how did you make this happen?"

"Your talent did all the work. I just took care of the paperwork."

"Thank you so much," I say as I rub my finger over the cool shiny metal. I place the badge on my hip.

"Alright, well let's get to work shall we?" I say with excitement. I begin to tell them about my most recent dreams.

Fredrick pulls out a file on the most recent victim. "Kayla White, 25 years old. She's a nurse and had just gotten engaged. She was stabbed once in the heart. The knife was longer than any knife I've ever seen. I think this killer gets them custom-made. We found a vial of blood on the scene but it's not the victim's blood."

My eyes jump from the innocent picture of the body to Fredrick. "What? Then whose blood is it?"

"It's of another female." My breathing quickens with panic.

"So what's going on? What is he doing?"

"He's obviously very smart in planning his attacks. The vial of blood is for the next victim. She hasn't turned up dead yet. He has her held up somewhere."

"Shit, if he already has the next victim, this is going to be a nightmare of a case. I saw the vial of blood in my dream lying on the counter. He told me in the dream that I'd have a hard time figuring him out and dreaming about him. He's doing this on purpose to see if I can catch him with my talent. This is bigger than I imagined."

"What's the name of the next victim?"

"Lori Chandler. She's 26, lives here in Charleston alone, and works as a hairdresser. Her co-workers said she hasn't been to work in the last two days."

"What about her family members?"

"No one who lives in the area. Her parents live in Virginia and they're on a plane here."

"So we don't know where she was taken or at what time?"

"No. We checked her house two days ago when she was reported missing from work but found nothing. Her DNA was the only one found in the house."

"What hobbies did she have?"

"We don't know. Her coworkers said she likes to stick to herself and they didn't share much. All I know is that she likes to go to the same yoga class four times a week."

"Have you checked there with the people? The more I know about Lori and her habits the more descriptive my dreams will be."

"We were going to do that today."

"Ride along with us?" Fredrick asks with a smile.

"Let's go!"

Abandoned Warehouse
Charleston, October 3
11:00 a.m.

"Oh stop your squealing, sweetheart, no one is going to hear you. We're in the middle of nowhere. No one is looking for you. Sit still and this needle won't hurt so much."

I place the vial of blood into my pocket and head to make

my next move. I circle around the block of this fancy, overpriced neighborhood to make sure no one is out on this dark, cool evening. I still don't know how a hairdresser can afford a place like this? Money must be in the family. I park a couple blocks down from the house of Ms. Lori, oh beautiful young, fit Lori. I can't wait to get my hands on her. I creep around the back and the wind chimes make the most obnoxious sound ever. I look into a big, clean kitchen. I am about to make that kitchen look like a madhouse. I touch the knife to my side and imagine it slicing through Lori like butter.

I see her in a long shirt that just covers her butt and it is getting me excited. When she leaves the kitchen I try the back door that is surprisingly unlocked. It's game time! I sneak into the living room where she is innocently watching a movie. I see her sitting on the couch, her back facing me. This is perfect.

I rush up to her and put my hand over her mouth. She squirms and tries to scream out loud. I pull her over the back of the couch and crack her neck, enough to put her to sleep, and her limp body falls into my arms. I drag her into the kitchen and pull out my knife.

One nice long stab into the heart is all it takes. Her blood is seeping onto the fresh, clean kitchen floor. I drag her body down the stairs. I want her body found in her home. I want the cops wondering how someone can kill a person in their own home and not leave a trace. I want Linda Jackson to wonder how I managed to pull this off without her catching me. Let the games begin!

As I walk out of the now-clean kitchen I place the vial of blood on the counter top. I smile and walk out the door feeling nothing but satisfaction.

Chapter 3

Get Fit with Yoga Class
11:00 a.m.

"Lori loved this yoga class. She never missed one even if she was sick. She always told me that it was her place to unwind and relax. This isn't like her to miss two classes in a row," the messy blonde explained to us. Her tight spandex and tank top was obviously a distraction to the boys here with their mouths hanging open. I can't believe Fredrick right now! Ugh, men.

"Okay, thank you. Do you know any place where she'd go after class?" Fredrick asks.

"No, the only place would be the grocery store. She usually goes straight back to her house on River Drive."

Fredrick and Arnold look at each other with concern. They say goodbye and thanks and we are out the door. We get into the car and I grab onto the head of Arnold's seat in front of me. "Why are you both freaking out? You already checked her house out, didn't you?"

"Yeah, but two days ago. We haven't been back since. We just figured she was kidnapped and is held up somewhere. This killer usually kidnaps them."

"You really think he'd kidnap her and then take her back to her house to murder her?" The images of the clean kitchen and the vial of blood pop up in my head. "Shit! The house in my dream has to be Lori's."

1428 River Drive
1:30 p.m.

We pull into the very familiar house. A sickening feeling takes

23

over when I picture the blood everywhere. "This is the same house I saw."

I stand behind Fredrick as they kick open the front door and the gun points ahead as we walk in. The smell of bleach fills my nostrils. "He has already killed her," I whisper.

We go into the clean marbled counter kitchen and the vial of blood is in the same spot.

Fredrick looks back at me. "Everything is consistent to your dream. So where would she be?"

I point to the closed door that leads down to the basement. We walk slowly down the dimly lit stairs. We search around some boxes and lying there in the open, not covered with anything, is the body of Lori. There is blood around her and the same stab wound through the heart. "Wow, this is awful. And now he has his next victim already. We need to run that blood asap and get an ID. Arnold call a bus, I want this place swiped for his fingerprints. He can't be that good," Fredrick says with anger.

I sit at the edge of the driveway with Fredrick as the forensic team swipes for fingerprints. We are both silent and I'm sure we are thinking the same thing. "Fredrick, how is this guy getting away with this? We're always going to be one step behind. Having the vial of blood for the next victim is sick and it's going to be tough to see."

"In all my years I've been working with the FBI, I've never seen or heard of anything like this. But I have faith in our department and in you. We'll catch this guy." I look into Fredrick's eyes and I see doubt. He's trying to hide it but I can see it, and it causes a burning sensation in my stomach. Whoever this man is, I have to stop him and I will do whatever it takes. *Whatever it takes…this seems all too familiar, and I haven't been back long. Here we go again.*

A few moments later the forensic team walks out. "Sorry to interrupt, Detective Fredrick." We both stand up hoping for good news.

"It's okay, what did you get?"

"I can't believe this but we didn't find one print that wasn't the victim's."

Fredrick's eyebrows raise and he shakes his head. "Not one?"

"I'm afraid not, Sir."

"Okay, thank you."

Fredrick turns back to me and Arnold joins us. "Linda, we're going to need to work this case 24/7. I'm going to need your full potential and focus. Are you up for that?" He sounds concerned and demanding at the same time. His dark eyes and blank face say it all.

I swallow and become nervous. "Yes, I'm all in. I'm signing over my contract of ownership to the store so I can work full time here. I want to catch this guy and I'm focused."

"Great, thank you. Because as of now all we have is this vial of blood. But he already has the victim and we have no leads on any suspects. As soon as we get an ID on this blood we'll visit family, friends, places of work, places of interests, everything."

"Got it. We know what he looks like. Well, almost. I need to see a sketch artist and we need to get the pictures out on all the databases," I say with hope.

"Shit, I can't believe I didn't have you do that sooner. I was so concerned with finding the victim, that blew right past me." He shakes his head with disappointment.

When we return to the station Fredrick tries to rush the blood sample so we can find out who the next victim is. I talk with the sketch artist and give them the description. I can't forget his weird long nose, his abnormally tall body, and how he walks with a hunch. I only wish I saw his face. I couldn't get his hair color either but it was shoulder length. Honestly there aren't many men with that description, so he shouldn't be too hard to find. But obviously he hides out well.

"I still can't believe I didn't have you do this earlier," Fredrick says with despair.

"Hey, don't be so hard on yourself. Your priority was to find that girl. And look, it's already finished!" The sketch artist turns the drawing around and chills immediately run through my body. For not knowing what his eyes, mouth, and hair color look like, this guy did a great job. His dull and large face has murder written all over it. He looks like a monster.

"His face even makes him look like a giant," says Fredrick with a confused tone.

"Tell me about it. He was really weird looking. He's big as in tall but he was really scrawny, he can't be hard to take down." Fredrick's phone rings and when he answers I head back to my desk. I look over and over my papers to see if I can find any clues from the crime scenes, to the bodies.

But I am lost.

Fredrick walks over with his shoulders high. "The DNA won't be back until tomorrow, dammit. They have a rush of blood samples. That's going to be too late!"

"Okay, we're going to have to do this on our own. We'll never get the blood results back in time on any of these poor girls."

He shakes his head. "What the fuck are we going to do?" I look around and space out for a minute trying to come up with answers. I see cops answering phones, shuffling through papers, and I see Arnold with his feet on his desk and his head in his hand.

"I have to do something," I say with anger.

"I'm going to focus on my dreams tonight to see if I can find any answers. All I know is the house he was in last. If I could go back there and follow him out of the house, maybe I can find out where he holds up."

Fredrick looks up with a sparkle in his eyes. "That's a great idea! If we know where he lives, then we have this fucker. I'm sure that is where he keeps his victims. Isn't that going to be hard though? I mean you usually see before things happen…how can you?"

"I stop him before he finishes. My gift is way more powerful than what anyone thinks. I've done it before. I'll be able to do it," I say with confidence. *At least I hope I can. Seeing the ray of hope in Fredrick's eyes is something I haven't seen in a while. I don't want that to turn into disappointment. I realize now that this case, this murder, is only going to be solved with my dreams.*

"Great. Well go home and rest before tonight. We'll meet in here tomorrow morning around 7:30 and hopefully discuss details. We don't have much time until the next victim."

"Okay, will do. See you in the morning, Fredrick."

He nods and I holler to the Sergeant and Arnold saying goodbye. I call Luke and tell him I'm on my way home. He is cooking dinner with Michael. I smile and can't wait to see my boys. I begin to think of the killer, the victims, and the crime scenes to keep my mind refreshed. *I've never had this much trouble before…Well I guess I did with Tom, but this is different. I don't know this man, but he obviously knows me. So is he doing the vial of blood to try and trick me so I can't see him coming? How in the hell is he planning ahead so quickly? What am I missing?* A million questions run through my head.

I walk in to the smell of lasagna and Michael running into my arms. "Mommy, I'm so happy you're home." I hug him tight. *Oh, this will never get old. I wish we could pause a few years before he gets older.*

Luke grabs me in his arms and kisses me. We head into the kitchen and begin digging in. "Wow, what a Monday it has been. It feels like it should be Friday already," I say with a yawn.

"I know what you mean. I had back to back cases, I'm just glad I got out of there early. Tell me about your day."

I begin to tell him about everything. Michael listens intently. I wonder if he is planning on trying to dream with me tonight. I hate that Michael hears this stuff let alone sees it in his dreams, but there's no point in holding back because he will see it anyway.

"Linda, this guy scares me. He sounds like another Tom but smarter. He knows who you are." *My protective Luke is coming out.*

"I know, Luke. We've been over this. Everyone knows about my gift. I'm probably going to be dealing with killers who think they can get around my dreams for life now. They see it as a challenge."

He shakes his head and takes a sip of wine. "It's sick, they're all sick. I worry about you constantly."

"Really, I'm fine. There are plenty of people to keep me safe where I work. It's what they're trained to do."

"Mmhm. That doesn't make me feel better."

"Speaking of training, I start my gun training tomorrow. Hopefully soon I'll be carrying a gun 24/7, so I'll be safe," I say with an excited tone.

"Yeah, I guess that's a good thing." Luke sounds unsure.

"We'll both have guns; no one is going to hurt us again, Luke."

He nods his head and Michael chimes in. "Can I learn to shoot?"

I look at Luke and we are both surprised. "Well hon-."

"No!" Luke interrupts me.

"Relax," I say putting my hand on his.

I turn to Michael and finish what I was saying, "Honey, guns are dangerous." He rolls his eyes. *I keep forgetting he is more mature than a normal six-year-old boy.* "Your dad and I will teach you to use a gun when you're older."

He puts his head down. "Okay, I guess that's fair. How much older? Like a year?" He smiles and we all laugh.

"You sure do have your dad's sense of humor." We all smile and begin cleaning up the dishes.

After we clean up and take showers we all sit on the couch and watch some TV. Michael is reading a book, Luke is glued to the TV, and I am looking through the files for the case; a pretty interesting combo in this household. I look at my family and smile.

***

I tuck Michael into bed and he looks up at me with his bright blue eyes. "I hope you find some information out in your dreams, Mom. Maybe I can help you."

I shake my head. "No Michael, please don't. Try to fight it and stay away from my dreams. I don't want you getting involved. I want to make sure you're safe."

"But Mom, they're just dreams. I can't get hurt in them."

"No, honey they aren't only dreams. They're real life, and if someone bad finds out you can do what I can do then you won't ever be safe."

He sighs and rests his head on the pillow. "Okay Mom, I'll try."

"Thank you sweetie, now get some sleep. I love you." I kiss him on the forehead and turn out the light.

"I love you too, Mom."

I climb into bed and join Luke. "Boy, that child is stubborn," I say with a wink.

"Hmm, I wonder where he gets that from," Luke says, grinning.

We lie face to face with our heads on the pillows. "I'm so worried about how his dreams are going to affect him mentally and physically," I say, choking up slightly.

"I know baby, but we've been dealing with yours for a while. We'll help him. He's a smart boy and he seems to already handle it well."

"Yeah, but if they're anything like mine then the older he gets the worse they'll get."

"True, but he'll be used to them. Who knows what's going to happen."

"I know, but we have to be prepared for the worst. I mean, if it gets out that my son has the same gift as I do can you imagine the press? Let alone the sick killers out there who would love to take advantage of that? If anything ever happened to Michael, I'd never forgive myself."

Luke grabs my chin. "Linda, nothing will happen to Michael. I'll make sure of that."

I nod. Luke brings me towards him and kisses me slowly. "Now, try to relax. You have a lot of work to do tonight. You need to focus."

I sigh. "You're right."

I close my eyes and Luke rubs my head. I picture the killer and the big clean house. It is time to find out some information.

I find myself outside of the house. I look in and see the bright kitchen splattered with blood. Well, he hasn't left yet, so that's good. Should I go inside or stay outside and wait? I decide to peek through the windows and I see the man walking up the stairs wiping his long knife with his shirt. He places the knife on the counter and wipes his sweaty forehead with the back of his hand. His long coal black hair sticks to his head. How can he get this place so clean? I see him leaning over the counter to pick something up. He pulls a bag onto the counter and begins taking out cleaning supplies and gloves. Well, I guess there's my answer. Shit, he's like a traveling maid.

After about an hour of watching him strategically clean, he places everything in a bag and begins to walk toward the back door. Here is my chance! I slowly creep around the back to follow him. I see him walk back behind the shed carrying his bag of cleaning supplies. Shit, I don't want to lose him!

I pick up my pace and find him walking down the street parallel to the house. This neighborhood is pretty dull and there are parallel roads with the same type of house lined along the streets. He walks down the street calmly as if nothing happened. He looks so out of the ordinary, why isn't anyone concerned? Then I look around and realize no one else is outside. He continues to walk out of the neighborhood and through the gate that is supposed to help keep strangers out; it doesn't help much when he can fit right through the bars of the gate. I look through the glass security box and the security guard is sleeping. Typical! I follow him out. He comes to a parked black SUV along the side of the road and opens the door. I quickly glance around – shit, there are no cars! I look at the license plate and try to memorize the number: BDS2587. I close my eyes and whisper the number many times. I open my eyes and the SUV is gone.

I close my eyes tight. "Linda, wake up."

I open my eyes to my ceiling and glance at my clock. It's only 2:15 in the morning. Before I forget the plate number I text it to Fredrick.

"I'm sorry it's late, but this is all I got from my first dream. At least it's a start."

Surprisingly, he texts back right away.

"Thanks Linda, great work. I'll send this in first thing in the morning. It's okay, I can't sleep anyway."

"We've got something. Try and get some sleep, as we'll have a big day tomorrow," I say in response.

"Will do, and same to you."

Before I head back to sleep I get up and use the bathroom and check in on Michael. He is sound asleep and looks peaceful. I smile at the sight.

Abandoned Warehouse
2:30 a.m.

I look at Linda's picture from one of the articles in the paper. "It's late now, Linda. Are you dreaming about me? I hope so. Can you see my next move?"

Chapter 4

Tuesday, October 4
7:30 a.m.

I take a deep breath as I enter the station. Today is going to be a long day. I hope we can find out some information and get a lead somewhere. *I can't wait to play this game with you, Linda.* His saying keeps popping into my head. *What exactly are you planning?*

I walk in and Fredrick is already at his desk shuffling through papers. I see a hot coffee next to him. He takes a sip and gets back to work quickly. "Fredrick, how long have you been here?"

He looks at me with crazed eyes. "Um, since you texted me this morning."

"What?! Dammit, I knew I shouldn't have texted you then. Fredrick, you've got to take a break and relax. If you keep this up, you'll end up crashing then becoming unfocused. It's better for us if you get some rest."

Arnold creeps in behind us. "Yeah man, she's right," he says yawing as he sets his coffee mug down.

"Right, like I'm going to take advice from you, Arnold."

"Hey, I get the job done, don't I? I just don't devote my entire life to it; that's where your problem is."

Fredrick stands up with force. "Don't tell me what my problem is." He stands close to Arnold's face.

"Look at you, man. Your hair is a mess, your eyes look bugged out, and your breath stinks!" I can't help but laugh quietly.

I decided to barge in before anything happens. "Fredrick, Arnold is right. Not about how you look, but how you need a break. When is the DNA supposed to be back of the next victim?"

"They said late morning," Fredrick says as he slumps back into his seat. He looks like he might pass out.

"Okay, well here's what we're going to do. I'm supposed to start my gun training at 8:00. I'm sure Arnold can teach me, right Arnold?"

He smiles. "Absolutely."

"Great, so Fredrick, you go home and get some sleep. Since it's going to be a few hours until the results come back there isn't much else we can do right now. You even put a hit out for the license plate number. All we can do is wait. While I'm training, you can go home and sleep."

Fredrick yawns, scratches his shadow of a beard, and stretches his arms. He is usually clean shaven. "Okay, okay, you're right. I feel like a zombie."

"And you look like one," Arnold chimes in.

I elbow Arnold and hush him. He gives me a wink.

"If anything comes up, you promise to call me?" Fredrick asks.

"Yes, we promise, now go," I say pushing him out the door.

Arnold and I get into his car ready for the gun training. I am beyond excited. I've always wanted to learn how to shoot and defend myself. "Have you ever seen Fredrick like this?"

"Once before. We've been partners a long time and even though he hates to admit it, I know him better than anyone. He's very strong and very good at his job, but deep down he's also vulnerable. This is the second time where the case has really taken a toll on him mentally and physically. He can usually solve the cases before it gets this far, but this case in particular is really getting to him and I'm worried."

"Shit, is there anything we can do?"

"Honestly, Linda there isn't. He has to overcome it on his own. I'm very surprised that he listened to you and went home. If it wasn't for you he'd probably still be there freaking out. He respects you."

"Well good, maybe I can help control him a little. I'm going to do everything I can to find this killer and fast."

"I know you will, Linda. You've already got most of the details we need. We know his description and we have a license number, which is a good start."

"True, but this far into the case we should have more."

"And we will."

"It's a good thing Fredrick has you as his partner, because you're very laid back and positive, and he needs that."

He smiles a big goofy smile. "Well thank you, Linda, and I guess in some far beyond way, I need his strict, play-by-the-book personality as well."

We pull into the gun range. "What about a wife? Is Fredrick married?"

"Nope, he's never been married and I can't remember the last time he's had a girlfriend. He's too into the job."

"Wow, that's awful."

"Yeah, me on the other hand, I have a beautiful wife and two boys."

"Really? I never knew that. I guess we've always just talked business."

"Yup, I've been married for seven years." He pulls out a picture of his wife and kids from his wallet. I see a bright glow in his eyes. His wife is beautiful. She has long curly blonde hair and a perfect smile. His boys resemble him though, both with long hair and nice smiles.

"You have a beautiful family," I say.

"Why, thank you. Now let's get this training started."

There are a few other cops there getting some practice in. It is a big open field with a wide range of targets set up. Arnold pulls out a few guns, but we start with the basic 9mm. He teaches me how to load the gun first. I put on protective ear phones and get a rush of adrenaline. He shows me the correct stance, how my arms need to be, and how to aim. He is mimicking the same motions and I follow his directions. He tells me to keep my wrists straight and locked and slowly pull the trigger. I aim for the closest target; I breathe in heavy and pull the trigger. I smile immediately following the first shot. I smile over at Arnold and he smiles back and nods. I proceed to shoot.

"Look at that...not too bad for a beginner. I'm impressed," Arnold says as he shows me the target with my bullet holes.

"Thank you, it sure feels good to shoot a gun. So when do I start martial arts training?" I say with excitement.

Arnold laughs, "We'll have to talk to the Sergeant about that. I won't be doing that training. Leon Zhu is our instructor; he'll train you."

"Oh boy, I can't wait!" As we pack up the gun I receive a phone call. I glance at the time and I can't believe it's already 10:30. Time passes when you're having fun.

"Jackson, it's Captain Sanders. We got a hit on the DNA and the license plate. You and Arnold need to come back now. Fredrick is on his way. The license number is heading towards you both, so get out of there now." I look wide-eyed at Arnold as I hang up the phone.

"Shit, we need to leave now. I'll explain in the car."

He puts the gun in the bag and before we can turn around we hear a whipping noise fly right by us. As we look forward at the target in front of us, in the bulls-eye is a long knife. Neither one of us says anything, but we turn around and all we can see is the back of the killer running into the woods.

"That's him!" I can tell by the awkward run and his shoulder length black hair.

"Let's go!" Arnold says as we run after him through the woods. I yell at the other cops to come and help chase him down.

Adrenaline pumps through my veins as I grab the gun and begin to run. I've lost sight of the killer, but I can still see Arnold ahead of me. My phone begins to ring and I ignore it focusing on the hunt. I can hear his high pitched laugh as if he were right behind me and if sends chills down my spine.

I'm getting closer to catching up with Arnold when he stops dead in his tracks, staring at the ground.

I yell to the cops behind me to keep the search going and call back up. Then I softly walk up behind Arnold and before I can speak, I look at what he is seeing. The body of a young female, and from the looks of her, she has been dead for a few hours. I see a blood stain through her shirt near her heart. I look closer as I see something popping out from her mouth. "What the fuck?! Arnold, do you have gloves?"

He hands me a glove and I put it on. I grab the small vial from her mouth, I hold it up, and watch the blood move inside. "That's sick!" Arnold says with shock.

I put the vial of blood down on the ground when I see something else. His long knife, I assume he used to murder this woman. On the handle of the knife the number 20 is written. "What do you think that means?" I ask Arnold.

"I have no idea. I'm calling forensics now. They need to bag up all this evidence and we need to return to the station." My phone rings again and I take off the glove and answer it.

"Linda, are you and Arnold okay?" Fredrick asks with worry.

"As okay as we can be. We found another dead body. Not only did he leave another vial of blood, but he left the knife he murdered the woman with next to the body."

"Come back to the station now."

"We're on our way. The other cops that were out here at the shooting range are still looking for the killer, but I'm sure he's gotten away. I'll take a picture of the knife and send it to you."

"Okay, be safe. We know he's still out there."

The fear sets in as I hang up the phone. Arnold and I stand looking around the wooded area, waiting for forensics team to arrive, and waiting to see if the killer makes his way back. The air is silent and I can hear the wind blow through the leaves.

After the forensic team finishes up, we head back to the station. They bagged the knife and they are sending the vial of blood off to get the DNA. I already know we are going to too late for the next victim. *How in the world am I going to stop him when he is always one step ahead?* Arnold and I drive in silence, both shocked at what just happened. We were so close to the killer and he still got away. I mean, we had him in our sights. I can't stand the silence anymore so I decide to break it.

"Arnold, what are we going to do?"

"I don't know. Maybe they got something off the license plate back at the station. If we can find out where the vehicle came from, that's our next step, and of course waiting for the blood sample to come back."

"There's got to be a way we can rush that, especially after everything that has happened."

"We can try to move our sample to the front of the line. I'll call them now."

"Good." As he talks with the lab, I put my mind at work to see if I can come up with a solution. Then the thought of Arnold's aunt comes into my mind. She helped me find ways to control my blackouts and panic, so maybe she can help me go deeper into my dreams. The thought disappears when Arnold hangs up the phone.

"Well, they're going to put the blood sample in front. I told them how urgent it is and how it can save a life."

"Okay, good. Hey Arnold, I have a question for you."

"Sure Linda, anything."

"I was thinking of ways I can dig deeper into my dreams to

be able to find information about this killer and there's only one person that can help me, and that's your aunt. Would you mind if I pay her a visit and talk with her?"

"Of course not! She'd love it. I'll text you her number when we get back so you can give her a call."

"Oh, great thank you."

As we get ready to walk into the station, we brace ourselves with the swarm of paparazzi outside. "Well, there's no way out of this one. Just walk forward and don't say anything," Arnold says.

There are flashes of light everywhere I turn. So many people are talking at the same time, but I hear a few questions out of all the madness. "Mrs. Jackson, do you think you've lost your talent? Why can't you and the CPD find this killer?" Arnold gently places his hand on my back and guides me through the swarm and into the building.

"Don't let them get to you, Linda."

"I know, I won't." *But in reality it does get to me. I mean, I've been able to help solve every case that has come my way. Maybe I'm losing my gift?*

Fredrick immediately walks up to us. "Guys are you alright," he asks with concern.

"Yeah, we're doing okay," Arnold responds for the both of us. Fredrick looks at me waiting for a response.

"I'm fine, I promise."

He leads us to his desk. "Welcome to the job," he says sarcastically. I smile in response.

Capitan Sanders walks up to us as we are deep in conversation. "Alright, what do we have?"

Fredrick answers, "Well, we got a hit on the license place. It was bought from the Chevy dealership that's only a few minutes away from a man named Jack Bolder back in 2011. From the records, the SUV has been with him ever since. Now the question is, is Jack Bolder the killer, or is the SUV stolen? There hasn't been a reported stolen vehicle that matches this description or license plate."

Captain speaks with a deep voice, "Is there an address listed?"

"Yes, the address is in the same neighborhood where Lori's house is, and the house is in Jack's name."

"Hmm, coincidence or not?" I ask.

"From the work this guy has done already, this is definitely not a coincidence. I guarantee that if we find whoever Jack Bolder is, he's not the killer, and if he is then he won't be at that house. He's too smart for that, but it won't hurt to go find out."

"Alright, let's go!" Arnold says with enthusiasm.

"Wait!" I yell out before everyone gets up. "What's with the number on the knife?"

"We aren't sure, but we think it might be either the twentieth woman he has killed, or he's counting down how many he's going to kill."

My stomach turns in knot. "Oh great," I sigh.

"Well, at least we have something. Go to that address now," Captain says. On the way to River Drive, we grab something quick to eat and discuss the possibilities and next steps to take.

1508 River Drive
3:06 p.m.

"Shit, I can't believe how close this house is to Lori's. I bet he knew her every move and habit," I say.

"If the killer really lives here then yes, you're probably right," Fredrick responds. We park down the street and slowly walk towards the house. The SUV is sitting in the driveway looking as clean as ever.

"He took care of cleaning the car already. I bet it's as shiny on the inside as it is on the outside," I say.

Fredrick bangs on the door. "Charleston Police Department, open up!" I have the warrant in my back pocket to check the house in case someone unexpected is here.

"Dude, just break in, we have a warrant," Arnold says.

Fredrick gives him a, "yeah I know" kind of look and kicks down the door. The instant smell of bleach takes over our senses. "What the hell is up with all this bleach?" I say with annoyance.

We separate and check the house. I have my gun pointed out as I search the upstairs. This house looks like something out of a magazine. Designer couches, paintings, furniture, and bright and vivid color schemes. There is something seriously wrong with this guy. I check each bedroom and there isn't a spot of anything. It doesn't even seem like anyone has slept in any of the three beds. I walk back down the shiny wooden stairs and meet Arnold in the kitchen.

"Anything?" I ask.

He shakes his head. "Nothing."

"Linda, Arnold, get down here," we hear Fredrick calling from downstairs. We make our way down the carpeted stairs to the basement.

"I've got something," Fredrick says as we come close to him. We stand next to him and look down at another body with a note that says, "You're too late, again!"

"You've got to be fucking kidding me!" Arnold yells out.

Next to the body is another knife with blood on the blade. It has the number nineteen on the handle. "Just as I thought, he's counting down the murders."

"What a sick bastard. Where's the vial of blood?" I ask.

"Over there," Fredrick says as he points to a table from across the room. Arnold makes another call to forensics.

"Two in one day? He works fast," I say shaking my head.

"I'm lost, and I don't know what to do," Fredrick says as he walks back up the stairs.

"I do. I'm going to take my dreams a step further."

He looks at me with one eyebrow raised. "How are you going to do that?'

"I'm not sure yet, but I'm going to find out tonight."

"Okay, I hope it works."

"Me too."

Arnold comes running up the stairs, "Guys wait, we missed something."

He hands us the note that says, "You're too late, again." "Yeah we've already seen it, what is it?"

"No," Arnold says with a sigh. "Turn it over."

Fredrick turns it over and reads it aloud, "Since the so-called police department isn't getting any closer to finding me, I'll give you all a head start. I won't kill the next woman, which I already have in my grips, for another forty-eight hours. Let the games begin."

We all look at each other. "Let's get to work," Fredrick says.

On the drive back home tons of questions arise in my head. *What if he already has all eighteen women he wants to kill? Who's going to be number one? Why can't I see him? What will happen to me if I dig deeper into my dreams?*

I become overwhelmed with thoughts and try to think of good things. I call Arnold's Aunt Maggie and she wants to see both Michael and I tonight. I can finally get some answers about both of us.

"Alright, I'm out of here for now. I'm going to find out some answers about how to use my dreams, which should be fun," I say sarcastically. Arnold laughs.

"Be safe, we'll call you if anything comes up. We should get the blood sample of the new victim back by tomorrow morning. We'll start from there," says Fredrick with a yawn.

"Okay, great. Make sure you both get some rest," I say as I begin to walk away. As I walk to my car I get the weird feeling that someone is watching me. I stop and look around and see nothing but cars and other police officers. I put my hand on my gun as I walk to the car. I know I've only had one day of training, but I learn pretty quickly and I am confident that if I have to use it, I will be successful.

I unlock my car door. I look ahead and standing next to the one lone tree is what looks like the killer. The tall man standing with a hunch gives it away. I can briefly see his long black hair and I swear I see him smiling. My heart pounds and I grab my phone out of my pocket and dial Fredrick's number. When I look back up the killer is gone. I rush and look at my surroundings with panic. "Fredrick, get down here now. I just saw the killer."

Seconds later I see Fredrick and about six cops running out of the doors. They all go off in different directions. Fredrick runs up to me. "Are you okay?"

"I'm a little spooked but okay. He was standing over there by the tree," I say pointing in that direction.

Fredrick runs towards the tree. After about fifteen minutes of searching the premises they came out empty handed. "Are you sure you saw him?"

"Yes, I swear! That's twice he has been in eye sight distance from me today."

Fredrick shakes his head. "This is going to take everything we have, but we'll catch him. I'm going to follow you home, to make sure you aren't followed."

"Okay, thank you."

I search around the area as I drive home. I don't see anything out of the ordinary but this guy knows how to hide. I pull into the driveway and Luke paces out the door. I get out of the car and see Luke look at Fredrick in the car behind me.

"What's going on? Are you okay?"

"Yes, I'm fine; Fredrick is just taking extra precaution."

"Extra precaution for what?"

I walk over to Fredrick as he rolls down the window. "Thank you for following me."

"You're welcome, please let me know if you hear or see anything."

"I will," I say as I nod and he drives off.

I walk back up to Luke who doesn't look happy. "Now what's going on?"

"I'll explain inside. Where's Michael?"

"He's inside reading his book."

"Okay, we need to take him and go see Maggie, Arnold's Aunt. I need some answers right away."

Luke grabs my arm as I try to walk inside. "Stop, I need answers now."

"Okay, but I need to tell the both of you." I sit down on the couch with both Luke and Michael and explain what has been going on. I describe what the guy looks like in case they spot him.

Luke shakes his head. "Is the Captain or Sergeant giving you extra protection?"

"No, I won't need it. Jack comes close but not that close he wouldn't risk it. He's got his big game going on and he won't do anything to ruin it."

"And what if part of the game is capturing you?"

"It's not." *But deep down I know it will be part of his game.*

Maggie's House
6:45 p.m.

"Darlings, thank you for coming," she says in her deep voice. Her curly hair is still out of control and the strong fume of incense makes me cough.

"Thank you for seeing us on such short notice. We really need some answers."

She motions for us to sit in her round table and she begins right away. "So Michael, my dear, you see the same things your mom sees in her dreams, right?"

He doesn't hesitate to answer; he is such a confident boy. "Yes, I do. It's like I'm right there with her but she can't see me. She can hear me though."

"Interesting," Maggie says as she looks at his palm and then mine. "See these lines on your palms?" she asks us both. We nod in agreement. "They're exactly the same, and I've never seen that before. Linda, it seems as though your gift has passed down to Michael, except he can't see the future, only through your dreams. So if you aren't dreaming then neither is Michael. He can't have his own dreams, he shares yours." I shake my head and tears form.

"I was afraid of that. Will this ever go away from him?"

"No, it won't. His gift will stay for life just like yours." Luke puts his hand on my back and I look over at Michael.

"I'm so sorry, Michael. I've cursed you."

"No you haven't Mommy. I can help you." We soak in the misery for the next few minutes.

Maggie chimes in, "Next order of business. What you asked over the phone is something I can't help you with. You're in control of your dreams. Mediation is the best way to go, which I already told you about. I was thinking of some other things you can try and I came up with one."

My ears are open wide.

"Well, you've proven that you can see the future and you can go back in the past, but what if you tried to dream as the killer?"

My mouth drops. "Wait what!?"

"Before you go to sleep, picture yourself as the killer. Maybe if you can see through his eyes and not yours, you'll get some answers. If you're the killer, then you know what your next move will be, right?"

I sit and try to soak in what she is saying. "I guess that could work."

"But impersonating another human being, especially a strong killer, can cause a great deal of pain when you wake up."

"Like the blackouts and flashes I was having before?"

"Worse."

I take a big gulp. Luke gets up fast. "No, that's it, we're done and leaving. I'm not going to see Linda go through worse. She's just getting back to work after a six-year long coma and she hasn't had any flashes or blackouts. She isn't risking this."

"I know it's tough, but this might be the only way," Maggie says with concern.

"What could happen to me?"

"Possible seizures, heavier flashes, and the inability to control what happens to your body."

"No, Linda, I'm sorry but you'll have to find another way," Luke says with anger. Michael and I get up and begin to walk out.

"Thank you for your time Maggie, I appreciate the help."

"Anytime darling, I'm always here."

We pull into the driveway and we all get out of the car. Michael goes up to his room to get ready for bed. I go and sit in the kitchen trying to grasp the concept of what just happened. "Don't even think about it, Linda. You're not doing that. The CPD is going to have to work harder to find this killer."

"Luke, I'm the Charleston Police now.'"

"I don't care, Linda! You aren't doing that!" He can say all he wants, but I am the one in control of my dreams, and I am going to do it.

As I put Michael to bed, I whisper to him, "Michael, mommy is going to do something very important, but very hard."

"I knew you were going to do what that crazy lady told you to do."

"I have to, I just have to."

"Do you need my help?"

"Yes, since you can dream with me. If something bad begins to happen in the dream, I want you to wake yourself up and then come and wake me up."

"What if I can't wake up? Remember you dream and I dream?"

"I know, but you can control it, trust me."

"Okay, mommy I'll do it, but please be careful."

"I will honey, now don't tell your daddy. He isn't happy about what I'm doing; actually he doesn't know I'm doing it. So this is between us and our special bond."

"Okay, I promise," Michael says with a half-smile.

"I love you so much honey," I say as I kiss his forehead.

"And I love you very much too."

Luke and I say our goodnights and I turn off the light. I can tell he is still upset, and I hate going to bed angry at each other, but this has to happen. I close my eyes and picture myself in Jack's shoes. When my eyes open in the dream, I have to be looking through his eyes; the eyes of a cold-blooded killer.

Abandoned Warehouse
10:30 p.m.

"Seeing you panic today was such a release. I know that I'm getting to you know and you're so far from finding me, this makes the game that much better." I stare in the eyes of Linda Jackson's picture I found online. Being that close to her in person gave me the chills...oh how I can't wait to make her my number one. "You have no idea what you're in for."

I look at the picture of my next victim, number eighteen, the beautiful Elena Jenkins. I will plan on kidnapping her after she comes out of Pavilion Bar this Saturday. She goes every Saturday alone, no friends, no boyfriends, such a sad story. That will soon change and she will never be alone again.

I lie down in bed and think of Linda and wonder what she is going to dream about tonight. How is she going to try and find answers? Then I grab the picture of the one man I idol. "I promise I'll do you justice, and I'll get the job finished. I love you, brother."

Chapter 5

I walk towards the Pavilion Bar with eagerness. It's about 2:00 a.m. and Elena should be walking out any second now.

Okay, I'm here, I can see through his eyes. Focus now, Linda.

I shake my head. What is that? I refocus when I see her stumble out of the bar. I walk over and pretend to help her. "Ma'am let me help you. Are you okay?" She starts to respond and when she looks at me, her eyes grow wide with fear, and she tries to run. I laugh as I watch her try and run away from me. She is falling all over the place and making this easy for me.

Please run away. Oh God I don't want to see how he kills her.

I shake my head to get rid of whatever annoying voice that is.

"Yeah, that's right. I'm in your head now."

"Linda, is that really you? Ah, I see what you're trying to do. See through my eyes, huh? Well I hope you like what you're about to see." I pick up my pace and take out the chloroform from my back pocket along with a paper towel. I quickly put some on the towel, ready to attack. I speed up and as I reach her she fumbles and I catch her as she falls. She's already passed out. I throw the paper towel away. Well she saved me some trouble there. "Like what you see so far, Linda?"

At least I know what he uses, so that's' a start. I now know who he's going after next. Keep focus!

"Are you ready for what's next?" I put her on my back like I am giving her a piggy back ride. I try to make it look playful.

Why does nobody think this is weird? I look around and the people walking are too into their own business or too drunk to realize what is going on. No one cares. How sad.

I walk over to my black, tinted car, open the back seat, and lay her down.

Something doesn't feel right. I feel sick. What is happening? "Mommy, it's time to wake up now."

I wake up and take a deep breath. "Shit, I was close to finding out where he takes her," I say out loud. I check my watch and it is 2:45 a.m. There has to still be a chance she is alive. I call Fredrick right away.

"Fredrick, I'm sorry it is so late, but we have got to move now. I saw through Jack's eyes. He kidnapped Elena Jenkins from the Pavilion Bar. They got into a black car and the windows are tinted. It was a Chevy Cobalt, but I didn't get the license number. This happened tonight, so she has to still be alive."

"I'm on it. I'll call the car in and have them run her name through the database to see what we can find."

"Thanks, do you want me to come in?"

"No, Linda, you did a great job, try to get some rest and we'll talk first thing in the morning. I'll see you at work. Goodnight and thank you."

"Good luck," I say and he hangs up quickly. I sit up in bed and try to relax. I feel pretty good considering how I dreamed. Maggie said it could affect my body worse, but I feel great. I decide to get up and check on Michael and figure out why he woke me up at that moment. I get up and then stumble a little. My head feels heavy and light headed. "Woah," I say out loud as I sit on the edge of the bed.

Luke wakes up immediately. "Linda, what's wrong?"

"I don't know," I say as I rub my head. "I feel really light headed and it's not going away." Luke walks toward me and sits next to me. I feel rumbling in my stomach and I rush to the bathroom and lift the toilet lid. Everything I ate the day before comes out and now I feel even more light headed than before. I sit back against the wall and Luke rubs a cold wash cloth over my forehead. The light from the bathroom seems to fade and my eyes become heavy.

"Linda, stay with me!" I can barely hear Luke.

Fight it. Don't let it take over you; take big deep breaths and try to relax. Open your eyes, slowly open them. Get confident, fight this... I say to myself as I slowly regain my eye sight and hearing. Luke is holding me by my face talking to me. It sounds like I am under water, but it is slowly clearing up.

"Oh, thank God. I thought I lost you," Luke says as he pulls me close.

"I thought I was going to lose it, but I fought through it and pulled myself together. That's the first time I've been able to do that."

"You're getting strong, Linda."

"I kinda have to because my gift is getting stronger. I dreamt through his eyes and saw what he saw. I was able to figure out some information and Fredrick is already on it."

"That's great babe. I'm proud of you," he says as he kisses me on the forehead. He helps me stand up. I stand in his arms for a few seconds so I don't overdo it. Luke walks me over to the bed and gently lays me down.

"Can you get me some water please?"

"Of course," he says with his beautiful smile.

Michael walks in a few minutes later. He looks so tired, my poor boy. "Mommy, are you okay? I heard you run to the bathroom and get sick."

"I'm fine, Michael. I got sick but I was able to control a worse outcome. Honey, why did you wake me up so early in the dream?"

"Not only do I see what you see in the dreams but I also feel what you feel. I felt like my stomach was getting sick and I knew you were too. If you had stayed any longer in that dream, I think we both would have felt much worse."

"Oh, Michael," I say as I pull him into my arms. "I'm so sorry you have to go through this. I had no idea that you felt what I felt."

"Mommy, don't be sorry. You say that too much. I'm fine and I know when to stop you." Luke walks in with the water and lies down next to us.

"Is everything okay?"

I shake my head no. "No it's not. Michael can feel what I feel in the dreams. I was getting sick in the dream and he knew to wake me up because he felt it too. There has to be something we can do."

Luke gives a blank stare. "We'll figure out something. I can't have the two most important people in my life suffering every night. I'm taking you to see Dr. Hue. He found out why you have the gift from the brain waves. Maybe he can do a test on Michael to see how his brain waves are. Maybe there's some kind of therapy we can give him."

"That sounds good but Maggie said-" and he cuts me off before I can finish.

"Screw what she says. She isn't a real doctor."

"Yeah, but she's helped me."

"Yeah, well you helped yourself; she just told you what to do. Dr. Hue will be able to help. He's a licensed doctor."

"Alright, I agree. I'll call first thing in the morning to make an appointment." *Except, this is way beyond what doctors learn in school. This is much more spiritual. Maggie is the only help.*

"Good," Luke says as he covers Michael and me with the sheets. Michael falls asleep on my chest and I don't want to wake him. Lord knows, we all need the sleep.

***

We all wake up the next morning to the sound of my alarm. I feel pretty refreshed. Luke gives me a quick kiss on the lips and Michael looks up and smiles. "How did you sleep, Michael?" I ask.

"Good, I didn't have a single dream, but neither did you," he smiles a goofy smile that makes his dimples show. He is the cutest six-year-old boy I've ever seen.

We all get ready for work and school. I make a quick breakfast of granola and Greek yogurt for us all. I pour orange juice for Michael and make to-go cups of coffee for myself and Luke.

I drop Michael at school and head down to the station. I get a phone call on the way to work. "Hey baby," I say because I see Luke's name pops up.

"Don't forget to call the doctor."

"I won't, but they don't open till eight. I'll call then."

"Okay, let me know what they say and when the appointment is."

"I will, have fun at work. I love you."

"I love you too, Linda. Be safe." His voice sounds off. I wonder what is going on with him. He sounds pre-occupied and concerned. It's probably just worry. I pick up the speed and head down to the station, anxious to find out if they got anything from last night.

I walk into the station at 8:00 a.m. sharp. I see Fredrick in Captain's office with Sergeant Gordon. The door is shut but I can see the tension from here. *Shit, this can't be good.* I see Arnold sitting at his desk on the phone. I walk over and place my coffee and purse on my desk and find a folder there. I open it and see the innocent face of Elena Jenkins. Then I see a picture underneath it of her dead body. "You've got to be kidding me," I say as I slam the folder down. I look over at Arnold and he is shaking his head. He puts the phone down.

"I'm sorry, Linda. We couldn't get to her in time. We managed to track her cell phone, but when we found the phone we also found her body. She was found inside the black cobalt, with the same stab wound, with the number eighteen on the knife."

"Did you find a vial of blood?"

"Yes, we're getting information on her now."

"This is never going to end," I say with a sigh.

"Yes, it will." But even Arnold doesn't sound as confident as usual.

I glance into Captain's office again, "So what's going on in there?"

"I'm not sure exactly. It's about the case and that's all I know."

"I feel that this is all my fault."

"Don't go there. You got us more information, more than any of us would. The good news is, we got another hit of DNA from the car that isn't the victim's. They're working on that as we speak."

"Good. If we can at least get his DNA from the scene we can get a warrant for arrest."

"Yes, that's if we can find him."

I look through the pictures once more to see if I can find anything, and then it hits me;

Flashes!

Flashes of me as Jack, of me watching Jack, putting Elena in the car, so many different images hitting me all at once. My head is pounding and I try to stop the pain.

Arnold is yelling over to me. "Linda, what's going on?" His voice sounds so far away as the pounding in my head takes over.

Control it, stop it, slow, deep breaths. I close my eyes and focus on darkness. The sounds of the station become clear again and when I open my eyes Fredrick is right there next to me with some water. He stares at me with concern.

"I'm okay."

"You don't look okay. Do you need to go home?"

"No!" I yell out. I'm not letting this ruin my work. "I really am okay."

"Was that because of your dream?"

How would he know that?

"That's a pretty good guess. Why did you ask me that?"

"Well, you told me you were going to try something new and you found out information yesterday for us. I put two and two together. I'm a detective you know," he says with a joking tone.

I smile. "Well good job, detective. But I really am fine. It was from the dream, but I'm able to control the outbreaks before it gets too bad."

"Are you sure you should be doing this?"

"This is my life now. Yes, I'm sure. Now what did you find out?" I change the subject before he can say anything else.

He begins to put up the pictures of the victims on the board and Jack next to all of them. "They've all been murdered the same way. In all the crime scenes he's left the knife with the number counting down and the vial of blood for the next victim. So far each victim has been in their early twenties, so that is his main target."

We get interrupted by Christopher, the Forensic Pathologist, who has been working his ass off to help find any evidence that could lead us to anything. "Sorry to interrupt detectives but I got the blood sample back from the vial."

Fredrick gets to his feet quickly. "Already? How did you get it so fast?"

He smiles so big that if lifts his thick glasses. "Well, I have my ways." He shakes his head and his look becomes serious. "Anyway, his name is Henry Ringer. He's twenty-three years old and finishing last year at UC as a teacher."

"He?" I say, confused.

"Yeah, this one is a male."

"And are you sure you tested the right blood?" asks Fredrick.

"Yeah, the one you gave me."

Fredrick nods. "Okay, thank you for rushing that sample, Christopher." He walks away with pride.

Fredrick slams the picture of Henry up on the board with the rest of the victims. "He must be trying to throw us off," I say.

"Yeah, and he's doing it big time. Unless he's tricking us and that isn't even the next victim's blood," Fredrick says with disappointment.

Arnold chimes in. "Here's his cell phone number and he still lives in a dorm at UC."

"Great, call his phone and trace it," Fredrick says with a stern tone.

"On it!" Arnold's smile turns into a blank look. He hands me the phone. "Uh, Linda, it's for you."

I glance over to Fredrick and he nods to take it. "Trace this phone now," he calls to Arnold.

"Hello," I try to say with confidence.

"Ah, Linda Jackson, how nice it is to hear that lovely voice of yours." Fredrick is glaring at the phone as he listens through the speaker. "I know I'm on speaker phone but that's okay, as I want your boys at the station to hear this too. Don't try and trace this phone, as it won't work." I glance over at Fredrick. He motions for me to keep calm. I nod and take a breath.

"What do you want, Jack?"

"I don't need anything from you, but I know I have something that you want."

"So why a male this time? Are you trying to throw us off?"

"I thought I'd mix it up for you all. I know you guys at the station are trying your best to catch me. How about I give you guys a timeline for this one?"

"Another one of your sick games, Jack? Why do you care so much about what we think?"

His high pitched laugh comes screaming through the phone. "Because you're the people who try to catch the bad guys. Why not make it a game? Don't you see this was his plan all along?"

My eyes move to Fredrick and Arnold quickly. "Whose plan, Jack?"

"You have twelve hours to try and save Henry or he's dead just like the others," and then he hangs up. I slump back into my chair and sigh.

"Well, now we know there's someone else involved," Arnold says breaking the silence.

"Unless he's crazy," Fredrick says. "Think of how many murderers we've caught who always thought they were working for someone higher up, when in reality they were just crazy, trying to put the blame on someone else. Or someone with a split personality who hears someone else's voice in their head."

Arnold raises his shoulders. "That's very true."

I chime in, "But this guy is smart. Look how he has tricked us many times already. I think whatever the plan is, is something Jack and this other guy has been waiting for, and when it ends, I don't think it's going to be small, I think they want this to end and leave a lasting impression. I think it's all going to come down to whoever their number one is."

Fredrick nods his head. "I think you're on to something. Let's keep digging. I know that Henry is a trap. He's probably already killed him, but let's look."

"I got a hit on the phone. It's showing that the phone is located right by Harper Elementary School."

Panic, fear, and anger explode inside me. "What!" I get up and yell out. People in the precinct stare at me. "That's Michael's elementary school. We need to go now."

Fredrick and Arnold scramble to their feet and we are out the door. I glance at my watch. "It's just after lunch and they're at recess now. That creep was probably watching my son and the other kids play. He said he wanted to play a game. Boy, has he started one; messing with my son isn't a good idea." My heart is racing and I call Luke. Luke gets upset too and is meeting us at the school now.

When we pull up to the school I can hear the children's laughter on the playground. I look around for Michael and I don't see him. "I can't see Michael," I say with panic and I jump out of the car and race up to the front door. Fredrick follows close behind and Arnold checks the surroundings. I run into the office and Mrs. Murphey, the secretary, looks up and smiles. "I need to sign Michael out now." Her smile fades. "Alright, Mrs. Jackson, is everything okay?"

"No, I need to speak with the Principal. She nods in agreement and calls Ms. Williams in and goes to get Michael from the playground.

"Mrs. Jackson, please step into my office." Fredrick follows me in.

"We believe there's a threat who's watching the school. You'll need to go on lockdown until we can catch the perpetrator," I say.

"We'll have officers patrolling the school for safety," Fredrick chimes in.

Her green eyes become wide with fear, "Who's the threat? Why would they want anything to do with our school?"

"That's confidential ma'am, but here's a photo of the man. Please be on the lookout and if you spot anyone that looks like him…tell one of the officers right away."

"Okay, how long will this take?" she asks with tears in her eyes.

"We aren't sure, but we're working hard," Fredrick says. Michael runs into her office.

I embrace him in my arms. "Oh Michael, I'm so glad you're okay."

"Mommy," he whispers into my ear. "I saw the bad man outside."

I gently push him back and look him in the eyes. "Where was he, Michael?"

"He was across the street watching us at recess." I look over at Ms. Williams and tears now fall from her eyes.

"Oh my, who is this man and what does he want with our school? I have to protect my children."

"Don't worry, myself and the rest of the Charleston Police Department are going to catch him," I reassure her. *I hope we can catch him. I don't want to let her down or let him harm any of these kids.*

"Wait, if he was watching at recess then he can't be that far away! Fredrick, we need to go," I say with panic. As soon as we walk out of the door Luke comes rushing up the stairs. I run into his arms and Michael joins us. Luke grabs my face and looks me in the eyes.

"Are you and Michael okay?"

"Yes, but the killer was here at the school and he's not far away now. We have to go. Can you take Michael back to the house?"

"Of course I will, but will you be okay?"

"I'm fine. I'll be better once we catch this guy. Keep the doors locked and keep your gun handy. I don't know what Jack is going to do, and the worst part is I can't see any of it coming."

"We'll be okay. You be safe and call me if you need anything," Luke says as he kisses me one more time and takes off with Michael. I watch my boys walk away and anger takes over. If Jack ever touched my family, I'd kill him with no hesitation.

"Let's go get this son of a bitch," I say to Fredrick and Arnold.

"Arnold, any hits on the phone now?" Fredrick says as we walk towards the cop car.

"Y-yeah," he hesitates and looks around with confusion. "It shows that he's still here." We all stop at the car and look around. Then I hear a beeping noise.

"Guys what's that-?" I can't finish my statement because fear takes over when I see the bomb under the car set to explode in five seconds. Fredrick grabs my arm and we try to run away. The bomb blows up and I feel the heat take over my body, and it's as if gravity takes over. We all fly backwards and as I'm falling I hear screams in the background. Then I hit the concrete so hard that my entire body is stinging.

Heat.

Pain.

Dizziness.

I try to get up but I feel pain everywhere. I cough up the smoke and I look at the smoke filling the sky. "Linda!" I hear vaguely in the background but it sounds like Luke. The ringing in my ear is all I can hear. Then out of nowhere kneeling down beside me is Luke. "Linda, babe are you okay?" I nod my head in agreement and try to talk but all that comes out is coughing. I try to get up but I feel too much of a stabbing pain. "Shh, relax, I'm here to help and the ambulance isn't far away." I hear the sirens in the distance.

I look up to see how Fredrick and Arnold are doing when I see Fredrick hunched over Arnold who's lying there still and lifeless. *No, no, not Arnold, please God.* "Fredrick," I try to call over to him. Luke is sitting me up because I'm so weak. He doesn't seem to hear me. "Luke, help me up please." I look around in panic. "Wait. Where's Michael?"

"I told him to wait in the car."

"You what!? Luke, Jack is still around here." His eyes become big instantly.

"Shit!" he says and goes towards the car.

I limp over to Fredrick and Arnold holding my bleeding leg. Fredrick is still hunched over Arnold, shaking his head from side to side. I now stand over both of them. Arnold's eyes are closed and his head is bleeding from the back. There is a pool of blood on the ground. "No, no Arnold," I say as I kneel down on the other side of him and tears fall from my eyes. I look up at Fredrick who's across from me and I see tear tracks down his dirty face. I've never seen Fredrick like this. "Is he-?" I can't finish my statement.

He is shaking his head. "He's dead."

"NO! No, this can't be. Arnold," I say shaking his arm. He stays still and limp. I put my fingers to his neck to check his pulse. Nothing, I feel nothing. He really is dead. I start to cry. The ambulance pulls up and the EMT's rush over to us. One of them bends down and checks Arnold's pulse.

"Get a stretcher now!" he shouts over to him. They rush and get Arnold on the stretcher and take him in the ambulance. "You both need to come with us. You're both bleeding and in need of assistance.

"I won't go. I have a killer to catch," Fredrick says.

"I'm with him," I say to the EMT.

His light brown eyes look at me. "Ma'am, your leg is bleeding heavily. You need assistance now."

"Linda!" I hear Luke's voice from afar. I turn around and see him running towards me without Michael and my heart drops. He stops in front of me breathing heavily. "Michael...he's gone."

"Gone? What do you mean gone?" I scream.

"Everyone, search the premises now for their six-year-old boy," yells Fredrick. I show the EMTs and the other cops that arrived seconds ago a picture of Michael.

They all run off and begin the search. Fredrick puts a call in for backup. "The more people there are, the better chance we have of finding him," Fredrick says as he places his hand on my arm. More tears fall from my eyes.

"Ma'am, if you won't go with us then sit over here and let me check your wound," the same EMT says to me.

"Listen to him, Linda. You need to be checked out," says Luke assisting me to the ambulance.

"Fine, but I'm not going anywhere until Michael is found." Luke nods in response.

The paramedic pulls up my pant leg over my knee. I look down and all I see is dried blood. "Well, the good thing is, it's not bleeding anymore," I say trying to lighten the situation.

"Yeah, but ma'am you have a very deep wound. He dabs the wound with a towel and it sings badly."

"Ouch!" I yell out.

He wraps the wound and then looks at my shoulder next and treats that wound. "You're going to need stitches on the knee," he says to me as he continues to tend to other scrapes.

"Okay, but I can't go now." I see Fredrick walking forward after about twenty minutes.

"We didn't find him."

"It's only been twenty minutes; we have to keep searching," I say with anger. I jump up from the ambulance, but I stumble and both Luke and the paramedic catch me and sit me back up. They give each other a weird look as if they know one another. *What's going on?*

"She needs to get to the hospital, Luke," says the paramedic. *How does he know his name?*

"Yes, I know, Jared, thank you for your input." They glare at each other. I sit there confused as to what is going on.

"We need to find Michael!" I yell out. I try to stand again when out of nowhere Michael walks around from the side of the ambulance.

"Mom, it's okay, I'm right here."

I stare in shock and open my mouth to speak but nothing comes out. "Call off the search, we found him," Fredrick says into his radio.

"Michael, honey where were you!" I say and I bring him into my arms.

"I'm sorry I scared you. Dad told me to stay put but I couldn't help it. I had to help."

"Michael, you're only six years old, you need to stay put and do what we say." He bows his head.

"I'm sorry, Mommy." I sigh and hold him closer.

"It's okay honey, I'm just glad you're safe."

"I saw where the bad man went. I followed him."

"You what?! Michael you could have-" Luke puts his hand on my shoulder to stop me.

"He's okay now, Linda."

Fredrick bends down on his knees to meet Michael's height. "Michael, what you did was very brave, thank you for helping us. Where did you see him go?"

"He got into a big white truck and then left."

"Okay Michael, thank you very much," Fredrick says and calls Sergeant Gordon. I am itching to get back out there and Luke can tell I'm antsy.

"Don't you even think about it, Linda; we all need to get to the hospital now." I know he is right but deep down I want to help. Arnold is now dead; we have to stop him before he kills anymore of us.

I sigh. "I know, let's go." We start to climb into the ambulance and Fredrick stops us.

"Linda, I'll be down at the hospital soon. I need to visit Arnold's wife and kids, and then I need to keep working. We only have a few hours left to save Henry." Tears sting my eyes at the thought of their reactions. I nod and lie on the stretcher in the ambulance. I look up and hope God is listening to me, *Please God, help us catch Jack before he hurts anyone else. Keep Arnold safe up there.*

Deep down inside I know our chances of saving Henry in time

are slim to none. I have to figure out another way to get ahead of Jack. There has to be something I can try.

Jared puts an IV in my arm and checks my vitals again. "How are you doing, Linda?" he asks with a gentle voice.

"I'm fine, thank you," I say. I still want to know the connection between him and Luke. Lying down on this stretcher and relaxing makes me feel tired. "Well, I guess I don't have to call the doctor now," I say jokingly.

Luke smiles. "Just relax babe."

I begin to close my eyes. I feel a small hand grab mine and I tighten my hand around his. *Thank you God for keeping Michael safe.*

I look at my watch and then I look down at Henry who is pleading for his life. "Well Henry, it looks like you only have about an hour to live. I don't think the police will get here in time." I look around at all the trashed cars piled high. "Plus, how would they even find you in this dump?"

"Pleas Sir, don't do this. I have a wife and a baby at home." I watch him on his knees, hands tied behind his back, blood dripping down his face, begging for his life.

"Shut up," I say and knock him in the head with the back of my knife. I begin to think of my next victim, number sixteen the sexy Jessica. I am sure she is just waking up in my warehouse. She will look around and see that she is trapped and she will scream for mercy. Ah, the thought makes me shiver.

I look up when I see a bright light in the sky. What the hell is that? Then I hear a beeping noise. I look around in circles confused about what is going on. The light gets brighter and I put my arm up to block the light.

I wake up in a panic but shut my eyes to the light. I slowly open my eyes and I realize that I am in a hospital bed with an IV, and I dreamt as Jack again. That sure is a weird feeling. "How are you feeling?" Luke asks as he and Michael sit right next to me.

"What time is it?" I say impatiently.

"It's 7:15, why?" I ignore the question and pick up my phone from the side table.

"Fredrick, get to the car junk yard now! I believe Jack has Henry there and he doesn't have much time left."

"On it now!" I set the phone down and look over at Luke.

"I had a dream just now. I saw through Jack's eyes again. It might actually work this time!" I say with a little excitement. "I guess it took getting blown up for my dreams to really start working," I say with a smile and a wink.

"Linda, that's not funny," Luke responds. I wink at Michael and he giggles quietly. "The explosion is already on the news. I've gotten like fifty phone calls from everyone making sure you're okay. The media is outside the hospital now waiting for you."

I sigh. "Lovely. They never stop." My stomach begins to rumble. I put my hand over my stomach and bend over. "I think I'm going to be sick." Luke rushes to grab the trash can and put it by my side. The burning sensation of liquid comes up and out instantly. Luke presses the button for the nurse.

Luke is pulling my hair back and rubbing my head. It burns so much because I don't have any food in my system. I finally finish when the nurse comes in. She checks my temperature and blood pressure. "Everything looks good and the IVs have been hydrating you. How do you feel now?"

"I'm a little weak, but okay." *I know exactly why I threw up.*

"Okay, just rest. I'll get Dr. Hue; I know he has been wanting to come check on you. He has been very busy."

"Thank you."

I look over to Luke. "I'm glad Dr. Hue is coming. Now I can talk to someone who really knows what's going on with me. Maybe he can tell me something about why I'm physically hurting from these dreams."

Dr. Hue's shiny head walks through the doors. His bright smile brings a calming effect to me. "Hello stranger, causing more trouble I see?" We all laugh. I begin to tell him everything that has happened today and with my dreams.

Dr. Hue turns serious. "Linda, your health is already in danger because of the brainwaves you have. Trying to use those waves in someone else's mind is beyond dangerous. You've already been in two comas, one lasting six years of your life. If you continue to dream like that, you could possibly face another coma." My heart starts to race. "You're going to have to find another way to catch this killer. If your normal dreams aren't working, then find another safe way. I'm telling you now, if you continue to dream through him, you're going to face serious health consequences."

"But the dream I just had, I didn't even mean to dream through Jack. It just took me there. I didn't even try to dream about anything,

I just fell asleep."

"That's not good. That means your Theta waves are working harder than they were before. This is the most powerful and dangerous state. That's what your brain was at the entire time you were in your coma."

"So what can she do to stop this?" Luke chimes in.

"I-I'm not exactly sure."

"But you're a doctor!" Luke says with a loud tone.

"Yes, but like I said before I've never seen anything like this. I don't know how to deal with it. It's almost inhuman."

"You're saying I'm not a human?"

"No, but this is nothing a human has ever had that I know of. You fought hard to be able to dream through Jack, so maybe if you fight even harder to stay out of his brain that might work. Try to dream as you were before and not through someone else. That's the only option I can give you. If you dig down deep you're the only one who can stop and control this. I'm so sorry. You can be released in a few hours after you relax a little longer." Dr. Hue leaves the room and we all remain quiet.

Luke puts his hand on mine. "We'll figure this out, Linda. I promise."

About an hour later of all of us are sitting waiting for me to be released and making small talk when I get a call from Fredrick. "Give me something good," I say as I answer the phone.

"Well we caught Jack off guard. He didn't think we'd make it in time. When he saw us all he ran."

"Did you catch him?"

"No, but Henry is alive and safe now."

"Good, but Jack got away again."

"Yes, but Linda do you see how close we're getting? Henry wouldn't be alive if it weren't for you. You're getting us closer and closer. How are you feeling?"

"I'm better. Ready to get back to work."

"Well go home, sleep in, and come in tomorrow when you're ready."

"Okay, thanks I will. How was Arnold's wife and kids?"

"They were heartbroken. That was the hardest thing I've ever had to do. I never want to lose anyone again. Jack is going to suffer and we're going to be the ones who make him suffer."

"And we will, Fredrick. Was there a vial of blood there?"

"No, there wasn't. I'm guessing it's because he didn't kill Henry. So we don't know if he has another victim and now we don't have a blood sample to test."

"He's got another victim already in his warehouse. Her name is Jessica. I saw her in my dream."

"Any idea where the warehouse is?"

"None, but I can try to find out."

"I'll do some research and see if we can find any buildings in the area that haven't been used in a while and start there."

"Okay, and I'll do my best to find out where it is as well. I'll see you tomorrow, Fredrick."

"Goodnight, Linda. Rest up."

When we get home we all go straight to bed. My body is so sore I don't want to move once I lie down. "Don't even think about dreaming tonight. You need to rest from all areas," Luke says as he tucks me in.

"Okay."

"I mean it," he says as he kisses me before lying down next to me. I close my eyes and begin to wander off. *I have to dream, it's my job to help. Arnold is dead, Jack has another victim. He is down to sixteen now and that is getting too close to one. I don't want to find out who number one is. I don't want to find out who number fifteen is. Jack needs to be stopped and it needs to happen now. I am the surest hope of catching him, so I must fight.* I close my eyes and begin the fight.

Chapter 6

I walk in to see Jessica lying in the cradle position on the couch. She is pale, shivering, and scared for her life. Just how I like them. I walk towards her with excitement. I have a good plan for this one.

Okay Linda, it's time to focus. You are here and you are looking through his eyes. Stay strong and fight this for as long as you can. Concentrate on details.

I shake my head of some weird buzzing noise I hear. Oh wait, "Linda, are you here with me right now?" Silence. Maybe she isn't here this time; maybe she decided to give up. I stop in my tracks and laugh because I know that isn't possible. "Well if you're here with me, I hope you enjoy the ride."

Don't let him know you're here. Focus. Fight.

I sit down next to Jessica and rub her head as she begins to awaken. "Good morning, you know my plan with Henry didn't go as planned. I didn't get to leave your blood with his dead body. In fact, he got away, the cops are getting closer, and I don't like that. So I need to throw them off again and that's exactly what I am going to do."

When she realizes where she is at her eyes widen and the look of fear shines brightly through. She wakes up quickly, breathing heavily. "Where am I? Who are you? HELP!"

"Oh honey," I say laughing. "No one can hear you. We're out in the middle of a field in an old abandoned warehouse. You can scream all you want."

She looks at me with her tearful eyes. "What do you want from me?"

I move closer to her face with my nose almost touching hers. I can feel her panicked breath against me. "Oh, what I want from you my dear is more than you can imagine." She begins to cry harder, tear after tear falling from her face. I bring her in for a hug, "Shhh, it's okay sweetie, I promise to take good care of you." I pick her up and she begins to fight me. It doesn't affect me much because she weighs about one hundred pounds "If you fight me it'll only make it worse. She stops squirming and lets me take control.

I take her outside since it is a beautiful clear night and lie her gently on the ground. She is silent now. She knows what is about to happen and she isn't going to fight. She wants it, I know she does.

Oh God no. I can't watch this, but I have to stay strong. Look at the details. A one-story rusted warehouse, one streetlight and gravel road, and yards upon yards of grass. This can't be too hard to find.

I scream out when the buzzing noise gets louder. What is that!? It is messing with me and I can't concentrate! Jessica's brown eyes look at me and she begins to smile. I slap her in the face! "Don't smirk at me. Don't think this is over yet." I pull on her long brown ponytail so her head is arched back. "Better hold on tight for this ride."

I throw her used body in the back of my white van and decide to take her somewhere to drop the body.

Concentrate on the drive, every turn, and every road.

After about twenty minutes of driving I end up exactly where I want to be. It is about 2:00 in the morning and I know the police station won't be so busy. I stop two blocks down and park the car on the road. I start to get out of the car when I stumble at some loud ringing noise. What the-.

"No! I yell as I wake up quickly to my alarm. I was so close!" Luke gets up and turns off the alarm.

"You dreamed last night? Linda, I told you not to!"

"You really think I'm just going to stop looking for this guy?" I begin to rant when I get the rush of nausea and I run to the bathroom and puke up everything I ate the day before.

Luke hands me a cold washrag. "I don't even feel bad this time. You brought this on yourself," and he leaves the bathroom. To be honest I don't blame him. I know what I did and I am glad I did it because I'm one step closer. I rinse my mouth out with mouthwash, grab a quick breakfast, and kiss my boys goodbye. "Luke, can you take Michael to school this morning? I have a hit and I have to go to the station now."

He nods his head without speaking. I know he is frustrated with me and I understand but we are getting so close to finding Jack. After killing Arnold, Fredrick and I can't stop. It's a good thing today is Friday; maybe I can spend some time with my family this weekend. Shit! I just realized tomorrow is the dinner with Sarah, Bobby, and their new baby. I totally forgot. I call Luke on my hands-free car phone. "Hey babe, just a reminder that tomorrow we're going to Sarah's for dinner. Could you pick up a few bottles of wine today so we can take it over for them?"

"I haven't forgotten. I'll get it done," he says with a cold tone.

I am not going to fight this right now. "Okay, thank you. You're the best. I love you."

"You too," and he hangs up.

I know I'm a pain in the ass right now, but once this case is closed I will be able to relax some more. I pull into the station, park my car, and speed walk inside. Fredrick sees me rushing in and gets out of his chair. "I have something. It is going down tonight."

"Great, give me details."

We talk about what Jessica looks like and the details of the warehouse. "I pulled up all the abandoned buildings within a thirty-mile radius. From what you described his drive from his place to our station shouldn't be that far. Here are the buildings I found."

He places the list and the map in front of me. "Now from your dream it seems like his place isn't all that big so we can cross out some of these and narrow it down." We go through and cross out about twenty different buildings that don't match the criteria.

"That leaves us with five different buildings," I say with relief.

Fredrick points to one on the map. "This one here would be about a twenty minute drive and this one over here in the opposite direction would be about the same distance."

"So we have a 50/50 shot finding this place."

"It's early in the day. Let's check out both places and once we find the right one, we find Jessica before he even harms her," Fredrick says with determination.

"Perfect." I fill up my coffee mug and we are on our way.

***

Twenty minutes later we pull into abandoned house number one and I can already tell this is not the one. "This isn't it. This one is too tall and there's no gravel road."

"Are you sure?"

"Yes, absolutely. There's no point in wasting time searching because I'm one hundred percent sure."

"Okay, then off to the next one."

As we are pulling into the gravel road that leads to the building shivers take over my body. My stomach begins to rumble. "Stop the car!" I yell. I open the door and puke.

"Are you okay?"

"Yeah, I'm fine." I shrug it off like its nothing. "This is the place."

"Okay, good. Let's stop the car and walk the rest of the way."

"Fredrick, we need to be extra careful. This guy is good. He probably has traps around here or something."

"We will, don't worry." We decide to walk in the grass about twenty yards from the gravel road, but honestly he would see us coming any way we try because this is literally a completely open field, not one tree. I don't see any cars, and no white van. Hopefully he isn't here and we can take Jessica and go, but it's never that easy.

We walk up to the rusted building. It looks like it might collapse any second. There is only one way in and out; one door that doesn't shut all the way. Fredrick peeks in the building and slowly begins to open it. He motions me to wait. I pull out my gun pointing it in front of me. My training is going well and I feel confident after only a few days. We both walk in pointing our guns.

"Over there on the couch," Fredrick says.

I run over to find a young woman who looks exactly like the girl I saw in my dream. "Jessica," I whisper. She is fast asleep. "Fredrick, something is wrong here," I say. "This isn't like Jack; this girl hasn't even been touched." I look back at her pretty face. Her long brown ponytail is lying over her shoulder almost like a blanket.

I try to wake her again when Fredrick stops me. "Linda, you need to see this."

I walk over to a plain metal table resting in the middle of the room where there are two vials full of blood. "No, what did I miss?"

"You didn't miss anything. He has tricked us once again."

"He must have known I was watching him in my dreams. He knew we were coming; he left Jessica here untouched on purpose. I fell right into his trap. I can't believe this."

"Look at this," Fredrick says as he picks up the vials. On the vials there are labels with the numbers seventeen and sixteen.

"He's already got them. We're already too late," I say with despair.

"Maybe. He usually doesn't kill them if he leaves their blood. They're still alive and Jessica may be able to help us. We need to take her back to the station for questions. She might be able to give us some details."

"Okay, but if Jack left her here unharmed for us to find, I doubt she knows anything."

"It's worth a shot," Fredrick says as we walk towards her.

I finally wake her up after a minute of gently shaking her. "Where am I?" she asks with a soft voice.

"Do you remember anything that happened to you last night?" I ask her.

"I was sitting at a coffee shop outside on the patio when I met a nice man."

"Coffee shop? What coffee shop?"

"Sweet N Spice."

My heart drops into my stomach and I look at Fredrick who is standing behind me.

"Okay, what happened next? What did this man look like?"

"Wait, where am I?" She gets up fast and rushes out the door.

"Wait Jessica." We follow behind her.

She turns around quickly and with anger says, "How do you know my name? What's going on? I want answers!"

"Keep her company for a few minutes. I'm going to call in a squad to tear this place a part to see if we can find anything that will help us get a lead on Jack," Fredrick says as he dials a number in his phone.

I nod and calmly walk up to Jessica. "Don't worry, we'll give them to you. I'm Detective Jackson and this is Detective Fredrick, and we're here to help you. Please come with me and sit in the car and we can talk about what happened."

Before she gets into the car she checks her jeans for her phone. "My phone is gone! My sister is probably worried sick about me."

"Do you remember where you last put it?" Just then Fredrick gets into the car as Jessica tells me what happened.

"I was showing that man pictures of the cruise I went on last summer with my sister. I got up to go to the bathroom and that was the last time I remember seeing it. Why can't I remember anything? Why is this happening to me?"

"We believe we know the man who kidnapped you and we hope you can help us find him."

"Did something else happen to me?"

"We don't know, but we'll take you by the hospital to get checked out. We can ask you questions there."

"Okay, but can I use your phone to call my sister?"

I give her my phone and she calls her sister. "Fredrick, let's take her to MUSC." He nods in agreement and drives off.

"Hello, who's this? Where's my sister?" I can hear Jessica panic on the phone. Fredrick and I look at each other; we both know who it is.

I turn around to look at her and she hands me the phone. "It's for you," she says with fear in her voice.

"Jack," I say as I grab the phone and put it on speaker.

"Ah, Linda and Fredrick, I believe you found a piece to my puzzle."

"What are you up to, you son of a bitch?" Fredrick asks with anger.

"Woah now, we don't need to get hostile now do we?"

"I have Jessica's sister and she's fine."

"We need proof, Jack." I can hear rumbling on the phone.

"Jessica, are you okay?" a soft, panicked voice says.

"Kristen, I'm fine but are you okay?"

"I'm scared, help me." Then the rumbling of the phone comes again.

"Okay, that's enough. You know she's alive." Jessica cries in the back of the car.

"What do you want Jack?" Fredrick asks.

"I want you to play my game."

"We already are, asshole," I say with a loud tone.

"Follow my instructions step by step and you'll get this beauty alive and the other one alive too." I look down at the two vials of blood lying in the dashboard with 17 and 16 on them.

"Alright Jack, you win. What do you want us to do?" I say. Fredrick and I glance at each other and take a deep breath.

"Good, I'm glad that you're willing to cooperate with me."

"Get on with it," I say with force. I look through the rearview mirror and see Jessica's horrified, swollen, red, and wet eyes as she stares forward in shock.

"I want all three of you to show up to the place I tell you unarmed and with no other cops or I'll kill everyone in sight."

"Okay, and then what?" Fredrick asks knowing there's more.

"I'll exchange Jessica's sister and this other blonde beauty for Linda." My heart drops deep into my chest and it begins to race.

"What! You really think I'd let you take Linda?" Fredrick yells.

"No, but I know Linda likes to try and save everyone and she knows if she doesn't come two more innocent girls are going to die, along with many more I have planned. Linda, if you come with me I'll stop killing for good."

"And how do we know you're actually going to do that Jack? You're a serial killer; it's your nature to kill. You won't stop now," Fredrick says with panic.

"All I can tell you is that I will stop…whether you believe me or not is up to you."

I don't even know what to think right now. *Why does he want me? Why is he using all this effort to play games with me?*

"And why is it you want me so badly, Jack?" I ask with confidence.

"It's not me who wants you. It's a promise I made to someone that I need to fulfill, and I tend to keep my promises."

"And who is it that you made the promise too?" I ask.

"Well," he says with his high-pitched laugh, "If I tell you, I'd have to kill you."

"You son of a-" I stop Fredrick before he continues and nod my head in reassurance.

"Okay Jack. You win. Where do we meet you?"

Fredrick pulls his car over and puts it in park. "Linda, what the hell are you doing?"

"Relax, this will all work out."

"Yeah Fredrick, it'll all work out," Jack says mockingly.

I feel a soft touch on my right shoulder and I jump, startled. "Linda, you don't have to do this," says Jessica. I'm surprised with her reaction.

"Yes I do. It'll save your sister and the other woman he has. If I don't do something he'll never stop killing."

"What about Luke and Michael? Linda, you have to think of them," Fredrick says.

"I am. The thought of one of them getting hurt because of me sickens me. May has already been hurt, these people or person or whoever won't stop until the conclusion finally comes to an end. I know they'll go after them. Look what happened the other day at Michael's school? I need to take care of this and I need to do it on my own."

Silence embraces the car.

Finally, Fredrick breaks the silence. "Jack, where do you want us to go?" Relief and nerves take over my senses.

"Meet me at the end of Towel's Crossing Dr. off of Savannah Highway at midnight tonight. This place is desolate so I'll know if there are other cops here and as soon as I get suspicious I'll shoot both of these girls in the head. Or better yet, use one of my precious knifes."

Fredrick hangs up the phone, sighs, and puts his head down. "I hope you know we aren't going through with this."

"We have to. I have to save these girls."

"And I have to protect you. I vowed to Luke that I would. I can't lose another one of my partners. We will play this game but we'll become the game makers. We have enough time to figure out a plan. We're heading back to the station now."

"Am I coming with you? I should really get a hold of my mother," Jessica says with her sweet voice. Her long brown hair is sticking to her neck and face from sweat and tears. I can feel her pain and I know it is going to get worse.

"Yes, we need you with us. We'll let you go back and get showered at your mother's and she can bring you to the station. If we don't show up with the both of you then your sister will die. I hate to put it that way, but you have to be here."

She nods her head and more tears fall. "Linda and I will go in and talk with your parents and assure them everything will be okay."

When we pull into a beautiful L-shaped one-story brick house a worried woman rushes out of the door and Jessica races out of the car and falls into her mother's arms. They both fall to their knees and sob, hugging each other tightly. Tears begin to form in my eyes. How am I going to tell her we are going to put her in danger to hopefully save her and her other daughter?

"Don't worry Linda, I'll do all the talking." I swear he can read my mind sometimes.

"I'll be okay; I just have to give myself a second to mentally prepare."

"This job is tougher than you thought…are you sure you want to continue? You could have your life back at the coffee shop."

"You're right, but if I leave now, Jack will never stop. I can't quit this job until this problem is over. It has been going on for too long. Plus, I'll live with my dreams for the rest of my life. I'll always see the crimes coming."

"I'm sorry. I wish I could make this easier for you."

"Believe me Fredrick, you do." His gentle yet tough smile assures me that I am correct.

"Alright, let's do this," he says as he smoothly gets out of the car. He takes off his black sunglasses and puts them in his black t-shirt. I don't think I've ever seen him in any other color than black, but it suits him. It's Fredrick. His tall body walks confidently over to the two women; his short black hair reflecting the sunlight from his gel. He really is a good detective and very trustworthy, unlike Tom. Just thinking about his name gives me chills all over.

I shake my head and re-focus. "Here goes nothing," I whisper to myself. The two women stand up as I walk over.

"Ms. Hensley, I'm so sorry to bother you on such a tough day," Fredrick says as he puts his hand out to shake hers. "My name is Detective Fredrick and this is Detective Jackson." He points to me and I smile and shake her cold clammy hand.

"Thank you for bringing back my daughter safely. Please come inside and I'll make some tea." *Yeah, bring your daughter back and then have to take her back out there.* A sick feeling arises in me.

We follow them inside a beautiful bright house. All the walls are a light yellow with bright blue accents of all kinds of furniture, paintings, and vases. She leads us into her kitchen and dining room that is surrounded by open windows. This house instantly makes me feel better. She turns the stove on and puts the teapot on top. She walks towards us nervously tucking her short brown hair behind her ears. She sits down in the chair next to Jessica and across from us. They look so alike. They are both petite but full of love. As I walked into the house I didn't see any pictures of a father or husband. I wonder how long she's been caring for her daughters by herself.

"Please tell me what happened to my daughter," she asks as she puts her hand over Jessica's on the table.

Fredrick begins to speak and tells her about Jack, the killings, the vials of blood, and everything else. I sit back in my chair remember every detail as he says them. I watch the horror in Ms. Hensley's eyes as she realizes what her daughter has been through and this is only the beginning.

She turns to Jessica and kisses her on the forehead. "Honey, how-how are you doing?"

"I'm okay Mom, but the story gets worse."

"How can it get any worse?" she says holding back her tears.

'Ma'am, we're so sorry to tell you this, but Jack kidnapped Kristen and has her hostage."

She begins to sob and Jessica holds her. "How can this be? What does he want with my daughters?"

I decide to step in. "Jack doesn't want your daughters, Miss. He wants me."

"What does wanting you have anything to do with my daughters?"

"Jack is a smart man who likes to play games. He has been after some of us at the Charleston Police Department and he knows I'll do whatever it takes to save people. So he wants to exchange your daughter and another woman for me."

"But why you?"

"We aren't sure about that and we're trying to get to the bottom of it," Fredrick chimes in.

"What will he do to you?" she asks as the tears begin to fade.

"I'm not sure, but I have an idea," I say as I look at Fredrick. It becomes silent as Ms. Hensley thinks about what was just thrown at her.

"I want my daughter back," says Ms. Hensley changing her tone from sadness to anger.

"You'll get her back. I'm forming a plan that will save everyone," Fredrick says. I look at Fredrick with a questioning look wondering what he is planning. I know if Jack suspects anything then everyone is dead.

"What are you going to do?" she asks.

"I'm going to need Jessica's help. Jack told us he needs to see the three of us in order to get Kristen and the other woman he has kidnapped back."

Jessica's mom stands up from her chair. "And put her back into harm's way? What happens if I lose both of my girls?"

"That won't happen, Miss."

"But you can't promise that. No, I won't let you do this."

"Ma'am, if we show up without Jessica he'll kill Kristen and the other girl without any hesitation. It's all part of his game we have to play or more people will die. I believe my plan will work and I'll be able to get both of your daughters out of there alive and keep Detective Jackson with us."

She becomes silent with a blank look on her face. "Mom, sit back down please," Jessica says as she touches her back for comfort. "I heard Jack myself over the phone – he'll kill Kristen if I'm not there and I don't want to be responsible for that. I want to get revenge on what this guy did to me and I want to help these detectives achieve that. I'm going with them."

Fredrick and I watch and listen as they discuss this decision. Finally, the mom gives in, "Okay fine, but I want updates every minute!" she says with a worried tone.

"I promise I'll text as often as I can. And I'll call you when Kristen and I are back in the car on our way home safe tonight."

Fredrick glances at his watch. Time is ticking away and we need to get working on whatever plan he has. "I'm sorry but we have to get going. I need to get this plan in action."

"Okay, please be safe honey," Ms. Hensley says as she kisses Jessica on the forehead and they hug so tight as if it were their last hug.

Ms. Hensley walks toward us with confidence. "If your plan doesn't work and the only option you have left is turning Detective Jackson over to him, you'll do it. We 're talking about my only children; they're all I have left in this world." Ms. Hensley may be petite but she has a big heart.

"I've already decided I was going to do that. You don't have to worry. One way or another you'll get both of your daughters back by tonight," I say.

As we close the doors to his Ford before putting the key in this ignition Fredrick turns to me. "You won't have to worry about turning yourself over to him. I'll make sure of it."

I nod my head and smile back. I know that I'll have to do it and I'm mentally prepared for this task. I put up a good fight with Tom and I can do it with Jack. *I just hope it doesn't come down to that.*

A few miles down from Towel's Crossing Drive in an empty house.

Friday 5:00 p.m.

I am getting closer to finally putting an end to this mission. I'll be happy when it's all done so I can stop taking orders from someone who isn't even in the picture anymore and get on with my life. But a promise is a promise and it is even more precious when it deals with family. I glance at the picture of the two of us side by side. "I promise you brother, I'll finish this. Soon there will be no more turning in your grave."

I put the picture back in my wallet and start working on my plans. I know Fredrick and Linda won't be coming alone. I have to make it known that I am always one step ahead of him. These traps will catch anyone coming from any distance around this street. They will try to hide behind the trees and use the darkness to their advantage but I will succeed in making sure that doesn't happen. I put rope in my bag and set out to make the traps.

I glance at Kristen and Sherry taped up with their hands tied together sitting on the couch. Their eyes are filled with fear, which is exactly how I want them. I shut out the lights, walk out the door, and prepare for the beginning of the end.

Jackson Household
5:15 p.m.

I walk into the house with nerves running through me. How am I going to tell Luke and Michael what I'm about to do? If I give Luke all the details he won't let me go and then innocent people will die. Luke gets up from the dinner table and rushes over to me. He can tell there is something wrong. I must be giving it away with my face expression but I can't help it. "Babe, what's wrong?" Luke says as he takes my arm and helps me to the couch. Michael is at the dinner table but I know he will be listening.

"I have to do something tomorrow that you won't like, but I have to because innocent lives are at stake if I don't."

He shakes his head. "What is it this time?"

"Fredrick and I are meeting with Jack to get back two girls he has taken. We're taking Jessica with us, the girl we found today. Jack has her sister and another female about the same age. Jack said he'll give them back if he gets to chat with me." *I can't tell him the whole truth.*

"What does he mean by chat with you?"

"I'm not sure. I don't know what he wants with me or why I'm so important to him, but I want to find that out for myself."

"I'm assuming Fredrick will have some kind of backup plan?"

"Yes. Fredrick is doing some planning now and after I eat with you and Michael I'm heading to the station to prepare. Everything will be okay and this is our one chance to get this guy."

"Okay, but I've had enough scares and I don't think I can handle anymore. If something happens to you after this case, you're done with the CPD and I don't care what you say because this job is too much. You have a family now and more important things to worry about. We constantly worry about your life and I don't know how much more I can take."

"What are you saying, Luke?"

"I'm saying you're going to have to make a decision once this case is over."

"What kind of decision?" My heart drops into my stomach pounds so fast I can barely stand.

"I'd rather not talk about it now, but you're going to have to think about where your priorities lie. Now go hug and kiss Michael and assure him you'll be okay again."

Is Luke making me choose between my family and my job? He's right though; I feel I've barely had any time with Michael since I came back from my coma. Am I getting too obsessed with this job? I can't stop now. I'm still in danger, and if I'm in danger so is my family. Luke may not see that right now, but I'm doing this for the protection of my family. Once this case is over it won't be like this ever again. At least I hope so.

I walk over to Michael and take a deep breath before I begin to speak. But he takes the words out of my mouth. "Mommy, I know you'll be okay. Just go and catch the bad guy. I'll be praying for you."

He gives me a big hug and kisses me on the forehead. Gosh, he is so grown up for six years old. And it's because of me. He's had to learn how to grow up without a mother and live with a mother whose dreams he can see. *Poor Michael, what have I done?*

"I love you Michael and I'll be back and here when you wake up tomorrow morning. I'll cook you a bunch of pancakes."

"Okay Mom," he says in a voice that speaks, "I don't believe you." I can't believe it's come down to this.

"I love you, Michael." I say again with a stern voice and I look him in the eyes.

"I love you too, Mom," he says looking back at me with watery eyes.

My eyes begin to tear up as I walk towards the door. *This has to be the end, tonight.* I turn around and Luke is standing behind me. He gives me a cold kiss on the cheek and then walks away. I walk out of the door feeling more regret and pain than I've ever felt. *It's almost over.*

Chapter 7

The car is silent as we make our way to Towel's Crossing Drive. I know their hearts are beating as fast as mine. "Fredrick, if this goes south, I'm going with Jack."

"No you're not. I won't let you do that."

"It's my life or three innocent lives. I'm not taking that chance. Plus, we don't know if he'll actually kill me. I can put up a good fight, from what training I've had from you and Luke, I can hold my own."

"I believe you can, but for how long? It doesn't matter anyway; you won't have to do that with the plan we've set up. Our men are already surrounding the road as we speak."

"You know Jack has his own plan too."

"Yes I know and that's why we're staying on top of him. As soon as they have sight of Jack, the two girls he has, and us they'll smoke the area. We'll grab the two girls and all get out of there safely. My men will attack and grab Jack and that will be the end of it."

I sigh, saying, "I hope this works."

Jessica stays silent in the back seat. I know exactly how she is feeling. That is what I went through when Tom kidnapped May. I could never stop worrying or get the sick feeling out of my stomach. I turn and look back at her. I can see her eyes are swollen even through her reading glasses. "I'll make sure you get Kristen back alive tonight. I promise you." She nods and her long brown ponytail sways forward. She ducks her head to try and hide the tears.

As we pull up close to the road, Fredrick backs the car down the road so we have an easy get away. He stops about 100 feet before the end. We look at each other and nod our heads. "It's time to put this to an end," Fredrick says with confidence.

Car lights suddenly appear bright behind us. We turn to look, squinting our eyes. "He's ready for us," I say nervously. *Stay strong, Linda. You have one mission here. Keep these girls alive.*

The three of us get out of our car and begin walking towards the car. Nothing but the sound of gravel beneath our feet and the sway of wind in the trees surround our senses. The piercing light from the car dims and I see three black figures standing only a few feet from us. As we move closer I begin to see their faces. Jack's unforgettable big nose, long black hair, and scrawny face along with two beautiful women whose faces are covered in dry mascara tears.

Jack steps forward. "I see you brought what I want."

"Yes, you finally have me, Jack."

"I want you to come with me first."

"No way. You don't think I know that line by now?" Fredrick says.

"Alright then, exchange at the same time."

I nod over to Fredrick and he slightly shakes his head. *Where are the smoke bombs?*

Fredrick glances around waiting for the smoke to appear.

"Why Fredrick, it appears you're looking for something. Men to help you? Well I doubt they'll be here. I already took care of that." He laughs his high-pitched laugh.

I begin walking forward and Fredrick shakes his head. Suddenly I see a figure appear behind Jack. Then I hear a gunshot that seems to echo through the woods and I see Jack's surprised face as he falls to the ground. The girls begin to cry with relief and Kristen makes her way into Jessica's arms.

The cop who shot Jack limps over to us. "That bastard had different traps set up. I tripped over a wire and was shot with an arrow." I see the arrow sticking out of the right side of his abdomen.

"Thank you, Officer Jordan. Thank you so much."

He nods. "Fredrick, you need to call ambulance and back up now. A lot of our men are wounded out there. I don't know what this creep is or how he got all the equipment for those traps, but he's one brilliant son of a bitch."

Fredrick makes the phone calls and I go to comfort the girls. I glance back and see Jack lying face down on the ground. It looks like the gunshot was to the back. Blood has already made its way into a puddle.

I can hear the sirens come closer and I speak with Sherry, the other woman Jack kidnapped, and ask her questions. Kristen and Jessica are reunited and already laughing about the memories they have had together. I am so glad this is all over.

The ambulances pull in and Fredrick and I assist the girls over to them. Sergeant Gordon struts over to us. "Good work, detectives. Now where is this son of a bitch?"

"He's right over there in front of that car." The three of us walk over there. I feel my eyes grow wide with fear.

"Where the fuck is he?' I scream. All I see is a pool of blood and Jack's body is gone.

"There's no way he could have gotten up, let alone survived! He was shot in the back."

"This can't be happening. He can't be that far away from here. He's severely wounded and on foot," I say with anger.

"Everyone search the premises now! No one goes home until we have Jack in custody!" yells Sergeant Gordon.

I follow Fredrick as he makes his way off the roads and he turns quickly and faces me. "Linda, go home," he says with force. I can tell he doesn't want to hear any of my complaints about going. I am now the target; I would be stupid to stay.

"Okay, but do me a favor and catch this guy."

"I'll try my hardest. Here, take my keys so you can get safely home." He hands me the keys and I look in his eyes. Even in the dark I can tell they are filled with fear and anger. I grab the keys and head home.

***

Jackson Household
1:30 a.m.

All the lights are off as I enter the house. Usually Luke stays up and waits for me but not this time. He isn't going to hang on much longer and I have to do something about it. I quietly walk into Michael's room and kiss him gently on the forehead. "I love you sweetheart," I whisper.

He slowly opens his eyes. "I love you too, Mom, no matter what." Tears form in my eyes as I watch his eyes slowly close. I go straight into the bathroom and close the door so it won't wake Luke. I turn on the hot shower and let down my long black hair. I take a quick look at myself in the mirror. *Who have I become?* I look at my tired green eyes and begin to cry. The scariest thought is losing my family but this isn't over yet and if I don't help stop Jack he will come after my family. Luke may see this as a vendetta that I want to end, but it is more about protecting my family. I wish I could get that through his head.

I wipe the tears from my eyes as I feel a warm hand touch my shoulder. I turn to face Luke and he embraces me in his arms. He turns on the shower and guides me through the glass door. I turn around and he slowly takes off his boxers and joins me. He begins rinsing my hair. The warmth from the water and his touch is soothing. I look into his seductive brown eyes, "Luke I-" He puts his finger to my lips and drops his hand slowly. He kisses me softly and it feels as if time has frozen and everything becomes numb. We don't have to speak to know what each another is feeling. I can't lose him, I won't. After this case with Jack is over I'm done with the CPD. I'm tired of putting my family in danger and my life on the line every day.

Luke begins washing my body, making sure to clean and rub all the right areas. He turns me around to face the water as he rubs off the soap. His touch makes everything else in the world disappear. He comes closer to me and kisses the back of my neck.

Abandoned Brick House
2:15 a.m.

"Linda, you bitch, you will pay!" I scream out in agony. I dial my cousin Kim who is a doctor. "Kim, I need you please. I've been shot in the shoulder from the back and I can't go to the hospital. Please hurry. I'm in an abandoned brick house 1309 West Highland Street." Her response was hanging up the phone. I know she will be here. I lie face down on the brown rugged couch kicking myself for letting this get out of control! I am much further away than what I want to be. I'm going to have to be patient, I will get Linda, and I will get justice for my brother's death. It's only a matter of time.

I feel myself fading. I hear a door slam and hands on my back. "Don't worry Jack, I'm here." I hear Kim's soft voice fading and everything is getting darker.

Saturday October 8
Sarah and Bobby's House

I sit on the blue leather couch admiring Michael and the baby. Everyone looks so happy and this is exactly what we needed. Sarah invited May and Charlie. It is time to talk wedding details. I take a sip of my fruity white wine as I listen to May talk. "I'm only having you and Sarah as my bridesmaids. I want to keep it small. I want to have the ceremony at the beach and then I thought maybe we could do the reception at the coffee shop. Would that be okay?" May asks Sarah and Bobby hesitantly.

"Of course! We'd be honored!" Sarah says with excitement.

"The coffee shop is the perfect place! There's a ton of room inside, and we could easily move chairs and tables off to the side to create a dance floor, plus we can open all the doors to the patio out back!" I say. I stop myself and laugh. "Sorry, sometimes I forget I don't own the shop anymore."

"Well, if you ever decide you want to be a part of the shop again, we'd love to have you," Bobby says with a slight tone of desperation.

"Well I might take you up on that in the near future."

"Really? Is everything okay at the station?" May asks.

"It's getting too dangerous. I'm stuck on a case right now that's hard to solve. Long story short, this man is worse than Tom." I look at them and they are speechless. I haven't said his name in front of everyone, especially May since the incident. Charlie rubs May's back.

"I'm sorry, I shouldn't have said anything."

"Are you going to be okay? Why can't you leave now?"

"It's complicated but I can't." I get up and walk outside for some air. May walks out a few minutes later.

"Sis, is everything okay? It has been days since you've contacted myself or Mom and Dad. We're all worried, including Luke."

I look up into the beautiful pink and orange sky. The reflection of the colors shine off the calming water from the bay. "How do you know Luke is worried?"

"He called me. That's the main reason I'm here."

"What did he say to you?" I turn to face her and watch her beautiful blue eyes turn sad with tears.

"He's worried that you're going to get yourself killed, and quite frankly so am I."

I start to cry. "I know, I'm worried too, but I can't stop now. Jack is too dangerous and vindictive. If I stop now, he'll get to me eventually, and he'll probably get to my family first. He won't stop until I'm dead and if he wants to, he'll make me suffer first. He likes the chase with me and if I stop he'll go to Michael, as he's already tried. If I stop, we're all dead."

She hugs me tightly and whispers in my ear, "I want this all to be over. I hate seeing you like this. You've been through hell and back."

I look her in the eyes. "This is worse than hell. Michael can see my dreams too."

"Oh my God, since when?"

"Since forever. He's living through this as much as me and there's nothing I can do about it. I've already been to the doctors and my brainwaves are almost inhuman, and Michael's ability is passed on from me. There's absolutely nothing I can do. Even when Jack is dead, our lives will never be normal."

May grabs my face with her soft hands. "You'll find a way; I know you'll fight until you do." She kisses me on the forehead. "Just deal with Jack and be done. Let everything else fall into place. If these dreams continue, do what you were doing before. Call the cops with the information and then let it be. You can't continue to be responsible for all the crime for the rest of your life or you'll lose the two most important people in your life." I look through the window at Luke talking with Bobby and Michael asleep on the couch. I look at Luke's face and I see fear all over it. I haven't seen him smile in days.

I look back at May. "You're right, May. Once Jack is caught or better dead, this is over." She lightly smiles and rubs my arm and we head back inside. Both the baby and Michael are asleep so we decide to head into their kitchen for one last round of wine.

We are sitting around the table talking more about me coming back to the shop and making some changes. Then a flash hits me with an instant headache. "Linda, you got away once but that won't happen again. I'll be seeing you soon." I hear his laughter piercing through my ears. I fall to the floor on my knees in pain. Luke rushes over to me but I am sidetracked from the cry out by Michael.

"Michael," I say as I rush up fighting the headache as I walk into the living room. He rushes off the couch and into my arms. I feel my shoulder get wet with his tears. "It's okay, sweetie."

"Mom, I heard him in my dream, I saw him. He said he'll be seeing you soon."

"I know, I heard him too."

"He's communicating through Michael's dreams even when I'm awake. I don't know how I'm ever going to catch him," I say as I look up at everyone standing around us. I hold Michael and rock him slowly.

As I get ready to fall asleep I think about how nice it would be if I could have a normal life. But God created me this way and there is a reason for it.

I am walking along Rainbow Row. It is a clear night and it seems like the stars are shining brighter than ever. I continue to walk when I hear a faint scream. I stop in my tracks and listen closely. I hear screaming and banging as if it's coming from inside a car. I walk towards the sound and find myself walking onto Vanderhorst Wharf, which is deserted except for one car. The screams become louder. I walk towards a blue Chevy truck where I can see clear signs of struggle. I look at the license plate and pull out my gun. I open the door and a man who's not Jack turns around and looks at me with shock.

"Please help me," the girl is crying out. She is kicking and her hair is moving all the over the place. The man hits her in the face and pulls a gun from his back pocket and points it at me.

"Get out of here now and you'll live." We point our guns at each other and before I pull the trigger everything fades.

I open my eyes to the ceiling. I turn over slowly to grab my phone. I'm upset that it wasn't Jack. I wonder what his next move will be as I call Fredrick. "What do you have for me?" Fredrick says.

"You sound wide awake. It's four in the morning. What are you doing up on a Sunday?"

"I'm at the office. I can't sleep much and I won't until Jack is caught. Plus, you would have woken me up anyway," he says with a short laugh.

It brought a smile to my face. "Tonight at 1:15, there will be an attack in a blue Chevy license plate MBY765 along Vanderhorst Warf. The attacker is a white male, with short black hair, from what I could tell medium height, and he wears a diamond earring in his right ear. The victim is female and all I could see was her long blonde hair, and that she was wearing a black and red skirt, black heels, and a white tank top." I take a breath.

"Wow, great work Linda. You're getting the hang of this."

"Yeah, too much."

"Listen, I know you didn't picture yourself in this kind of a career, but you're good at it, and a great partner." The feeling of guilt takes over as I imagine myself telling him I'm quitting.

"Thanks Fredrick."

"Go back to sleep and enjoy your Sunday tomorrow. I'll see you Monday morning."

"I'd say the same for you, but I know you won't stop," I say with a smile.

"You know me well, partner." I hang up the phone and put it back on the table. I'd miss working with Fredrick, Sergeant Gordon, and Captain Sanders; they've treated me well. I turn to look at Luke who is sound asleep. But I don't want to lose the love of my life. I kiss him on the forehead and close my eyes.

***

Monday October 16
CPD

"It has been over a week and not a single dream or sign of Jack," I say to Fredrick with frustration.

"Maybe he's dead."

"He isn't. He came to me through Michael's dream the other weekend. He must be taking his time and scheming a plan. He'll come back and with even more vengeance than before."

"And we'll be ready for him. Until then we have a bank robber we need to catch. He's hit two banks in the last two days. Today would mark day three and we need to stop him before he hits again."

"On it." I grab some coffee and begin doing some research on the last two banks he hit and what his patterns were. I get a flash and know what is about to happen. I control it, listen, and close my eyes. I can picture the bank robber going into Chase. It is bright out but I don't know the time. The flash is over and I open my eyes only to catch Fredrick staring at me.

"Is everything okay?"

"Yeah, Chase bank downtown. Let's go now," I say as he grabs his keys and we head out. As we get into the car I get a phone call from Harper Elementary School. This can't be good.

81

"Mrs. Jackson, this is Ms. Williams. I'm calling about Michael."

"Why, what's wrong? Is he okay?"

"He's fine except for the fact that he fell asleep in class and woke up in a panic. He broke out into a cold sweat and was crying. He's here with me now and says he's fine and wants to go back to class. But I'd advise you to take him to a doctor." I know exactly what happened with Michael. That is why I had the flash, as he was dreaming it.

"Okay, thank you. I'll be there to pick him up."

"I'm sorry Fredrick, you're going to have to catch this one on your own. It's Michael, I have to pick him up from school."

· "Is he okay?"

"Yes, but unfortunately, he takes after his mother too much."

"Well then he's a lucky boy. Take care of him today and don't worry about coming back. I'll see you tomorrow."

"Thanks, Fredrick. Text me after you catch the robber."

He nods his head and I walk to my car. I call Luke on the way.

Harper Elementary School
9:30 a.m.

Luke and I enter Harper Elementary School hand in hand. I can see Michael in the chair across from Ms. Williams with his head down. He hates getting in trouble and I feel like it's my fault. I knock and she waves us in. Michael gets up and gives me a hug. He whispers in my ear, "I'm sorry Mom, I didn't mean to get in trouble."

"Shh, don't be sorry, you helped catch a bad guy today." I look in his eyes and see a sparkle and a small smile grows on his face." Luke and I sit in a chair along with Michael. Ms. William's green eyes are staring at us with concern. She pushes her short black hair behind her ear and clears her throat.

"I'm shocked with Michael's recent actions in school. Falling asleep in class isn't like him. I'm worried that there's something going on at home that's keeping him from sleeping." *Oh no, I hope she doesn't think we are bad parents. This is too hard to explain to her and she will never understand.*

I clear my throat, "I know and I'm so sorry about this. As you know, Michael is a very good boy. He has been experiencing night terrors and he hasn't been sleeping much. We've taken him to the doctor and they're working to help him."

She slightly raises her right eyebrow and looks at us as if she doesn't believe the story. "I'm sorry to hear that. Mrs. Jackson, if you don't mind, you currently work for CPD, correct?"

I gulp. "Yes that's correct."

"Do you think Michael overhears some of the stories you tell Mr. Jackson and that could lead to the night terrors?"

"I try not to speak about work to anyone, including Luke, but sometimes I say things and I make sure Michael isn't around. Michael is a very creative and imaginative boy. He's smart for his age and understands things most six year olds don't."

"I completely agree Mrs. Jackson, but a mature boy who has night terrors? Obviously something is bothering him."

"You're right and as I said he's currently seeing a doctor about it," I say as I begin to get frustrated. Her tone seems to be accusing me.

"I'd like to see the doctor's notes when he goes. I'd like to keep a record of his visits since he's experiencing night terrors at school."

"Okay, I'll be sure to get a copy for you."

"Great. I'm only concerned for his well-being. I know he's in good hands," she says as she looks at Luke and smiles.

I stand up holding in my anger. "I'll be sure to get you those doctor's notes. I'd like to go ahead and sign Michael out."

She takes her glare away from Luke. "Sure thing, Mrs. Jackson." As we walk out the door the anger begins to show.

"What's wrong?" asks Luke.

"Really? You didn't see it? She was basically interrogating me while she was all starry eyed with you. She doesn't think I'm a good mother...I can tell."

"Don't you think you're over reacting?" Luke asks as he opens the car door for me.

"No I'm not, but she doesn't matter. What matters is that Michael is safe."

I look at Michael in the back seat and smile at him. "Thank you for helping us today, but I don't want you to make a habit out of this. I can't get any more phone calls from Ms. Williams."

Michael's innocent bright blue eyes stare back. "I know Mom, but I can't help it. I sleep at night and I'm not tired when I'm at school. I'm sorry."

I rub his short soft black hair. "I know, honey. I love you." We spend the rest of the day together as a family, which is exactly what we needed.

***

I am walking down a dark road when I see something on the ground glare from the streetlight. I walk closely towards it and stop dead in my tracks when I realize what it is. I quickly glance around to see if anyone is near me, but it is in the dead of the night and no one is out. I bend down and pick up the vial of blood that has the number 17 on it. "He's back," I whisper to myself. I look ahead and see another vial of blood and another. There are tons of vials of blood all leading somewhere. I follow the vials picking them up as I go. My stomach becomes sick thinking of all these innocent victims. The last vial of blood, which has the number 2 on it lies on the doorstep of some abandoned brick house. The door is a little open already. I take a big gulp and I open the door fully.

Candles are lit providing just enough light for me to see. There are couches and tables covered with sheets. In the middle of the living room is a small round, brown table. There is a picture frame and a piece of white paper. I lay the vials of blood down and pick up the picture frame. My heart is racing with fear. "No, no this can't be," I say out loud and stumble. It's a picture of Jack with his arm around another man. A man I'll never forget. A man I'll never be able to truly run away from. The man I never thought I'd see again….

Tom.

Above Tom's picture are the letters in red, B-R-O-T-H-E-R. I drop the picture frame on the floor and watch the glass shatter.

Now I see why Jack won't stop until he has me. I can't believe this. I look down at the sixteen vials of blood lying on the table. I know his number one is supposed to be me. I pick up the note and begin to read:

My dearest Linda,

You are probably suffering from shock after looking at that picture and that is exactly how I want you to feel. I made a dying promise to my brother Tom that I would finally put an end to you. I won't stop until my promise is fulfilled. Tom was my last close living relative and now I have nothing to live for. Well, I have one relative but she is a doctor and has her own life and I'm nothing to her. Tom told me to make sure you suffer and to finish

what he started. You have sixteen lives at your disposal and I can murder them all with one touch of a button. If you even think about telling your partner what has happened, they will all die. If you do exactly as I say, I will personally call Detective Fredrick and give him the location of all the girls and how to release them. Meet me at this exact location tomorrow night at 11:45 p.m. Don't even think of coming with someone else or everyone dies. I will put this to an end tomorrow. See you then, Mrs. Jackson.
  With Love,
  Jack

  I close my eyes hoping to wake up. "Wake up, Linda."

  As I open my eyes tears form instantly. *How am I going to get away with this? If I leave the house at night Luke will ask questions. I will have to make one convincing lie. Leaving my family is going to be the hardest thing I've had to do, but there is no other way.* I close my eyes and I can feel the tears fall down my cheeks. There's only one thing I can do: kill him.

Chapter 8

"Y̶ou're awfully quiet this morning. Is everything okay?" asks Luke as he pours coffee for me.

My stomach is in knots as I answer back, "I'm okay. This whole thing with Jack has been bugging me ever since it started."

"You haven't heard from him in a while though. Maybe he has moved on?"

"Yeah, I don't believe that."

Luke sits next to me and grabs my hands. "Linda, leave the job please. Look at what it's doing to you and to us."

Tears begin to form in my eyes, "I know and I'll leave as soon as Jack is either dead or in jail." He sighs in return. "I'd prefer him dead to be honest, then you could really move on."

"Yeah, you and me both." Luke bites a piece of his peanut butter toast as his phone rings.

"Yeah, I'm on my way," he says as he hangs up the phone. "I'm running late for a knee surgery. I can't believe I forgot. I'm too worried about you." He shakes his head with disappointment.

"Go, I'll take Michael to school."

"Thanks." I go to kiss Luke but he kisses me on the forehead instead. I slump back down in my chair. *What am I doing? What should I do?*

Michael walks over with his backpack on. He is dressed in blue jeans, a white and grey stripped shirt, and Sperry's shoes. He is so handsome and so mature; I don't think I'll ever get over that. I see him and I start to cry.

He comes and gives me a hug. "Mom, it's going to okay. Dad will understand. You have to save those women."

I look him in the eyes. "Michael, you saw my dream?"

"Yes, and I heard your thoughts as you read the letter from Jack."

"I can't leave you and your Dad. He's already so upset with me."

"He loves you Mom, he just needs time. I promise, everything will be okay."

"I'm so sorry you're dealing with all of this. No six-year-old boy should ever see these things."

"Stop saying you're sorry. I'm made this way and I'm handling it. If you don't do what he asked you won't forgive yourself if all those women die."

"Yeah, but maybe Fredrick could find information about missing women and track them somehow. Their computer technology is great and sixteen women all missing at the same time? How is it not already on the news?"

"Because he's a bad man, Mom."

I nod my head in agreement. "You're going to be late for school. Come on, let's head out."

Michael gives me a hug and kiss before he gets out of the car. "I love you, Mom."

"I love you too, Michael and don't worry, I'll be back and when this is all over, and I'll dedicate my time to you, Luke, and the coffee shop. Things will get back to normal." He smiles and walks towards the school.

Abandoned Brick House
7:30 a.m.

I clear a table and chairs to get ready for what is going to happen tonight. She better show up or I will have to take the next step and turn to her family. I glance at the sixteen TV monitors and watch those pretty women beg for their lives. No one can hear them and no one will find them. I sharpen all of my knives and line them up on the table from shortest to longest. I intend to use every one of these knives on Linda. Tom wanted me to make her pay and that is what I will do. "I promise you, big brother, I'll end this just the way you want."

I lay the empty vial with the label that reads #1 and set it next to the knives. "I can't wait to see Fredrick's reaction when they find out whose blood this is." I laugh.

I get in my blue van and stop at the store to get some trash bags and plastic. I can't wait for the fun to begin!

***

I call in sick today because I know Fredrick will know something is wrong with me and I can't lie to his face. I go the Waterfront Park and clear my head. I have to come up with a plan to kill Jack, save the women, and get out alive. I've had training and I know how to use my gun, but Jack is beyond the training I've had. He is smart and out for justice. As I sit and ponder I text May, Mom, and Dad to tell them I love them. I don't know if I'll make it out alive but I know I would never forgive myself if I didn't tell them I loved them. I send one last text to Luke. Then I sit and admire the beautiful view of the bay wishing I had never been blessed (or cursed) with such a dreadful talent.

Abandoned Brick House
11:40 p.m.

I grab my gun and place it in my ankle holster even though he will probably check my entire body. I place a small knife inside my hip that is strapped in by my underwear and shorts. And then I place a small knife that is protected by a case in my sports bra. I look at my watch as 11:44 turns into 11:45. I take a big sigh, close my eyes, and get ready. I begin to walk up the concrete steps and I notice the door is slightly open.

"Linda stop." I hear a whisper. I turn in confusion and I see Fredrick standing behind me.

"No! Leave now! You're going to ruin everything. There are sixteen innocent lives at stake! Please go."

He grabs my arm and pulls me aside. "Listen," he whispers. "The women are already safe. Michael told Luke and I everything. He knew where this house was. We were able to track the women from the cameras Jack had set up. We came by earlier when he was out. I'm here now to stop him because he still thinks you're coming."

"It's past time. If he suspects anything he'll be gone."

"Stay here, I have back up surrounding the neighborhood, so he isn't getting away this time."

I do as I'm told and I pull out my gun ready to go. Only a few minutes later Fredrick walks out of the door. "He's gone. He left everything out like he was ready. He couldn't have gone that far."

"Dammit! He must have seen us outside. He's always one step ahead. I'm just glad the women are okay."

"All units report. Jack is missing; search the entire neighborhood and go house to house. He has to be here somewhere."

I walk up behind Fredrick. "Where's Michael and Luke?"

"They're safe at the station with Sergeant Gordon."

"Okay good."

"Detective Fredrick, you need to come over to the end of West Highland Street, there's a dead end and you need to see this."

Fredrick and I look at each other and jump in his car. It is only two blocks down. I hear ambulance sirens in the distance and I see the cops standing over something. My heart begins to race as we walk towards the circle. Tears form as I see three dead bodies lying in the street, blood still pouring from their heads. Three innocent women that were walking minding their own business; three innocent women dead because of me. They are lying on their stomachs and the backs of the shirts are ripped open and engraved on their skin with a knife is 17 and on the other woman is 16, and 15 on the third woman. Blood is dripping from the numbers. "This is fresh as in a few minutes ago. How the fuck did he get away with this?" In between the bodies is a vial and a piece of paper. I bend down to get it.

"A vial filled with blood," I say as I show Fredrick the number 14 labeled on it. "He must have had this woman already, preparing for a change up. I didn't see any of this coming." I look at Fredrick, "Why did you have to stop me? Because of me, now I have three more women's blood on my hands. Now we're starting back from scratch."

I open the piece of paper. "You bitch, you're going to make me have to do this the hard way, aren't you? You're going to pay even more now." I crumple the paper and throw it down at Fredrick's feet.

"Linda-" I walk away before he can speak.

CPD
Midnight

When I walk into the station I see Michael asleep on the chair and Luke standing beside him staring out of the window. Sergeant Gordon walks up to me. "Are you okay?"

"You realize because of what just happened, Jack is going to torture and kill more innocent people? And now my family's lives are even more at risk." My heart is racing with anger.

"I know and I'm sorry but when Fredrick told me about this I couldn't let you risk your own life. I thought our plan would work."

"Yeah, but it didn't. This was my one chance to end everything and now we have no idea where he is or what move he'll make next. I want cops surrounding my parents' house, May's house, and our house at all times. I want a cop at school with Michael and one following us wherever we go. I can't lose my family."

"Understood, and I've already talked with cops about protection for everyone in your family."

"Thank you, now I'm taking Michael and Luke and going home."

Jackson Household
1:00 a.m.

I tuck Michael into bed and jump in the shower. Luke hasn't said one word to me and I know a fight is brewing. I walk into the room and Luke is sitting up in bed staring into space. "Luke I-" He stops me.

"No, don't say it. You lied to me and didn't even give me any information about what was going down tonight. You were just going to commit suicide without even telling me! How can I trust you?"

I put my head down and tears begin to form. "You don't understand where I'm coming from," I say as I stand in front of him.

He gets up from the bed and is now standing face to face with me. "You're right, I don't get where you're coming from because you never tell me anything anymore. Once again my family is at risk."

"It's my family too Luke, and you don't think I feel like shit because of everything that's happening? Well, I do! I didn't tell you about any of it because I knew you'd try to stop me and I was doing this to protect our family! I have no choice right now. Jack is going to do whatever it takes to hurt me and kill me. I can't just leave and forget about what is happening. He'll continue to kill until he's killed you, Michael, May, my parents, and me. I can't live with that. I can't live with always watching over my shoulder, always worrying about protecting our family; it's taking a toll on me. I just want this to be over."

"It's taking a toll on me too," Luke says as he walks out of the bedroom.

I fall to me knees bawling. "Why is this happening to me… why?" I say out loud as I continue to cry. Everything is falling apart around me. My world is slowly dying and this is exactly what Tom wanted…he promised…and he's winning.

***

I look over at the clock and it reads 5:15 a.m. I haven't slept at all and I know I won't get any sleep. I get out of bed and put on my black pants and black t-shirt. I stare at my badge asking myself why I got involved in the first place, and then put it on my hip. I pull my black hair into a ponytail and brush my teeth. I walk into Michael's room and kiss him on the forehead. "I love you," I whisper.

I walk downstairs and I see Luke asleep on the couch. My heart aches for what is going on, but I know I can put an end to it. I just have to kill Jack. I grab a protein bar and head to the station.

CPD
5:50 a.m.

I walk in to see Fredrick sitting at his desk. "I'm guessing you couldn't sleep either?" I say to him as I set my purse and jacket on my desk. I go over and pour some coffee into my mug.

"Linda, I'm so sorry for what happened yesterday."

"I'm sorry, Fredrick. I shouldn't have yelled at you. I know you were trying to do the best thing by saving everyone, but Jack is too good for that. You know he's Tom's brother?"

"I saw a picture of him and Tom on his mantel when I searched the house, and I put two and two together."

"Tom is dead and still controlling my life. He promised me he'd do that. I just didn't think he had that much power. I should have known better. I feel like my dreams are worthless now. I can't even see Jack coming. I can't concentrate on any other crimes that are happening in Charleston. I feel like a big failure."

"I understand how you're feeling. But we won't stop until this is

91

over. This is the hard part, overcoming the stress, fear, and anxiety. It's time we step up our game and beat Jack before his next move."

I swallow the sweet coffee. "Okay, let's get working."

"I had Christopher run the blood sample of the next victim," Fredrick says as he hands me the paper.

"How did he do it that fast?"

"I called him and he came in early. He wants to help catch Jack just as much."

"Wow, that's nice of him." I look down at the paper of the victim. "Carry Bromer, twenty-five years old and a school technologist for Harper Elementary School. Shit, what is he playing here? Is this a warning sign? He's even closer to Michael than before."

"But we can follow up with her family, friends, and the school. We might be able to find her before he does anything."

"As soon as the school opens we're going to go chat with Ms. Williams. Is there anything else from the crime scene that will give us a lead on where Jack is?"

"Christopher is back there testing samples of everything gathered. As we wait, let's go back to the brick house and see if we can find anything."

"Sounds like a plan."

"Did I hear that you're going back to the house?" Christopher asks as he walks out from his office.

"Yes, do you want to come with us?" I ask.

"Yeah, you'll need a forensic scientist there to really gather the good stuff," he says with a soft smile that raises his glasses up his face. I thought his spiky black hair was excessive but that is nothing on his flamboyant smile.

"What about the stuff you're testing now?" Fredrick asks.

"I'm testing the blood from the wounds of the victims now to see if there was anything on the knives; other than that, there's nothing. It'll take a little while for the tests to be done."

"Okay, come on then." Fredrick says.

Christopher lights up like Christmas Day, grabs his briefcase, and follows closely behind. As we pull up to the house, I feel like we are in a scene of a scary movie. It is still a little dark out and there is a fog that surrounds the house. It gives me chills that run down my whole body.

"This is definitely a killer's house," says Christopher with a soft voice.

"Yeah, just wait until you get inside," I say.

"Let me go in first so I can check the house. Who knows, he could have a secret room in here where he's staying. I doubt it, but we can never be too careful."

Fredrick goes in first holding his gun and I follow behind him holding my gun as well. Poor Christopher is breathing so heavy I can hear it. We walk through the dark house with the small light from our flashlights. The creaking of the wooden floors beneath our feet makes the adrenaline pump. So far there is no sign of anyone, in fact all the candles and things that Jack had in here before are gone. It's just covered old furniture.

"This place is clean, well clean from Jack's items. I bet he didn't leave anything behind," I say with frustration.

"Alright, Christopher go ahead and get to work. Linda is right, there's no one here, but I'll go ahead and check the next floor."

"Okay, where should I set up and start?"

"Start in the living room because that's where he had me go and where the table was."

"Okay!" he says with excitement. I search the other rooms as well to see if I can find any signs, but there is nothing. Fredrick and I stand on the bottom of the stairs watching Christopher do his thing. He has gloves on, a black light, and his briefcase full of tools and baggies is out. He pushes his glasses up with the back of his hand. "I found some hair samples, so I'm going to bag these and I'll test them when I get back. I also found some fingerprints. I'm going to take all fingerprints. Maybe there was another victim or another person involved."

"Great work Christopher," Fredrick says. After about twenty minutes, Christopher packs up his equipment and we are out the door. Once we get back to the station more police are there. Sergeant Gordon comes out of his office and approaches us.

"Where were you all?"

"Linda and I both came to work early because we couldn't sleep and we decided to check out the abandoned house, and we have some samples to test."

"Oh, great work," he says surprised.

"Once the school opens we're going to go talk with Ms. Williams at Harper Elementary to see if we can get any leads on where and when Carry was taken."

"Okay," he says and nods his head as he walks back into his

office. Christopher is already in his office running the tests. I walk in to see how he is doing.

"Hey Christopher, how long will it be before you can make and ID?"

"About an hour. I'll come to you as soon as I get the results back."

"Great, thank you."

Harper Elementary School
7:30 a.m.

When Ms. Williams sees us walking in her smiles turns into a frown. "She hates me by the way."

"Well, she's going to have to deal with it," Fredrick says with a smile.

She stands up from her chair behind her desk as we walk into her office. "Detectives, I'm assuming you're here because of Carry Broman?"

"Yes, we have a few questions," Fredrick says. I try not to talk as much. Being here at the school makes me want to see Michael.

"All I know is, she hasn't been at work all week. She's never missed one day and now this is her third day missing."

"Didn't you call home to check on her or call her family? Why didn't you call the police when you found out?" I ask with a stern tone.

"I called her parents in Florida but they haven't heard from her. She has a brother in the area and he hasn't seen her either. I was going to call the police today if she didn't show up, but you're all already here." Something about Ms. Williams seems off to me but I can't put my finger on it. I know Fredrick can feel it as well by the way he is staring at her with his eyebrow raised.

"Can we have her address please?" Fredrick asks.

"Just one second, let me get our secretary to help." She walks back in and her ponytail is waving back and forth. She is walking as if the whole world revolves around her. I can't stand her.

"Thank you," Fredrick says. I just smile and nod.

"Shouldn't you be concerned about the well-being of Michael instead of catching killers, Mrs. Jackson?" *She did not have the nerve to say that to me*! I turn around concealing my anger.

"I'm always concerned about my son, thank you."

94

"Well then, I'm surprised you haven't said anything about his absence at school today."

My heart drops into my stomach. "What? He isn't here?"

She laughs. "Just as I thought, you didn't even know."

I can feel my face getting red. "Did Luke call in today and say he was going to be absent?"

"No, he didn't."

I look at Fredrick. "This isn't good. Luke would never let Michael skip school without a good reason and without informing the school. We have to go to my house now."

We storm out of the door. "I hope everything is-" We leave before Ms. Williams finishes her statement.

I call Luke as we get in the car. "There's no answer. Oh my God, I hope nothing has happened," I say with panic.

"It's okay, we'll find out Linda," Fredrick says with a refreshing tone.

"I swear, if Jack harmed them or took them I'm killing him myself."

"And I won't witness a thing." Fredrick knows this is very personal; he would stick up for me no matter what.

Fredrick's phone rings. "Hey Christopher, what do you have for me." Fredrick is quiet as Christopher tells him. I look over and his face is surprised. His eyes grew bigger by the second. "Are you sure that's right? There's no mistake?" He pauses for a second, "Okay, thank you."

Fredrick pulls off to the side of the road and now I am freaking out. Tears form in my eyes because I know what he is about to say is something bad. "What is it, you're scaring me?"

"Christopher got the results back from the hair samples and fingerprints."

"And?"

"He found Jack's, Carry's, and one other person."

"Who is it?" My hands are shaking.

"Luke's."

"What? It can't be! There must be a mistake."

"It's not a mistake. Christopher ran the fingerprints multiple times. They're his."

I shake my head and begin to cry. "There has to be an explanation."

"I hate to say this, but do you think there's a connection as to why Michael isn't in school and why Luke isn't answering his phone?"

I look at him with shock. "No, this isn't happening. There has to be a reason and I need to find out. Call Christopher back and have him track Luke's phone."

He calls Christopher as I run so many reasons through my head. *I know Luke inside and out; he's not a bad person. God please help us.*

"Okay, he tracked him. He's at the Waterfront Park."

"What's he doing there?"

"Let's go and find out."

"What about Carry? You need to go and check out her place."

"I'll call some of the police officers to check it out for us. I'm not leaving you, not after the information we just found out."

"Luke isn't a bad person. I know he has a good explanation for this."

"Okay, but I'm still not leaving you alone." I am silent for the rest of the ride there.

Waterfront Park
9:00 a.m.

I quickly get out of the car as we race around trying to find them. Then I see them. They are sitting at the edge of the pier staring out into the water. "There they are!"

Fredrick looks at me, "Do you want me to go with you?"

"No, I'll be okay."

"Okay, I'll be standing right here if you need anything."

As I walk down the boardwalk my heart races fast. I am afraid of what he is going to say. "Luke?"

Michael turns around and grows a big smile on his face. "Mom!" he shouts as he runs up and gives me a hug.

"Honey, are you okay?"

"Yeah Mom, I'm fine. Dad let me skip school today. He said he wanted to spend the day with me."

"Okay honey, do you see Detective Fredrick down there?" I ask pointing in his direction.

He nods his head in agreement. "Okay, good. Will you go stand with him for a little bit while I talk to Dad?"

"Yes Mom, I love you."

"I love you too, sweetie."

I sit down next to Luke. "You had me so scared! Why didn't you call the school or let me know you were keeping Michael today?" I say with a loud tone.

"I just wanted to spend a day with my son. He's been having trouble at school and I wanted him to have a relaxing day. A six-year-old boy shouldn't have to deal with this." Luke's tone implies that it's my fault.

"And you don't think I know that? You act like it's my fault. I can't help that he got the awful traits from me. I wish I could help him." Luke blaming me is really making me angry.

"You can help him by quitting this job. Now you have to find the criminals and you have to dream about the killings. He sees everything you dream."

"You're right, but I also dream of these crimes without trying as well. This will never end because I'll always dream of the crimes. Speaking of crimes, Fredrick and I went to check out the house Jack was staying at and we took fingerprints and hair samples. Your fingerprints were found there. What were you doing there?" I say with precaution.

He turns and looks at me with a grim look. "I was trying to help so you could stop this. You said once this case was over you'd quit your job. I want that to happen more than you know," he says with a stern tone. Relief floods through me.

"Luke, you could have gotten hurt. What if Jack was there? You have to stay out of this. He wants nothing more than to hurt my family. That's why I'm working so much to keep you all safe. Why can't you just see that?"

"What about you, Linda? You're so worried about keeping us safe, but who's going to keep you safe? Michael and I can't lose you again." Tears start to form in his eyes.

"Luke, I'm protected by Fredrick and all the cops. I'm not afraid of Jack."

"That's what I'm afraid of. You aren't afraid and that could get you killed. You want him so badly that you're willing to sacrifice yourself. Don't tell me you don't because I know you better than anyone."

"You're right. I'd sacrifice myself for you and Michael because you mean the world to me."

"Michael tells me about the dreams and how he worries about

you. That's how I found out about the house. He keeps me informed, so I'll know what you're doing. You can't expect me to sit back and let you go through hell."

"Okay, but I don't want you getting involved or going to any of the crime scenes because that's how Jack will get you both. You're safer at home with your gun. I'll let you know what I'm doing all the time from now on. Only if you promise me that you won't interfere unless I ask?" *All I know is that this needs to end fast for my family's sake.*

He sighs. "Okay, that's a fair trade. I'm sorry for taking Michael away from school. We both needed to stop and take a minute."

"Trust me babe, I understand that more than anyone." He turns to me and kisses me softly. "I'm so sorry. I don't ever want anything to happen to you because I love you too much."

"I love you too and nothing will happen, I promise."

We get up and walk back to Michael and Fredrick. "Is everything okay?" Fredrick asks.

"Yes, everything is fine," I reply with a smile and nod.

I say my goodbyes to Michael and Luke. "I'll be home for dinner. You two get back to relaxing for the rest of the day."

They nod their heads and Luke gives me one more kiss goodbye.

On the car ride back to the station I explain to Fredrick everything Luke said.

Abandoned Factory
2:00 p.m.

I carry in the rope, shovel, and pickaxe that I bought from Lowe's. As I walk through the door I see Carry's wide eyes sparkle with tears. "Oh yes honey, this stuff is for you. I bought it especially for you. You should feel special. I'm going to take you somewhere nice to do the job. I figured you deserve at least that. I mean, I didn't originally have you in mind, but plans change and unfortunately it had to be you." She is shaking her head rapidly, trying to scream through the duct tape.

I go over and hold her head. "Shhh, it'll be okay. I promise it won't hurt a bit," I say as I kiss her on the forehead. "As soon as the sun goes down, we'll begin."

CPD
2:30 p.m.

"We've got something. Carry's credit card was used earlier at Lowe's. Jack must be getting supplies. Let's go," Fredrick says.

Lowe's
3:00 p.m.

Fredrick pulls out Jack's picture and asks the workers if they have seen him.

"Yeah, I saw him. He bought rope, shovel, and a pickaxe. He was one of the creepiest guys I've seen," responds a young woman.

"Great, what time was it and did you see a car he was driving?"

"It was around 1:30 and I didn't see his car, but his shoes were filthy as if he had been in the woods or something."

"Thank you for your time," Fredrick says as we walk out the door.

He calls Sergeant Gordon. "Look up any kind of abandoned building within ten miles of this Lowe's and ones that could be in the woods please."

I feel as if my head is going to explode with all the flashes running through it. I hang onto Fredrick and I focus on what Michael is dreaming right now. I see what looks like a large, old factory. I see Jack and Carry in the building. Jack is putting the supplies into the back of his blue van and he shoves her in. The license plate reads YT 9831. Then the flash is gone and I stand straight on my feet.

"Have Gordon track this license plate now!" Just then I get a phone call from Luke. "Did you see what Michael saw? He was napping on the couch and he told me all about it."

"Yes I did and we're on it now. Tell Michael I said thank you and he's such a strong boy and that I love him."

"I will, Linda. I love you."

"I love you too, Luke."

"He's only about five minutes away. His van is parked right now. This could be our chance, let's go!" Fredrick says and we run into the car.

Abandoned Factory
3:20 p.m.

We drive through a gravel and dirt road with trees surrounding us. "He loves to pick the craziest places, doesn't he?" I say to add a little humor.

"Well, that's what killers do so they won't be tracked."

"This is the first big mistake Jack has made. He knows better than to pay with her credit card."

"Unless he meant to do this," Fredrick says. We drive through some bushes and find ourselves in front of an old factory, the same one that I saw in my flashes.

"This is it, and there's the van." Fredrick stops the car and calls for back up.

He looks at me and nods. "Let's go." He walks around the back as I go to the front. The door is locked, so no surprise there. I shoot the handle and it cracks open. I slowly open the door to see Carry tied to a chair. Flashbacks appear in my mind as I imagine myself tied to a chair. I shake my head and walk in.

"It's okay," I say as I show my badge. I take off her duct tape and begin to untie her. "Are you okay?"

"Yes, thank you so much. He said he was going to kill me when the sun went down."

"Do you know where he is now?"

"He said he was going for a walk." *This is too easy. What is he planning?*

Fredrick rushes over. "There's nothing here and I don't see Jack anywhere. Let's get her out of here now."

We take her to the hospital for a checkup and ask her questions on the way. "He must have followed me from work, because I stopped to get some groceries after work and he came up to me with a gun shoved to my back and said if I didn't follow he'd shoot me. I got so scared, I followed him back to his van. I should have screamed because there were a lot of people in that store," she said crying.

"It's okay Carry, you were scared for your life. Don't blame yourself. The good thing is you're safe now."

Carry calls her brother while we head to the hospital. "He's getting sloppy," I say.

"Once he finds out we saved her, he'll find a new target. It's been a long day, go home and rest," Fredrick says to me.

"Okay, I'll try and dream tonight. Maybe I can see who he'll take next. We're getting closer; this is a good sign."

Jackson Household
9:30 p.m.

As Luke and I lie in bed we talk about what happened. It feels back to normal. He is happy and so am I. I am glad we finally talked and cleared the air. I don't know what I'd do if I lost him. All of a sudden Luke rolls over on top of me and kisses me hard. "You're a strong woman and as much as I worry about you, the way you handle yourself is a big turn on. So let's see if you can handle what I'm about to do to you," he says with a seductive voice. *Woah! A complete 180 from earlier today. He must feel bad for yelling at me. I can't say I'm not glad that happened now!*

My body starts burning as I become hot. "That was one of the sexiest things you've said. Show me what you've got babe." He rips off the shirt I was wearing and it exposes my breasts.

"I hope you weren't attached to that shirt," he says with a wink.

I shake my head and grab the back of his head so he is kissing me hard. I take his shirt off quickly. He stands and takes off his boxers and then takes my panties off so quick I didn't have time to even move. He shoves himself inside me and begins to pound.

I see Jack walk into the old factory and I follow. I stop when I see him storm out and slam the door. I guess he found out Carry is gone.

"You little bitch!" he yells out. For a moment I thought he could see me but he is walking around in circles panicking. "How did she get out? There's no way she could have gotten out on her own." He pauses for a minute and stands still. "Linda, she got a step ahead of me but how? I must be more careful; she's way too close."

You're right, I'm too close, closer than you think, I thought to myself. Okay, keep close and follow where he goes. I know he will find his next target. I walk away from the factory towards the trees. I hid my car behind some trees so he wouldn't see it. I open my door and I see his car leaving. I wait a little bit and follow, leaving my lights off. I check the time on the clock and it is 10:00 p.m. I can take a wild guess as to where he is heading, definitely downtown somewhere. He likes his young party women.

He parks out in front of the Victor Social Club. This is a different scene for him. I guess he wants it classy. What is his plan here? Does he just pick out a woman he likes and then follows her? There has to be another way I can catch him. I see in the past, present, and future. There has to be a way I can catch him in the act. Then it dawned on me, Michael. I bet he is watching and dreaming as well. Maybe I can wake him up and have him tell Luke to call Fredrick to get him over here now, because this is going down tonight and this can be the only way we catch him.

"Michael, are you listening?" I pause for a moment. No response. "Michael, honey can you hear me?"

"Mom, I can hear you. Are you okay?" I pause for a second because I still can't believe we can talk through our dreams.

"Yes, I am. I need you to do me a favor. Can you see what I see?"

"Yes, I see a building across the street that starts with a V."

"Good. I need you to wake up and tell your Dad to call Fredrick and send him to the Victor Social Club."

"But how can I wake up when you're still dreaming?"

"You can do it, honey. Just close your eyes and tell yourself to wake up. You can be a hero tonight."

"Okay, I'm going to try now." I wait a few minutes and I don't hear back from him. It must have worked. I hope Jack doesn't find anyone soon, because this could be our chance to catch him for good.

It has been twenty minutes and there is no sign of anyone and Jack is still there. I hope Michael got the message through. Suddenly I see Jack get out of the car and walk towards the club. He is dressed in a black suit and his hair is back in a short ponytail. How did he change? Did he have clothes in the car already? I guess he's always ready. He is a member of this club? How is that possible? Gosh, even in the dark I can see his big nose sticking out. As soon as he walks up to the door the security guard opens it as if he knows him. How long has he been coming here?

It looks like this is the place we will be coming tomorrow and interviewing every staff member. I see Fredrick's black car pull up in front of me. I yell out as if he can hear me, but he can't, as this a dream. Wait, it worked! Michael got the message through. This is how we are going to catch Jack, I just know it!

Fredrick walks up to the door and shows him his badge. The guard lets him inside. I wait anxiously at what is going to happen next. All of a sudden people start running out of the club. Oh no! What is going on? My mind starts buzzing. I close my eyes to make it stop.

Then I wake up in bed. "No!" I yell out.

"What is it?" Luke asks as he quickly sits up in bed.

"I need to go now. I think Fredrick is in trouble."

"Okay, I'll drive you. Michael told me everything."

"Good, I'm glad it worked but you have to stay here with him."

"Are you sure?"

"Yes," I say as I quickly put on a shirt and pants. I grab my gun and head out.

"Be careful, I love you," Luke says. I yell it back at him as I race down the stairs.

On my way over I call Fredrick. No answer. Shit! I call Sergeant Gordon and he didn't answer either. I am still ten minutes out. I get a phone call from Luke. "It's all over the news."

"What? What are they saying?"

"Right now they're videoing a bunch of cop cars and people standing outside the club."

"Do you see Fredrick anywhere?"

"No, they're trying to get reporters to get people to talk but no one is."

Finally, I see what he is saying as I park my car across the street. "I'm here, I need to find Fredrick. I'll call you back. I love you."

I get out of the car and search all around for Fredrick. I go up to one of the officers and ask if he has seen Fredrick.

"He's inside talking with the manger." I rush through walking around the fallen chairs. It looks like there has been a big fight. Chairs are overturned and glasses are broken on the floor. Fredrick is writing down notes as he talks with the manager.

"Fredrick, what's going on?"

"Linda, how are you-?" He pauses and shakes his head and smiles. "Never mind, I'm getting statements right now."

"Did he murder anyone?"

"No, when he saw me he made a huge scene by yelling GUN at the top of his voice. It caused everyone to panic."

"So he got away?"

"Yes, but he didn't kill anyone."

"Did he take anyone?"

He clears his throat. "I don't know. I'm asking everyone in the club if he saw him and if he was with anyone."

"Any luck?"

"Everyone is saying they saw him sitting over there." He points to a black couch, "Sitting and drinking, but he wasn't talking to anyone. A few of the women told me they thought he was creepy."

"Hmm, no surprise there. Okay, well I'll help you ask around."

He nods his head and I walk around to find someone to interview. A girl rushes through the door and she is crying. "Carol!"

I walk up to her. "Miss, calm down. Is Carol your friend?"

"Yes," she says shaking her head. Her mascara is running down her face but her black bangs are almost covering her dark eyes. "When that man yelled, we both got up and we were panicking and shuffling through the crowd to get out. I lost her in my sights but I figured she'd run outside with the rest of us. When I got outside I couldn't find her. I called her phone and she didn't answer, which is unusual because she always has her phone. I came back in here to find her, and she isn't here. I'm worried."

"Okay, I'm Detective Linda Jackson and we're going to help you find her. Does she usually run off alone?"

"No, we always stick together. If she goes home with a boy she always tells me then texts me when she gets to his place so I know she's okay. I haven't received any text from her."

"Okay, can you give me her cell phone number? I'm going to have someone track her phone."

She nods her head and gives me the number. I text it to Christopher, as I know he has a fancy computer at his house that he can track from. I'm not sure if it is legal, but no one says anything about it. "So Miss, what does Carol look like?"

"It's Mary, and she's the total opposite of me. She's tall and thin with curly light brown hair. She dresses in tight clothes and she wears glasses."

"Okay, great Mary, thank you."

"You're welcome," she says biting her black nails anxiously. I walk over to Fredrick.

"I got some information on the girl who was taken. I texted her number to Christopher to track her."

"Okay, good work. I haven't gotten anywhere with anyone else. So how did you do it?"

"Do what?"

"With your dreams? We were so close to catching him, so whatever you did worked."

"I talked to Michael in my dreams, had him wake up and tell Luke."

"Wow, that's amazing. Can you imagine the press and stories you could get?"

"No," I said with a stern voice. "I won't let anyone find out about Michael. He isn't going to be an even bigger target than he is now."

"Okay, okay, I'm sorry."

"It's okay." My phone is buzzing. "It's Christopher," I say with relief.

"Were you able to find her?"

He yawns through the phone. "Yeah, she's on the move." I tap Fredrick on the shoulder and point to head out the door. "She's heading down Spring Street."

I hop in the car with Fredrick. "Spring Street now," and he drives off.

"Wait, she's stopped somewhere on Spring Street."

"Okay, thank you. Call me if anything changes."

"She's stopped on Spring Street. Is there anything around there?" I ask Fredrick.

"Just a bunch of houses and apartments. At two in the morning it'll be dead."

"That's not good," I say.

A few minutes later we are driving slowly down Spring Street looking for something out of the ordinary. "Wait, stop!" I say. "Look over there in that parking lot." It was a dimly lit parking lot in the middle of two apartment complexes. Only a few cars are around, but one of those cars is his van.

"Let's go," Fredrick says as he pulls out his gun. We walk slowly towards the van and I notice the sliding door is cracked open. I look at him and nod. He carefully opens it then points his gun.

"Shit," he says lowering his gun.

I walk around him and look inside. It's Carol lying there lifeless, blood seeping through her cream blouse, and her green eyes wide open. The number 14 is carved on her chest and lying next to her is a vial of blood.

"Fuck, how in the hell did he get another victim this fast?"

Fredrick picks up the vial and on it is labeled 13. "He's back," he says with slight fear in his tone. Under the vial is a torn piece of white paper stained with blood but it says, "Not close enough."

"Mother fucker!" I scream and slam my hand against the door. I storm away as Fredrick calls in the forensic team.

Fredrick comes up to me as I stand by his car. "Linda, I know I say this all the time, but we will catch him. Look how close we were tonight."

"Yeah, but not close enough."

"The way you dreamed tonight worked. That kind of dreaming is what's going to catch him."

"I hope so. Can you take me back to my car?"

I call Luke once I get in my car on the way home. I know I won't be sleeping tonight.

Abandoned shelter
4:00 a.m.

"Oh Linda, you won't be able to stop me. I mean. yeah you were close and all but I'm still smarter and I always will be. It looks like we will go back to the way things were. The next victim is already begging for her life. Let's get this countdown really going so I can finish what I started, well what he started." I stare at Tom's picture and smile.

"Who are you talking to?" I turn and see that little Miss Lila has woken up.

"Oh, you shouldn't be worried about that right now honey, because what you have coming is going to be brutal. I have to pick up my game."

"You don't have to do anything. Please, what do you want? I'll do anything, just don't kill me please." Her hopeless blue eyes are filled with tears. I see a tear drop right onto her cleavage. Gosh, that low cut, tight red dress got me the moment I saw her. How could I resist? She starts to cry harder.

I bend down and grab her face gently. "Oh, don't worry honey, I promise you'll enjoy every moment of it. Just sit tight. I'm going to go grab some friends to enjoy this game too."

CPD
Thursday 7:00 a.m.

Fredrick and I walk in at the same time. Phones are already ringing off the hook. I set down my bag and sip my coffee. Officer Gerald comes up to me with a concerned look on his face.

"Detective, we've been receiving phone calls since about 5:00 a.m. this morning. Two nurses from MUSC were kidnapped during their night shift. We aren't sure how it happened except the receptionist said a tall man with a big nose came in complaining about stomach pain. Next thing she knows she was passed out and woke up a little later and the nurses were gone."

"What? Where were all the other workers?"

"One receptionist was in the bathroom and the other was signing in a patient in a different room. When they came back, they saw Gina the receptionist on the floor and they called 9-1-1. By the time they got there the man was gone along with the two nurses."

"How does he get away with this?"

Fredrick overhears and grabs his keys. "Let's go."

I follow behind him. "How can he kidnap two girls at the same time? From a well-protected and secured hospital?"

"He must have connections within the hospital. I mean he's good, but he's not that good. Have you shown Luke his picture?"

I raise my eyebrows with surprise. "Well he's seen the drawing the sketch artist did just like everyone else since it's posted on the news and around town. Why?"

He pauses for a second. I look over to see his reaction. He raises his shoulders. "I don't know. It might be good for you to show him again so he's aware. Now we know that Jack isn't afraid to kidnap women from anywhere. We want to make sure all eyes are looking for him."

"Okay, I will," I say with concern. "By the way, Luke wasn't working last night."

"Okay," he says slowly. "Wait, you don't think I was asking because I think Luke is a suspect do you?"

"I'd hope not."

"No, never. I know Luke is a good person and would never do anything like that. I was honestly looking out for his well-being. He said he wants to help us so showing him Jack's picture is a good idea. Just hearing the hospital made me think of him, and that's why I asked."

"Okay good," I say with hesitation.

Medical University of South Carolina (MUSC)
7:30 a.m.

We park in the garage and head into the hospital. There are news stations outside the hospital waiting for answers. One of the receptionists comes up to us right away.

"Have you found Tori and Kendra yet?" Her eyes are big in concern.

I have to look down at her to speak. "No ma'am, we haven't. That's why we're here. We want to get some answers."

"Okay, I'll help you out as much as I can but Gina is in a room here. She's getting some tests done to see what he used to sedate her. She can help ID."

"Oh, that's great ma'am, thank you," I say even though we

already know what he looks like, but all details will help.

"So go ahead and tell us what you saw."

She sits down on one of the waiting room chairs. Her feet barely touch the ground. "Well when I came out of the bathroom I saw Gina lying on the floor. I went over to her to shake her to see if she would wake up but she didn't. I called 9-1-1." She takes a deep breath after saying that.

"Is that all?" Fredrick asks with an annoyed tone. "Did you check around the hospital for anything suspicious?"

"No, I-I was too scared," she says shyly.

"Um, okay. Did you hear any weird noises? Any screams?"

She shakes her head from side to side quickly. "No, but when I told Terry what had happened, she made an all call for everyone to come down to the patient waiting area. When all the staff members came down, that's when we noticed Tori and Kendra were gone."

"How long did it take everyone to come down to the waiting room after Terry did an all call?"

"Oh," she lingers trying to find an answer. "About ten minutes. Yeah ten minutes," she says, panting as if she's nervous.

"Okay, thank you for your time, ma'am. We're going to talk to Gina now," Fredrick says and we walk away quickly.

I look at Fredrick and we both roll our eyes. "Well that was interesting," I say. We quietly laugh.

When we walk into the room Gina is sitting up dressed getting ready to leave.

"Oh, I'm glad we caught you. We have a few questions about what happened last night," I say.

She sighs. "I saw this creepy man with a big nose come in. He complained about stomach pain. I was on the computer getting ready to type in his name then all of a sudden he was behind me. A cloth was covering my mouth and then I passed out. That's all I remember. Now can I go home please?"

We step aside as she storms out.

"Well, this visit didn't give us anything," I say aggravated. "Wait, what about the cameras?"

"That should have been the first thing we asked. Let's go and see the footage from last night." We walk into the security office in the hospital and see two bulky men sitting there watching the camera.

"Excuse us, I'm Detective Fredrick and this is Detective Jackson and we're here investigating the incident that happened last night."

They both stand up and I have to look up at them. "Detectives, thank you for coming. My name is Mark and this Josh. We were both working the night everything happened."

"Oh, that's great maybe you can help us out then," I say. "We'd like to look at the camera footage from that night."

"We had a feeling the cops would be here asking so we took the liberty of looking through it ourselves."

"Good, did you see anything unusual?" asks Fredrick in a deep tone.

"Actually we did. Here take a look at this," Mark says as he sits down and pulls it up.

I can see the receptionists sitting behind their desk on one camera and on the others nothing abnormal in the hallways yet.

"Okay, this is a few minutes before everything happens. The cameras are working fine but then all of a sudden they all go out." The screens are all blurry like the cable went out on a TV.

"What the hell? How did he know how to do that?"

"We aren't sure but he somehow did that to all the cameras all at once."

"He must have had help, unless he's smarter than we think," Fredrick says rubbing his chin.

"Thank you for showing us this. When you saw that the cameras went out, what did you do?"

"We both went out and searched around. We heard screaming coming down from the check-in desk so we ran there and that's when we saw Gina on the floor."

"So you didn't see anything out of the ordinary?"

They put their heads down as if they are ashamed. "No, we didn't. We couldn't believe someone could walk in here and kidnap two nurses."

"Okay, thank you for talking with us. Could we go ahead and take the footage from that night anyway? We'll look through it and see if we can't find anything."

"Yes, of course."

Mark puts in a USB drive and copies the footage on there. "Here you go. I hope this will be better help than us."

"Thank you. Oh, before we leave, did either one of you know Tori or Kendra well?"

Josh's face becomes red. "I knew Tori, we were an item. We weren't dating but we knew each other well. We were supposed to meet up after work that morning."

"We're very sorry," I say.

He nods his head and I notice his eyes begin to water. We shake their hands, thank them again, and head out.

"I bet Christopher can work his magic and find something out from this tape," Fredrick says.

"I hope so, but we're already too late. I mean, he has them kidnapped. He'll probably kill them tonight. He doesn't want to wait around anymore; he's becoming impatient."

"You're right and that's where you come into play."

I look at him with a questioning look as he turns on the car. "Do you think you could go home and sleep?"

"You want me to sleep and try and dream to find the girls now?"

"Yeah, like you said he'll probably kill them tonight."

"True, but I'm too anxious to sleep."

"It could save two lives."

"Okay, okay, you're right. I'll try, but I can't make any promises."

Harper Elementary
10:00 a.m.

Before I head home I stop by Michael's school. I can't let Michael be in school right now. If I dream he will have another outburst.

"Mrs. Jackson, why are you taking Michael out from school so early?"

Ms. Williams, of course, that nosey- "Oh hi, Ms. Williams, yeah I'm taking Michael for a doctor's appointment, just like you asked," I say with smirk.

She smirks back. "Oh, well that's good news. I'll be ready for the doctor's slip tomorrow."

Michael comes up and gives me a big hug. "Goodbye," I say as we head out the door.

"Mom, what's going on? I don't have a doctor's appointment."

"I had to tell a small lie because I have to get you out of school today. We'll have Daddy write you a note." I feel bad inside for lying and using my husband's job as reinforcement. But not really. Ms. Williams deserves it.

"So what are we really doing?"

"Well, I have to dream to find a bad guy and I know what happens to you when I do. I didn't want you to have another outbreak at school."

"Oh, thank you Mom. I don't like doing that in school. The other kids stare at me."

"Oh sweetie, I'm sorry," I say as I rub through his soft, short, black hair.

I give Luke a quick call on our way home to update him.

Jackson Household
10:45 a.m.

I decide to lie on the couch while Michael sits on the recliner watching TV and doing his math homework he is going to miss today. I close my eyes and focus on Jack and those two nurses. I see their young faces in my mind and I see Jack's evil grin. I take deep breaths to focus on my anxiety and relax.

I walk up to an eerie abandoned cottage in the middle of a bunch of trees. How does he always end up finding the creepiest places? I can see dim light through the cracked windows. If this place would get some remodeling done it would be a cute place. I shake my head. That's beside the point – focus. I walk up to the window and peek in. I can see three women sitting all tied to chairs. What is it with chairs? My focus shifts when I see Jack come up to the women and talk to them. I go closer to the window to see if I can hear anything. I can't hear a thing! I turn around to look at my surroundings. I have no idea where in the hell we are, which is not good. I am going to have to play the waiting game and watch his next move.

I turn back around and I still see the four of them. Jack pulls out a big black case and sets it on a table. As he opens it I begin to panic. I see a mass of shiny, pointy objects. Shit! He's back to his knives. He has so many of them. Long ones, short ones, and oddly shaped ones. Then I see the fear on the women's faces. Their eyes become big and tears form quickly. Tears form in my eyes just watching, but I can't stop it because this is happening tonight. I can stop it tonight if I know where the hell I am! It is imperative that I keep a watch on him because if he leaves I can follow and find out where this place is. I glance at the clock on the wall behind one of the women. It reads 12:25 a.m.

He takes off the duct tape on their mouths. It's as if he wants them to scream. Gosh, what a freak! He takes out a long, skinny knife and walks over to one of the blonde girls first and he places the knife in front of her. I close my eyes so I can't watch but the agony I hear from her voice makes me shake. When I hear the screaming stop I look up and on her chest is the number 13.

Oh my God, he carves the numbers on them first? That is horrible. He makes his way over to the brunette and does the same thing. I close my eyes until he is finished. My stomach turns to knots thinking about what he is going to do next.

When he is done carving the numbers he wipes the blood off the blade and sets it down. He picks up another knife that is thick and shaped like a hook. I begin to cry and stop myself from running inside. I hear scream after scream for the next ten minutes. I turn and face the trees because I can't take this anymore. I have to save these girls. Then I see something in the distance. The light from the moon is bouncing off it.

I walk quickly and quietly towards this object. I feel a ray of hope when I notice it is a car. It's not his blue van but a white Escalade. I go to the back and check out the license plate. I memorize it and make myself wake up. This is enough to catch him before he murders these innocent women. "Linda, wake up."

I wake up by a big breath. "Mom, are you okay?"

"Yes Michael, I found out some information," I say as my stomach rumbles and I rush to the bathroom to throw up. I don't know if that is from dreaming or from what I saw in the dream. Either way, I need to save those women.

I call Fredrick right away. "I've got something," I say as I rub my head. I am feeling light headed. "Run this license plate." I give him the number and hang up.

I sit down slowly on the couch holding my head. "Mom, what's wrong. Do I need to call Dad?"

I shake my head, "I'm okay, I think." I begin to dial Luke's cell phone when I see hundreds of black spots and then nothing.

I wake up in shock to a very pungent smell. I open my eyes and see Luke sitting in front of me. "Linda, are you okay?"

I hold my head and my stomach. That smell made me nauseous instantly. "I'm okay. What happened?"

"Michael said you passed out after your dream. I came over immediately and gave you these smelling salts. I bought them a while back when you were having symptoms from your dreams before. They came in handy," he says with a small smile.

"That's so weird. I haven't had symptoms in a while. I did see a lot in my dream though, well too much. It was very disturbing, but I think I gave Fredrick a lead in finding Jack."

"Good, I'm glad you're okay. How are you feeling now?"

"I'm okay, but a little famished. I haven't eaten in a while." I glance at my watch. "It's already 3:00? Gosh, my dreams seem much shorter than what they really are."

"You relax on the couch. I'll make you a chicken wrap."

"Thank you babe," I say as I kiss Luke on the lips.

I look over at Michael sitting on the recliner. "Did you see any of that dream?"

"No, I've been awake the whole time."

"Oh, thank God." I kiss him on the forehead and make my way into the kitchen.

"Are you going back into work?" asks Luke.

"No. I'm still not feeling the best and Fredrick should be able to take care of it now. I did my part. I'll be glad when this is over."

Luke sets the plate in front of me and the wrap looks so delicious. "I've been thinking. Once this is all over, I say we take a trip. We should go somewhere we've been wanting to go."

I swallow before I answer. "That would be wonderful. Where are you thinking?"

"Italy?"

I jump up with excitement. "Italy, really? I've always wanted to go there."

"I know and you deserve it. I can't even imagine what you're going through and what you've gone through. I want to take you somewhere you can totally relax and get away from everything."

"That sounds great. What about Michael?"

"I've asked your Mom and Dad already about watching him and they agreed to it."

"Wow, thank you babe. I don't know what to say. I hope this doesn't go on much longer. Italy sounds way better than what I'm doing now," I say as I laugh.

Just as I'm thinking about paradise I receive a call from Fredrick. "I've got some news."

I begin to worry. "Okay, what is it?"

"Christopher got some samples back, and not only does Jack murder his victims with his crazy knives, but on the knives is a rare poison. There isn't even a name for it. Jack has to get this poison from somewhere or from someone. Christopher dug a little deeper and found the name of a Russian man who sells poisons and knives on the street. Why the cops haven't caught him yet, I have no idea. He is about to get caught now though. I have men searching the place now. We got a hit on the license plate and I'm heading there now. Do you want to come?"

"That's so weird about the poison. I've never seen him use the poison in my dreams. How does he do that?"

"I don't know but we're going to find out. We have enough to arrest the man selling the stuff. Once he's in our custody we can interrogate him."

"Okay great, keep me posted. I'm going to pass on going with you. I haven't been feeling well since I woke up from that dream."

"Okay, no problem, I'll have Detective Raymond go with me. You get some rest."

"Will do, and please call me as soon as you find out something." I have been so involved with this case that I forgot they hired another detective, John Raymond. He seems like a good person. He will be a good person to take my spot when I leave too.

***

A few hours have passed and I have been enjoying time with Michael and Luke. We decided to walk down to Cumberland Smokehouse to enjoy some great barbeque. I call May and Charlie and invite them as well. We have to start discussing the wedding shower, as May 13 will be here before we know it.

"I was thinking we can have the bridal shower at your house?" May asks.

I glance over at Luke to see if he approves. "Go ahead. I'll take Michael to the beach for the day. We can spend some quality time together," he says with a smile.

"Thanks, honey. Well then our house it is. Go ahead and give me the names of people you want to invite."

May hands me a list already made with addresses and phone numbers. I laugh because that doesn't surprise me at all. "Great, not too big of a list."

"Nope, just family and a few friends from my work."

We continue to talk about the wedding and how they have been doing. I feel like I never get to talk to May because of how busy I've been. My phone rings as we are finishing up our meals. I leave to take it.

"Fredrick, what's going on?"

"I'm sorry to bother you. I have bad news." I take a big gulp. "Tori, Kendra, and the other woman are already dead."

"What?! That can't be. I saw them being murdered at night."

"Forensics says they haven't been dead long. Jack must have become more impatient than we thought."

"Then my dreams are useless. I can't believe all three of them are dead. Was there a vial of blood?"

"I'm sorry Linda, and yeah with the number 10 on it. Christopher is getting the sample tested now. The Russian guy is now in our custody. I'm going to go back and see if I can get anything out of him."

"Okay, I'll be there soon." I hang up the phone and start to cry. I can't believe those women are dead. I walk back and wipe my tears hoping no one will notice.

Luke gets up out of his seat when he sees me walk back. "What happened?"

"Those women are dead," I say as I begin to cry.

He hugs me. "I'm so sorry. Let's get you out of here."

When I get to the table I apologize to May and Charlie. They are very understanding as usual and we agree to get together again soon. We begin to walk home.

"My dreams were wrong. He murdered them sooner than I saw. He wins every fucking time."

I turn towards Michael as soon as I say that. "Oh Michael, I'm so sorry." I shake my head and realize I am losing it. I can't do this job anymore. I can't control myself. I begin to think of the dream and hearing those screams of the poor women. Then the flashes begin and the screams get louder and louder. I hold my ears and fall to my knees.

Chapter 10

CPD
Thursday 7:00 p.m.

I sit across from this Russian man appalled by his lies. His thick beard and accent stand out but his lies stand out even more. "Why don't you save us your time and tell us the truth," I say as I stare into his dark brown eyes.

"He's got you all confused, hasn't he?"

"Excuse me?" I say as I slam my hands on the table and stand up.

"If you think I'm going to talk about Jack or tell you where he is, you're wrong."

"You better talk, you're looking at 25 to life," Fredrick says as a threat.

"You think I'm scared of going to jail? I've seen and been through much worse." I hear a knock at the window and Fredrick and I get up and walk out.

"He's not going to talk," I say with frustration.

Sergeant Gordon nods his head in agreement. "Obviously this man isn't afraid of threats or going to jail. There's no breaking him. The DA is going to put him away for good."

"That's good, but doesn't help us now! Jack has his newest victim and he has nothing: no leads." I throw my hands in the air and walk back to my desk. I sit down and put my hands over my face.

Fredrick comes out and stands next to me at my desk. "Jack has been quiet towards me. He's going to kill ten more people and then who knows what? He's planning something big and I don't know what to do."

He puts his hand on my shoulder. "There isn't much left to do right now. Go home and sleep. Maybe you'll see something tonight. Come back in tomorrow morning."

"Okay, see you tomorrow." I grab my jacket and bag and leave.

Before going home, I stop at Waterfront Park and sit near the fountain. It is beautiful in the evening. I have to take some time to think before I go home. I have to find a way into Jack's head again. There were consequences before but it worked. As I begin to think my phone rings. "Linda, sorry to bother you this late, but we got the blood sample back on victim ten. Her name is Lindsay Turner; she's a young hair stylist that works at Master Cuts. Her parents put out a missing person's report. I figured this information would be good to give you before you go to bed. I am texting you a picture of her now. She got off work yesterday at around 5:30 p.m. and never returned home."

"That's good news. I can put myself at the Master Cuts around that time and I can at least see where they are now as long as he doesn't kill her first."

"Positive thinking, Linda. I know it's hard right now but it'll help."

"You're right, Fredrick, thank you. I'll get some information tonight and call you whenever I can."

"Thanks, goodnight Linda."

"Goodnight," I say as I hang up and take a big sigh. I look out into the dark, tranquil water. Tears begin to fall. I want this misery to end.

Jackson Household
10:30 p.m.

I crawl into bed because Luke is already sleeping. He is lying on his back with the sheets just covering his boxer line. His muscular chest and stomach are shining from the moonlight seeping in from the window. This mess that seems to continue on is tearing me up inside. I am stressed more than I ever thought I could be, and all I want right now is to be loved and comforted. I want to forget about what my life is right now and I want to fall to another place. I lean over and gently kiss his stomach and make my way up. His eyes are open and a small smile appears. He pushes my hair behind my ear. "Hey beautiful."

I start kissing him passionately as I lie on top of him. "Make me forget about the bad things please."

He takes off my tank top and kisses my breasts and looks me

in the eyes. "Of course, baby." He gently puts me on my back and starts kissing my neck. I start to become lost in the moment.

***

I look at my watch and it is 5:15 p.m. Lindsay should be getting off work soon. I don't see any sign of Jack yet. I would love to know how he kidnaps women while the sun is still out. I see Lindsay walk out in her black high heel boots. Her red hair is too bright to miss. This is a little out of his taste, but I guess it doesn't matter anymore. All of a sudden I see Jack walking right towards her. I freeze with panic as I watch what is about to happen. Jack bumps into Lindsay and makes it look like an accident. She drops her bag and he picks it up for her. A big smile forms on her short, round face.

They shake hands and I can see them talking. They are both smiling and look like they are hitting it off. She shakes her head up and down and they walk off together.

Okay, now I just have to follow them. They go to a small sandwich shop. I sit outside and watch them through the window.

There has to be another way I can focus myself to the present. I need to know what is happening now. I close my eyes and picture Jack. I remember what it felt like to be in his head. I can hear the echoing of his voice and the racing of my heartbeat. I shut my eyes hard and hear the humming sounds.

I open my eyes and I see Lindsay chained to the wall. This is it, I'm in his head. Focus now.

Oh Lindsay, you look radiant under that light. Your eyeliner is stained down your face and you look frightened beyond belief; just how I like them.

You sick bastard.

What is that buzzing noise? I shake my head and go to grab my bag of knives.

No! He can't do this now. Look around the shelter and find something that tells me where I am. Nothing! There's nothing! Now I have to watch another murder!

I shake my head again. Wait a second, I remember that buzzing sound. Linda? You're here with me again. I hope you enjoy the show. I walk up to Lindsay and rip open her shirt. I grab the small long knife and begin to carve 10 into her chest.

Jack, stop! Please!

I shake my head and laugh. I stop when I hear a loud buzzing sound. I set the knife down hard. "What the hell is that?"

I jump out of bed and turn off the alarm. I put my hands over my face. "I messed up. I'm too late with this victim again! Jack wins every fucking time," I say to Luke as I storm into the bathroom. I dab my face with the water. After I get dressed for work I head downstairs for breakfast.

My phone is buzzing on the counter, "We got a call. A dead body was just found in the fountain at Waterfront Park. Bystanders said they saw the number 10 carved into her chest."

"Great, I'm on my way."

I look at Michael and Luke innocently eating their oatmeal. "I have to go."

"Call me if you need anything," Luke says as he kisses my forehead.

"I love you, Mom."

I smile at them. "I love you both."

Waterfront Park
7:30 a.m.

I arrive at the crime scene and the reporters are already surrounding the area. Through the crowd I spot Fredrick and Raymond. Forensics is already checking the body. Fredrick comes up to me right away.

"Another vial of blood, you already know what's labeled on it. I received a phone call from Ms. Williams. Her third grade teacher, Ms. Riley didn't come into work today and didn't call a substitute. She's worried."

"You don't think the vial of blood his hers?"

"I have a very bad feeling."

"Great, he's targeting Harper Elementary on purpose." I begin to talk more when my cell phone rings. I raise my eyebrow in surprise that it is Sarah calling.

"Sarah, hey are you okay?"

"Um sort of. You need to come to Sweet N Spice right away." My stomach turns. "Why, what's going on?"

"There's a body in the dumpster."

"What!" I freeze in the moment as this brings back bad memories. *What is Jack playing at here?* I hang up the phone.

"Fredrick, we need to go now. A body was just found at Sweet N Spice."

Sweet N Spice
8:00 a.m.

We rush out and arrive at the shop a few minutes later. There are no other cop cars or press yet. Sarah and Bobby rush out of the door when they see us. "I didn't call anyone else yet, I figured you'd want to handle this."

"Thank you, Sarah. Do you know who the victim is?" I ask as we walk behind the store to the dumpster.

"No, but she has a teaching badge on from Harper Elementary."

I look at Fredrick in panic. I then look in the dumpster. "It's Ms. Riley. On top of her chest is the next vial of blood. That motherfucker is killing off the entire staff at Harper Elementary. We need to get that school shut down now!" I yell as I storm off.

They come out from around the shop. Sarah comes up and sits next to me along the sidewalk. "Linda, I'm so sorry all this is happening. If you need anything please let us know," Sarah says with a soft voice.

"How about a job?"

Sarah freezes and her eyes become big. "What? You really want to come back?"

"Yes, more than anything. I promised Luke and Michael that once this case is over, I'd come back here. If, of course, you'll have me?"

She gives me a big hug. "Of course, there's never any question."

"Thank you. I'm sorry about the body in the dumpster. This is like de-ja-vu."

"Yes, it is. Well, keep us posted and good luck with everything."

"Thank you Sarah," I say as I give her another hug.

Harper Elementary
9:00 a.m.

We arrive at Harper Elementary School along with so many reporters I can't even see the front door. Ms. Williams runs out. "Mrs. Jackson, another one of our teachers has gone missing."

"What? How can he be moving this quickly?"

"Who is it?" asks Fredrick.

"Mrs. Smith, one of our second grade teachers." Her puts her hand over her face and begins to cry. "This has always been one of the best schools in town and now people won't step foot inside unless it's a damn reporter."

"I'm so sorry. This is all my fault."

She looks at me with a scolding look. "You're right, it is. Ever since you've been out of the coma, shit is going in the hole!"

I step back from her in shock at her words said but she's right. "This will be fixed, but for now I suggest we shut down the school for a few weeks until this man is caught."

Her eyes become bigger and tears begin to form. "I've put my life into this school: there's no way you're shutting it down!"

"Three of your staff members have been kidnapped. Don't you want them to be safe?"

She throws her hands in the air. "There has to be another way. I'm not shutting down this school and putting these students' education in jeopardy. Think of what that would do to them mentally?"

"Is it better than putting their lives at risk?"

She pauses for a second to think. "More security. That's all we need. Can't you provide us with more security?"

I begin to protest then Fredrick stops me. "Ms. Williams, that can definitely be arranged. Since today is Friday, send the students home early and then when you reopen on Monday, there will be police officers surrounding the outside of the school and one on each floor."

"Oh, that would be great. Thank you so much Detective Fredrick," Ms. Williams says as she slowly touches his arm.

She walks past me with a cold stare and doesn't say a word.

I sigh. "Great, I'm the worst person in the world and this is all my fault."

"Stop, look we're going to get this guy. I know it sounds redundant."

"I know we will. I only hope we can before he takes the whole town down around me and everyone I care in it with him."

He touches my shoulder. "We won't let that happen."

I hear, "Mom!" coming from behind me. I see Michael walking with Luke. I am glad Luke got him out of there. I give him a hug and then kiss Luke on the lips.

"Thank you for getting him out of there. Will you take him

home now?"

"I would but I have two more surgeries today. I'll take him to your parents."

"Okay, thank you. It might be a late night."

"Don't worry, everything will be taken care of at home."

"Thank you. I love you, Luke."

"I love you, too."

I give Michael another big hug. "Have fun at Grandma and Grandpa's."

"Oh, I will. Grandma's brownies will keep me busy," he says with a big grin on his face.

I roll my eyes and laugh. "Don't eat too much!"

"I'll try not to," he says as he chuckles. I watch them walk off together and wish we can have a normal life soon.

CPD
4:30 p.m.

"Is there any location on Mrs. Smith? Did you track her phone?" I ask Fredrick

"Christopher is on it, but he hasn't found anything."

"No one saw Jack around the school at all?"

"Everyone was too scared about another teacher being kidnapped that no one paid attention," Fredrick says.

"Wow, he's playing this right." I say shaking my head.

"Tell me about it. This is the toughest case I've ever worked on."

Coming from Fredrick who is a "by the book" kind of detective, that is surprising.

I look at Fredrick leaning back in his chair with hands on his head at his desk. "Fredrick, how are we going to catch him?"

He sighs. "I don't know, but maybe we could go see Maggie again."

I raise an eyebrow. "We haven't seen her since Arnold's funeral. Do you really think she'd help us? Plus, what could she tell us?"

He shrugs his shoulders, "I don't know, I'm out of answers and she helped you last time."

"That's true. I mean she has séances and talks with the dead. I'm sure she can somehow use her skills and my dreams and come up with something. I might be crazy, but it's worth a try."

123

"Great, I'll call her now."

When we pull into the driveway, I swear I can smell the incense from inside the car. She opens the door before we even open the car doors. I see her standing there with her big crazy hair and a maroon and purple long sleeve dress that has peace signs all over it. We walk up and she gives me a big hug first.

"It's been too long since I've seen you." She gets teary-eyed. "You were a part of Arnold and that makes me feel better."

"Thank you Maggie, that's sweet of you to say. Arnold was one of the best detectives I knew." She smiles and gives me another big hug.

She boils water for chamomile tea. "So, what can I do for you today?" she asks as she lights her candles on the round table.

"Well, I'm having trouble with my dreams."

She moves her glasses down and looks at me. "Let me guess, Jack Bolder?"

I take a big gulp. "How did you know?"

"I'm a psychic, remember?"

"Yeah, I shouldn't be surprised about that." I shake my head. "Anyway, it feels like dealing with Tom all over again. I can't see him coming. When I do get a lead, he always finds a way around it. Now we have no leads whatsoever and I have no idea how to catch him. I have tried dreaming through his eyes like we discussed last time, but not only did it affect my health, it didn't work well enough. Now I'm out of ideas. I'm sorry to burden you with this."

She closes her eyes and shakes her head. "Oh honey, please don't worry about being a burden. I love the company, especially from you both."

"Thank you so much." We hear the teapot whistling. I walk through her beads and into the purple kitchen to help. I look up and see glow in the dark stars on the ceiling of her kitchen.

"You have good taste."

"Well, I have to keep the mood for my customers, and it relaxes me."

"I can see why," I smile. I carry our teas out to the living room and hand Fredrick his cup. Maggie brings the incense onto the middle of the table in between the candles.

"Okay, let's see what we can do. One of my specialties is doing a séance. I could try to speak to the spirit of one of the victims."

I look at Fredrick with fear. "Um okay."

"I know it sounds scary, but you deal with victims in your dreams and in your waking life, this will be a piece of cake, I promise.

"Okay, if you say so," I say rubbing my arms as a cold chill passes through me.

"Give me the name of one of the victims to contact."

"Fredrick, who do you think we should contact?"

"How about the most recent victim, Ms. Riley? She could give us his newest location."

"Good idea. We'd like to contact Ms. Riley. She was a third grade teacher at Harper Elementary."

"Okay, let's begin." She turns off all the lights and the only thing lighting the ominous room are the flickering candles. She grabs our hands so we are forming a triangle around the table.

"Spirit world, we enter you to communicate with Ms. Riley. Please allow us to speak with her," Maggie says aloud in a deep, soft voice. Hearing her gives me chills down my entire body. I squeeze Fredrick's hand a little harder and he responds back to give me comfort. She remains quiet with eyes closed. I keep my eyes closed as well and concentrate on what she looks like.

"Ms. Riley, if you are listening, please give us a sign that you are here. These two detectives are in dire need of your help and would like to speak to you." We are silent for a few seconds then a wave of cold air rushes by us, which makes me jump in my seat.

"Okay Linda, she is with us and listening. Go ahead and ask her something." I look over at Maggie and her eyes are wide open staring at the ceiling.

"Ms. Riley, first I'd like to say how sorry I am that this happened to you. My partner and I need your help finding Jack. Do you know where he is located?"

Maggie has her eyes closed now and her head is gently circling, and then she looks at us. "She said when he kidnapped her, she was blindfolded and she couldn't see where they were going, but she heard train tracks at some point. When he took off her blindfold all she could see was wooden walls and a dim light."

Shit, nothing. He cleans his tracks well. "Okay, tell her thank you."

"Wait, she has something else to say. What is it?" Maggie asks the air. "She's trying to tell me something but there's a struggle. She's running away from someone; she's trying to warn us but I can't make it out."

My heart is racing in fear. The wind around us is moving quicker. Then all of the candles burn out at the same time. I gasp and tighten my grip on Fredrick.

"What was that?" I hear nothing. "Maggie!" I say shaking her hand.

"It's not Maggie anymore." I let go of her hand and back my chair up.

"What the hell is going on?" I look at Maggie then at Fredrick and he looks just as confused as I am.

"Oh, don't be scared Linda." I see Maggie's mouth moving but her voice turns deep, cold, and manly. Maggie has no idea what is happening to her right no. I have to help her.

"If you're not Maggie then who are you?" The candles are all of a sudden become lit again. I see Maggie's eyes, and they are completely black. Shit!"

"Oh, I think you know. What we had between us was real."

"Oh fuck," I say with a shaky voice. My hands begin to sweat and shake. I look at Fredrick. "It's Tom."

"Aw, Linda you remember me. I was afraid you had forgotten me by now. My brother Jack is doing such a fine job; don't you think?"

"You're still a fucking lunatic."

He laughs, *"I made you a promise and I intend to keep that promise. Unfortunately, I'm a little dead to fulfill it myself, but Jack has that part covered.*

"What is it that you want?"

"You already know that, Linda. I want you forever. If you're dead, then you can be with me forever."

"Right, but you'll be in hell so I would be so far from you." Fredrick sits in silence. He has no idea what to do right now.

"That's what you think. Just wait, I'll get you one way or another."

"You don't scare me. I'm going to kill Jack, then you both can be together again."

"You have no idea what is coming, my dear. I'll be waiting."

The candles blow out and the lights turn on. Maggie gasps for air and wakes up. "Are you two okay? I hate when that happens!"

"That has happened to you before?" I say with surprise.

"Yeah, the spirit world is a tricky place. It's not filled with just good spirits and sometimes the evil spirits can overpower."

"Aren't you afraid that one day one of the evil spirits won't leave you?"

"Yes, but I have to please my customers." I shake my head in response. She's crazier than I thought.

"Did it help you out at all?" she asks with concern.

"No, it made me more scared and brought back a bad time in my life."

"I'm so sorry, dear. Maybe this will help." She gets up from her chair and walks over to a big black bookcase and opens one of the drawers. She hands me a glass jar filled with what looks like mashed up leaves.

"This is my own homemade sleeping remedy. The ingredients are all natural and it is supposed to help the restful sleep. This will clear you mind before you go to bed. You can focus on one thing and one thing only. This will help you control your dreams more than you ever have before. But if you're not careful and you take too much at once or multiple days in a row you can be stuck in your dream for a long period of time."

I shrug my shoulders, "Not like that hasn't happened before," I say jokingly.

"Linda, this isn't a joke. I keep this stuff hidden because if it gets into the wrong hands it can do damage. I don't want to be responsible for your death, or for you to be stuck in a dream state that you'll never be able to get out of."

I swallow hard. "Okay, I promise I won't overuse it."

"Save it for a time when you really need it. If you can't find any information about Jack and he keeps killing, then use this, but only the very last resort. I think you should give your dreams another chance before using this."

I shake my head in agreement. "Okay, I will. What do I owe you?"

"Nothing, believe me."

"Okay, thank you. Is there any advice you could give me about my dreams? Is there something I should try and do?"

"You've tried a lot. Don't let the fact that this is Tom's brother distract you from using your gift to your full potential. I believe you're holding back without realizing it because you're scared."

I am scared to death. I nod my head and give her a hug. "Thank you."

"I'm sorry I couldn't be more of a service, and I'm sorry I brought an evil entity to you."

Fredrick drives us back to the station. "Well, Tom hasn't

changed," he says to break the silence.

"That was fucking weird. I never thought I'd have to hear his voice ever again. My stomach is still turning from it."

"I'm sorry."

"It's okay, I'm just glad it's over. I don't want to go back to Maggie's unless there's an absolute need."

He smiles. "I agree. So are you going to use that sleep stuff she gave you?"

I pull it out of my purse and look at it. "I don't know. Using something like this with my past history of comas and health issues, I'm not sure it's a great idea. But I'll use it if I have to."

"Well let's hope you don't." *I have a feeling I'll be using it more than once. It's the price I have to pay to catch Jack. I'd rather be stuck in a dream than see my family murdered.* Knots form in my stomach just thinking about it.

Maggie's House
7:00 p.m.

I wait anxiously as I see Linda and Detective Fredrick walking out from this woman's house. Tom led me here for a reason and the plan is going to work out perfectly. Linda pauses before she goes into the car and looks down at something in her hand. I can't tell what it is from here but I'm sure it is important. Whatever it is, I need to get my hands on it. I can't let her be a step ahead of me. She puts it in her purse and then ties her long black hair into a ponytail. Oh, I can't wait until I can see the look on the pretty thin face of hers once this is over. "Tom, you'll be pleased, I promise."

After their car leaves, I see the woman with crazy hair walk back inside her A-framed house. I get out of the car. "It's time to play," I say as I walk across the street and up to her front door. I grab the knife out of my pocket case and hold it behind my back and knock on the door.

"Coming!" I hear a sweet voice, which is about to turn into fear. "Did you forget-" She stops as she sees me. Her eyes get big and she gasps as if she knows who I am. "What are you doing here?"

"I must be famous around here," I say as I step forward into the door of her house.

She stands straight in front of me. "You're not coming in here," she says with confidence.

I quickly hold my knife to her neck. "Are you sure about that?" I say as I knick her neck. I shove her inside and slam the door. I point the knife at her and look around her incense cluttered home. "I want what you gave, Linda." I say straight and to the point.

"I don't know what you're talking about." She is confident right now. She is going to be hard to break.

"Don't give me that bull shit, Maggie. I saw it in her hand."

"I don't have any left."

I glance around and I see a big wooden cabinet with many drawers and I slowly make my way over there. "Oh yeah? Are you sure about that?" I open some drawers. Her look turns to worry.

"You don't know what you're looking for. Go ahead and try one of those herbs and see what it'll do to you."

I grab her by her hair and pull her close. I slit one of her wrists. "You better tell or you'll suffer."

She falls to the floor and holds her wrist. She looks up at me. "You're going to kill me anyway. I know it's part of your plan. Well, your dumbass brother's plan."

I look at her with confusion.

"I'm a psychic. I can see and hear many things, Jack. So go ahead and kill me. I'll never tell you what I gave Linda. I want her to kill your sorry ass."

Hmm, she needs an incentive. I glance at the pictures of her family on top of the cabinet. "Okay, so what about these two children here. Who are they to you?" I say as I grab the frame and show her.

"Nothing that concerns you. "I'll never tell you where they are!" Tears form in her eyes. Good, I'm getting to her.

"You don't have to tell me who they are. They mean something to you so I'll kill them in your honor."

She shakes her head and cries. "No, please don't."

"Tell me what you gave Linda. Don't try and con me either and give me something else, because if it's the wrong herb, I'll kill them slowly and painfully, I promise. Read my mind and you'll know I'm serious." She begins to cry harder.

"Okay, but please promise me you won't hurt them."

"I cross my heart," I say and smile at her.

"The very last drawer on the right. It's in a plastic container."

I get a rush of excitement as I open the drawer and hold a container that looks like a bunch of cooking herbs. "This better be the real deal."

"It is, but I can't promise it'll work on you. Linda has a gift."

"What can it do?"

"Enhance dreams so you can change anything, make anything look real, and other qualities you can figure out on your own."

She looks up to the ceiling and starts to pray or something. I walk over to her. "Thank you for your service, Maggie. I truly hope you have a good life on the other side." I stab her through the heart. She's panting; the life is slowly disintegrating from her face and body. I quickly remove the knife and blood drips onto the floor. I pull a vial from my pocket and lay it next to Maggie's head.

I look down at the herbs in my hand. "Now we're on the same level," I say as I begin to laugh.

***

Fredrick follows me home and I wave goodbye as I enter the house. Luke and Michael are wide awake watching TV. Michael runs up to me and gives me a hug.

"Hey sweetie, what are you guys watching?"

"Since it's Friday and I got an A on my math test, Dad let me choose, so I picked Superman!" His face lit up.

"You got an A? I'm so proud of you. That's my boy!" I say kissing him on the forehead. I go over and kiss Luke.

"Boy, do I have a story for you."

"I smell the incense. Let me guess…Maggie?"

"Yeah," I say quickly. "I'm going to go shower and I'll tell you everything after."

The hot water feels amazing running down my body. I close my eyes as I wash my hair and all I can hear is Tom's voice. Flashes go through my head of what happened when I was in my coma; Tom tying me to the bed. Then I see him die in front of me and instant relief flies through my body. Little did I know that he would still haunt me. Even if we kill Jack, will Tom ever leave me alone? Does he have any other siblings or friends who can finish the job for him? Will I ever be able to forget about him and what he did to me? Tears fall down my face and I cry out in pain and fear.

I head back downstairs and Michael is now asleep in Luke's lap. I smile at the beautiful sight. Luke carries Michael to bed and I turn off the lights. I kiss Michael goodnight and head into the bedroom.

"So what happened at Maggie's?"

"She performed a séance."

Luke looks at me as if I am kidding. "What?"

"Yeah, and I thought I was crazy." I go into detail about what happened. Luke has his mouth open in shock.

"Baby, I'm so sorry you had to deal with that. That must have been horrible," he says rubbing my head.

"It brought back everything I went through. She also gave me this," I say as I pull the sleeping herbs from my purse. I explain to him what they are and what they can do.

"No, absolutely not."

"I know; I won't use them."

"You promise? I know what you'll do in desperate times. You go to the extreme Linda, and I won't lose you again."

"I promise. I'll go and flush them down the toilet now." I walk into the bathroom, open the toilet seat, and pause. I couldn't do it knowing this could help me catch Jack once and for all. I decide to hide them in the linen closest. I flush the toilet pretending I did it.

I walk back into the bedroom. "Good, now get into bed," Luke says with a smile.

I go to close the curtains and that is when I freeze. "Luke, did you notice a white van parked across the street?"

"What van?" he says as he gets out of bed. "No, I don't remember that being there."

My gut is telling me that is supposed to be there and we are supposed to find it. "I don't think this is a coincidence. We need to go check it," I say as I put on my shoes.

Luke grabs my arm. "No, remember last time there was a van outside our house? It blew up. I'm not having you walk anywhere near that van."

"It's fine," I say as I take my gun and head down the stairs. Luke follows me with his gun. He looks at me before I open the door.

"You're crazy if I thought I'd let you go out there by yourself."

I smile at him. "I'd be worried if you didn't."

We walk slowly across the street looking at our surroundings. There isn't a person in sight; funny how that always happens. Luke looks under the van for any abnormal parts or bombs. I look through the front windows but there is nothing there. I look through the back windows but they are tinted and it's too dark to see inside.

"We need to open the door." Luke nods and begins to slowly open the door. We both back away quickly as we are overcome with a rotting smell. He opens the door all the way.

There is Mrs. Smith dead, drowning in her own blood. Her arms are wide open along with her eyes, and the number 8 is carved on her chest. Next to her is a vial of blood and a note. I grab the note.

"I'm closer than you think," is what the note says; it's his new saying that I'm getting sick and tired of reading. I hand it to Luke, furious and sickened by this game Jack is playing. I am no longer sad, I am fucking mad.

Chapter 11

Halloween Night

A few weeks has passed since there has been any sign of Jack and victim number seven. The blood that was tested is a match for a woman named Holly Murphey. Her last known address was the streets. She has no family who cares she is missing. This victim is very out of his usual targets, but I can't even try to piece Jack together anymore. There haven't been any more victims of Jack's so far. We have caught other murderers but not Jack. He is keeping quiet again. Usually that means something big is coming. Police officers surround our house day and night. I wanted to keep Luke and Michael in a safe house, but Luke wouldn't have it. He won't let someone scare us out of our own home. It is a dark and clear night for trick or treating. Sarah and Bobby brought over their baby girl, Anna and we are all going out together.

Michael runs down the stairs in his Superman costume looking adorable. "Mom, I wish I could really fly like Superman. He's the best superhero ever!" he says as he imitates flying around the house. I've decided to dress as wonder woman, which is Luke's choice of course.

"So, we have Superman and Wonder Woman," Sarah says with a big smile. "Who's Luke going to be?"

"Well, I'm Thor," Luke says as he holds his hammer in the air. We all die laughing. Sarah looks at me from across the couch.

"Let me guess, this is your doing, Linda?" she asks as we laugh.

"Oh, you bet ya!" Sarah and Bobby are dressed up as the angel and devil and little miss Anna is Cinderella.

"We're quite a diverse group!" I say as we walk out the door. We stop at every house and there's so much candy. It is a warm evening and the moon is shining bright. A full moon on Halloween isn't a good sign. I enjoy hearing the children's laughter as we walk down the streets. It is nice to see so many people participating and so many houses decorated.

After hours of collecting candy, we sort through it together back at the house. I get Sarah, Bobby, Luke, and myself some wine as we watch Michael help Anna look through their candy. I talk with Sarah a little about May's bridal shower while the boys talk guns. No surprise there. Sarah and I decide to make it a tropical themed shower.

"Mom, there's a man standing outside our house," Michael says. Luke and I jump to our feet. I grab my gun from the counter and go to the door. Luke and I look out of the door and we see a tall, lanky man standing in the street facing our house.

"He has the nerve to come here! Where are the cops?" I ask.

"Over there. They're getting out of their car now and walking towards him," Luke says. Sarah is holding Anna and Bobby is behind us.

"He's running!" I start to go out the door but Luke stops me.

"Stop, the two policemen are going after him. Let them do their job."

"Luke, I'm a detective, so it's my job."

"Not right now it isn't." I stare out the door waiting for a sign, when my phone rings.

"Linda, I'm assuming you know Jack was at your house."

Fredrick sounds disappointed.

"Yes, I was about to run after him myself. Did either policeman get him?"

"I'm afraid not. They lost him in the chase."

"Of course!" I yell out. I hang up the phone.

"He got away." Luke calms me down since we have guests.

"Well we better get home, as Anna is falling asleep in my arms," Sarah says with fear in her voice. I can tell she is uncomfortable and I don't blame her. I tried to have a good time with my friends and it always ends up badly.

"Okay, I'm sorry that happened."

"Don't be. Please be careful," Bobby says. We watch them as they get into their cars and then we lock our door.

"Luke, what are we going to do? It has been weeks and we let our guard down and look what happened?"

"Linda, he just wanted to scare us. We have protection 24/7."

"Yeah and look what good that did.., they lost him. I want us to be in protective custody."

"And live in a hotel or safe house for who knows how long? No, I won't do that to Michael. He'll be fine here with us and the added policemen."

"Luke," I start to protest and then he stops me.

"We've dealt with this before and we won."

"If you call May getting kidnapped, our house burning down, and myself being in a coma for six years then yeah we sure did win. We have Michael to protect now. Jack showed up tonight without any problem, so what will he do next?"

Michael is sitting in the recliner keeping quiet. I can sense his fear. Luke is staring at me. "Fine, we'll go into protective custody. The last thing I want is Michael to be harmed."

"Oh, thank you, I'm calling Fredrick back now."

"Michael honey, I want you to go and pick out some clothes for a while."

"Luke, will you help him pack while I call Fredrick?" he nods his head and follows Michael up the stairs.

"Fredrick, Jack knows where we live and he was able to get right in front of us. It isn't safe for my family at this house. Can we get into protective custody?"

"Absolutely. I was wondering when you were going to bring that up. I was going to ask but I figured when the time was right you'd come to me. I have the perfect place. It's a little cottage next to a lake. There will be hired bodyguards who were in the military at the cottage at all times. There will be guards outside as well. A few hundred feet behind the cottage is a hidden house where the policemen will stay so there's plenty of protection close by. You'll have walkie-talkies at your cottage that automatically reach the officers in the house. You're literally a button away from safety if something goes wrong at the cottage."

I sigh with relief. "That sounds perfect. Thank you so much."

"How about I escort you all myself? We'll give you an unmarked car that can't be tracked. Your cars will stay at your house. Your cell phone will stay at your house too. We'll give you a cell phone that can only be traced by us, so you can still contact your family and friends. But be very careful who you give the number to."

"Sounds like great protection to me."

"Oh believe me, the best in Charleston. Michael will be escorted to school every day and an officer will stay parked outside the school and will escort him home."

"Great. What about Luke?"

Fredrick pauses for a moment, "Will he be up for an escort?"

"I'll make him be okay with it. I want everyone protected. I also want daily protection around my sister's family and my parents."

"Done."

"Fredrick, I can't thank you enough for everything."

"There's no need to thank me. We're partners and that is what we do. I'll be there along with other officers to escort you in about thirty minutes."

I head upstairs to start packing. I stop by Michael's room and see him packing all of his favorite clothes. "Hey Mom, Dad told me we're going to a place where we'll be safe. I'm excited to go somewhere new for a while."

"Oh Michael, you always see the positive in the worst of things. That's a gift. Pack a lot. I'm not sure how long we'll be gone."

"Can I bring some books and toys?"

"Of course, bring anything you want."

I head into our bedroom to start packing. I have a lot to pack in thirty minutes. Luke is shuffling around shoving things into his suitcase. He looks panicked and scared. I walk over to him, stop him, and grab his face with my hands.

"Luke, you need to relax. This is for the best. We'll be fully protected. Fredrick told me all the details. Plus, we can think of this as a nice getaway."

He lowers his head. "I know, I just don't like the fact that we have to leave our home because there's a risk our family could be hurt."

"I know and I don't either but we can't change it. We need to embrace it and realize this is the best situation for us. I already feel less stressed and I can focus on catching Jack. Knowing you're safe 24/7 is relaxing."

He grabs my hands. "Yeah, I guess you're right. Can you do one thing for me please?"

"I know you want me to be careful."

"Well yes, but I want you to bring this along with you." I watch Luke walk over to my dresser and pull out a black lace lingerie outfit.

I instantly smile and I can feel my face getting red. "Of course I can bring that with us, and anything else you want," I say as I grab the lingerie from his hands and gently kiss his lips. We start to get off track from packing.

I pull away. "We better finishing packing babe. We only have a few minutes until they get here."

"Alright, alright."

About fifteen minutes later Fredrick walks through the door. "Linda, are you all ready?' he calls out. We rush down the stairs with our suitcases.

"I think we've got everything."

Fredrick smiles as he looks at all of our suitcases. "It looks like you guys are moving out of the country?" he laughs. It's always good to hear Fredrick laugh as it makes for a calming mood.

I look around. "Oops, I guess we over packed but we weren't sure how long we'd be there. It's better to be safe than sorry!"

He smiles. "It's not a problem. A car full of bodyguards will be following us. They'll be staying with you all. There's another car driven by one of the guards staying with you that is driving your car. Remember, everything is only traceable by us so we can keep track of you. We have canvassed the area and there's no sign of Jack or any unusual unmarked cars. We should be safe leaving. On the drive to the cottage we'll make a few stops and go off track a little just to make sure we aren't being followed."

"Okay, sounds good. Let's get this show on the road." Luke and I leave our cell phones in the kitchen drawers and Fredrick hands us our new ones.

On the drive to the cottage, I call May and my parents to let them know what is going on and the new number they can reach me at.

"Luke, what are you going to tell the hospital?"

"I'll give them a brief explanation and give this new number to only a few people at the hospital who I can truly trust for emergencies. I'll tell them when I go into work tomorrow. I have a long day of surgeries starting at 7:30 in the morning."

"Okay, and it'll be a long day for me as well. Now that we know Jack is back and close, we have a lot of work to do." Luke grabs my hand with comfort and my other hand is rubbing Michael's head, who has now fallen asleep on me.

Protective Custody Cottage
11:15 p.m.

After what seems like hours of driving due to all the stops and detours we finally arrive at the cottage. It is dark so it is hard to see all the details but from what I am seeing through the car headlights it is beautiful. The cottage is surrounded by trees and to the side is a big lake. The moonlight shines off the water and it is so serene.

"Stay in the car while we check the area and inside the cottage," Fredrick says with his serious tone.

I calmly wake Michael up. "We're here," I whisper. He looks outside and his eyes grow wide.

"Wow, this is awesome!" This is the happiest I've seen Michael in a while. I'm in a happy place because I know we're all safe. Maybe this is what I needed all along, for my family to truly be safe, while I focus on my dreams and finding Jack. All signs are pointing up.

Fredrick comes back and lets us know it is all clear. We get out of the car and I look at the cottage all lit up. I stand in clarity for a minute. This cottage looks like something out of a fairytale – the stone siding, the windows glowing with a dim yellow light, and the lake adjacent glowing with moonlight gives a very inviting feeling. This is not only a safe house but also a place of simplicity and hope.

The three bodyguards who will be staying with us escort us into the house. Entering, I feel an aurora of tranquility. I feel the warmth from the stone fireplace and the glimmering yellow light that shines through the living room. There is oak wood furniture and two sofas that face each other, which look cozy with the light blue soft material. Fredrick shows us the kitchen that has antique stove and kitchen appliances but it is refreshing. Everything in here is antique but homier than anything I've seen. There are three bedrooms down the hall from the kitchen and one bathroom. All the bedrooms have huge beds with long wooden bedposts and rugs near the bed that look like they were handmade. I never want to leave this place. I turn around and look at Fredrick.

"So, is this place for sale?" After I ask, Luke and Fredrick let out a small laugh.

"Well if this place was for sale it wouldn't be much of a safe house, would it?" Fredrick says.

"I guess, but this place has so much character and story. I love it."

Luke comes up to me and kisses my forehead. "Well, maybe when Jack is caught and there's no present danger towards our family we can persuade the police department and FBI to sell us this house. Everything has a price."

I wrap my arms around Luke. "Oh, thank you so much."

"You're welcome. Now let's focus on the current issue and then we can plan."

Michael comes running in. "Mom, have you seen my room?" he asks with excitement. "There's a wooden chest full of neat toys!" I glance at Luke and Fredrick and smile as I follow Michael into his room. He shuffles through a big wooden toy chest and pulls out different toys onto his colorful rug.

"I hate to break up this moment, but I need to officially introduce you to your bodyguards and explain the communication system with the house behind yours," Fredrick says.

We all go into the kitchen. Three tall, hefty men stand before us. Fredrick points to the blonde one first. "This is Mick Reynolds, former CIA with military background." We shake hands and introduce ourselves. He then points to a dark-haired, clean-cut man. "This is Ryan Matthews. He served in Afghanistan." We shake his rough hands. Fredrick points to the last man. He has a soft, kind face with light brown hair. "This is Ronald Belview. He was in the Navy. The three of them will take turns watching out. One will be in the third bedroom and the other two will be outside surrounding the cottage. They will be in and out of the house using this back door only," Fredrick says as he points to the door behind the kitchen table. "They do have guns, but they keep them on them at all times unless needed. They'll escort you all to work, school, and to the store. It's best for now to keep the traveling to a minimum in case of you all being followed, we don't want to take any risks. Mick will go to the grocery store tonight so the fridge and pantries will be stocked. Do any of you have questions?"

The three bodyguards stand tall, shoulders straight, and arms in front. They look like they could all move in sync. "I think we're good for now," I say with slight hesitation. That is a lot to take in.

"Okay good." Fredrick hands us the walkie-talkie. "This is to be used only for emergencies. To call out to the officers in the house a few hundred feet from here, all you do is hold this big black button and talk. They will respond in seconds," he explains to Luke, Michael, and myself so we all know how to use it.

I grab the walkie-talkie. "Okay, thank you Fredrick, I think we got it," I say as I look at Luke and nod at him. I glance at the clock on the wall that sits above the stove and it reads midnight.

"I think we're all exhausted, so we should get some rest. We all have big days tomorrow," I say as I yawn.

"Of course. I'll see you at the office first thing tomorrow," Fredrick says as he walks out the wooden front door. Ryan and Ronald take first watch outside and Mick heads into the third bedrooms. We unpack a small bag with all of our toiletries and get ready for bed. I secretly packed the herbs.

Luke and I tuck Michael into bed and head into our room. I shut the beautiful wooden door and climb into the big, soft, comfortable bed.

"Exactly how tired are you?" Luke asks me with a seductive voice and smile.

I take off my tank top and roll over on top of Luke's bare body. "Not tired enough," I whisper and I begin to kiss him.

Abandoned Shelter
Monday November 1st 2:00 a.m.

I was so close to her. I know where she lives now, which will make my mission come to an end quicker than expected. That's good. I glance over at Holly who is sitting patiently in the chair. She is tied with rope but hasn't shown any restraint or fear. I guess I should have known better, picking a victim of the street. Well, she will be an easy kill. For my next target I need to find someone close to Linda, but not too close. I can't give all my tricks away this soon. I still have six murders to go, well five after today. I slap Holly across the face. "Why won't you cry or scream?" I yell out.

Her eyes are dark. "You think I'm scared of you? I've lived on the street for half my life. I've seen and done things way scarier than you."

I brush her red hair behind her ears then grab the back of her head with force. "Oh, you will be afraid of me when this is all over." I throw her head back and storm into the next room. I begin to revise my plan I had originally written. Linda is smarter than I thought and I've had a few setbacks but I will get back on track this week.

After about an hour of planning I decide that I need to get some rest. I hear a shuffle coming from the living room. "What the hell is that?" I slam open the door. "What are you-" I stand in shock. Holly has escaped. I glance at the front door as it sways. "That bitch!"

I run outside and glance into the dark forest. "I will find you!" I scream out.

***

I'm running so fast. It's dark but I can hear the ruffling of leaves under my feet. I am jumping over branches. My heart is pounding so fast and the adrenaline is pumping through my veins. Wait, this isn't me? I can see clearly and I can feel the emotions of this woman and she is scared to death. Okay, focus on what she needs and help her. I feel like we have been running for miles. She is breathing heavily. I can't believe she hasn't stopped for a break. She must be scared from whomever she is running from. I look ahead and I see a dim light. It has to be a streetlight! She picks up her pace as if she is fighting for first place in a marathon. I begin to feel her relief.

"I will get you, Holly! I will find you! You can't hide from me!" I hear a high-pitched screaming voice. I know exactly who that is. Jack. This is victim number six, Holly. I can't believe she escaped. I wonder if she can hear my thoughts or maybe I can speak to her some way.

"Holly, go to Charleston Police Department and ask for Detective Fredrick and Jackson."

I don't get a response but I hope she heard. She continues to run towards the light. She comes out on a street. I have no idea where the hell we are. She looks left and right but road is all there is. She runs down the street. She gets tired. She stops, bends over, and takes deep breaths. The sound of a car slowing down pierces our ears. The car pulls next to her.

"Ma'am, are you in trouble? Do you need a ride?" a nice young woman asks. Oh, thank goodness! I can feel Holly's relief.

"Oh, yes please. Thank you so much. A man captured me and I escaped. I need help."

"Come on in. I'll help you."

Holly opens the door and looks at the kind woman. "Please take me to the Charleston Police Department."

She heard me! Finally, someone I can help!

The alarm wakes Luke and me up. "I've got something! Finally, my dreams are helping. I have to get to the station now. I'll explain tonight I promise," I say as I kiss Luke, jump out of bed, and quickly get dressed. I grab a protein bar and I see Ronald sitting at the table drinking coffee.

He stands immediately as he sees me. "Mrs. Jackson, is everything okay?" he asks with a soft and kind tone.

"Yes, I need to go to CPD."

"Okay, I'll drive you there."

I nod. "Thank you so much."

It is a quiet drive but I do get a little information from him about his time in the Navy and his family. When we pull into the CPD I anxiously get out of the car. I hope Holly is there.

"Thank you for the drive. You can go back to the house; I'm fine here."

"Okay, my number is programmed into that phone. Call me if you need me."

"Thank you, Ronald."

I race up the stairs and rush into the station. I see a woman sitting in the chair next to Fredrick's desk. Her red hair shines in the light. Holly. Thank God.

Chapter 12

CPD
Tuesday November, 2nd 7:00 a.m.

I slowly walk over and Fredrick stands up and meets me before I reach his desk. "This is-"

I stop him before he finishes. "Holly."

He gives me a puzzled look. "How did you know?"

"I had a dream last night. It wasn't like my normal dreams. In my dream I was Holly. I felt all her emotions and pain. In the dream I told her to come here and it worked! I can't believe it."

Fredrick softly smiles. "You did it. You saved her life and she has information about Jack." He motions for me to go over there and talk to her.

I walk around Holly and grab Fredrick's chair and move closer to her. "Holly, my name is Detective Jackson, but you can call me Linda. I know you have a lot on your mind and I know you're feeling overwhelmed, but we need your help." She looks at me with her big brown eyes that seem full of anger. She has no trace of tears. She is strong, and she is our key in finding Jack. "How did you know to come here?"

She clears her throat. "It's hard to explain. When I escaped from Jack, I was running so fast and my gut told me to come here. It was like someone talked to me in my mind. I know it sounds crazy."

I smile. "It doesn't sound crazy, trust me. Jack is going to try and find you. You're his first victim that has ever escaped and I have a feeling he's upset that about. We're going to put you up in a hotel with officers outside your door until this is over."

"Wow, I haven't slept in a bed in years. That will be nice for a change. Thank you so much."

"You're welcome. Before we take you to the hotel I have some questions for you."

She nods her head ready to listen. Fredrick and Sergeant Gordon join us in our discussion. She looks around as if she feels suffocated by everyone.

I put my hand gently over hers. "It's okay. You don't' have to worry; you can trust us. We've been on the hunt for Jack for months. We're desperate to find him."

She nods her head and clears her throat again. "I don't know where he was holding me. All I know is that it was in some kind of old home in the middle of a forest. When I was running away it felt like I was running for at least five minutes until I reached the road. Then a woman picked me up and drove me here."

"Okay, good. Did you see any signs or stores that you could pick out on your way here?"

"Yes, we passed a Sunoco gas station, a few hole-in-the-wall shops, and we came to a stop light and turned right and passed under a bridge. Then we drove for a few miles and came into town here."

"That's great. We can find his shelter from that information," Fredrick says.

"Did he say anything to you about his next victim?"

She shakes her head. "No, but he was mad at me because I wasn't afraid of him. He said his victims are usually scared for their life, begging him to let them go. I wasn't afraid, I have seen a lot on the street and he didn't like that. He went into his room to come up with a plan for his next victim. That's when I escaped. He did tell me I was different than his other victims, as he usually likes them scared and delicate. He said he wouldn't get another woman like me again and that he was going to have a fun time killing me. He saw it as a challenge, but didn't want another challenge. So I guess his next victim will be like his others. He mentioned how he liked blondes the best. He talked to this picture a lot. He was weird. He told the picture that he was closer to his plan and he promises he will end it."

I roll my eyes. "Yeah, that's his dead brother he was speaking too."

She raises an eyebrow. "And I thought I've seen a lot," she says with humor.

I smile. "Is there anything else he said to you? Any other minor details?"

She thinks for a minute and her eyes widen with excitement. "He did say that after he killed me he was going back to the Pavilion Bar to do what he does best."

"That's great! Thank you, Holly. Now let's get you to the hotel and freshened up. The hotel is on us so please use room service for food. But we advise you not to leave the hotel until we tell you it's safe. If you have to go somewhere take Officer Douglas with you," I say as I take her to him.

"Oh, I don't want anywhere to go. I'm just happy I'll have a bed, TV, and real food. Thank you so much." She gives me an unexpected hug.

I hug her back and smile. "You're welcome. Here's my phone number in case you need me."

She smiles as she takes my card. I can tell there is good in her. She has a story, and maybe all she needs is a friend. I feel as if I need to help her. I watch her as she walks away with Officer Douglas.

I walk back over to Fredrick's desk and he is giving me a pondering look. "I know what you're thinking, Linda. You can't save everyone."

He knows me well. "This is the first of Jack's victims I've saved and she has nothing to go home to. I feel the need to help her."

"She has done fine on her own."

"Living on the streets isn't fine. There's more to her and I'm going to find out what and then I'm going to help her."

He shrugs his shoulders. "Okay, that's fine but Jack comes first. She's safe."

"I know. Let's go find that shelter."

Abandoned Shelter
8:30 a.m.

"Let's pull over here," Fredrick says as he thinks we have reached the point on the road where the shelter could be.

I look to my left. "There's the forest, and Holly said she ran about five minutes before coming to the road. Since it's daytime we should be able to find the shelter easily."

"I hope so, and I hope Jack is waiting there for us." We both know that isn't likely, as nothing comes that easily to us.

We walk slowly through the forest. I hear nothing but the sound of crunching leaves. I can smell the mildew from the damp leaves.

Then my stomach begins to turn. I pause and rub my hand over my stomach. "There's something wrong," I say as I hunch over in pain.

"What is it?" asks Fredrick as he rests his hand on my back.

"I don't know but I got a wave of nausea." Then flashes of my dream last night run through my head. I hold my head in pain.

Flash!

Images of Holly running through the forest.

Flash!

Holly breathing heavily and fear running through her veins. I stumble as I try to catch my balance. Fredrick grabs my arm.

"Linda, are you going to be okay?"

"Yeah, this is definitely the right area. I think my flashes are coming because we're getting closer to the shelter. Let's keep going," I say as I swallow a big gulp and take deep breaths to calm my nausea down. We begin moving forward. "I hope you know that when we do finally catch Jack, I'm not letting him go. I'm going to kill him," I say with anger.

"I didn't hear you just say that."

"Fredrick, you can't believe this will be over if he just goes to jail. He's part of Tom's family and they always get out or have connections."

"I know and you're right, but that's going above the law."

"Not if it's self-defense," I say giving him a grim look.

"And you're right again." He lightly smiles at me as I do the same.

"We have to be getting close," I say. Fredrick pauses and holds his hand out for me to stop as well.

"Did you hear that?" he asks me. I freeze and listen closely. I hear birds chirping but that is about it. We stand there stagnant. Then I hear a small ruffle in the leaves. We both turn our heads towards the sound. But all I see are more trees. Then I hear his screeching laugh that echoes through the trees.

"He's found us," I say quietly.

"Stay low and watch out," Fredrick says.

Whoosh!

It sounds like something flew by me at an incredible speed. I turn to look behind me and on the tree is a knife. "Shit! Where is he?"

"I don't know but we're going to have to get out of here now. He knows this terrain too well."

Whoosh!

Another knife flies by me and lands on another tree.

"If he wanted to kill us he would have already. He's trying to scare us away."

"Yeah, which means his next throw could be through either of our hearts," Fredrick says with anger.

"No, we can't let him get away," I say as I stomp on.

Fredrick follows quickly to catch up. "Linda stop; you're not thinking clearly."

I turn around with force. "This has been way too long of a game for him. We need to end it." Then something happens.

Pain.

So much pain.

Warmth.

Pain.

I look at Fredrick in horror then I look down at my leg. There is a knife sticking out from my calf muscle. I see the blood dripping onto the leaves and I can feel the warmth of the blood trickling down my leg. The pain is too much to bear. The forest is moving quickly. I am feeling dizzy. Black spots are taking over my eyesight.

"Hang in there, Linda." I can faintly hear Fredrick's voice. He is guiding me through the trees. There are so many trees and they are moving. My head is becoming foggy.

Darkness.

MUSC
10:00 a.m.

I slowly begin to open my eyes. I can hear the beeping noise from a monitor. I know exactly where I am. I have had way too much experience waking up in a hospital bed. I squint to adjust my eyes to match the brightness of the room.

"Linda?" I hear Luke's voice faintly. I turn my head and he is right by my side sitting with perfect posture in the chair. His blue eyes seem to shine even more.

"Luke," I say with a smile.

"How are you feeling?"

"Well, I can't feel much right now," I say as I chuckle.

"They gave you some pain medications through your IV." I look down at my leg and see it wrapped with white gauze. "They took out the knife and stitched you up. It was a pretty deep wound."

"It hurt like hell," I say.

"I don't doubt it," Luke says with a soft tone.

"Where's Fredrick?"

"He's trying to find the son of a bitch. He told me to call him when you wake up."

"Please tell me he didn't go back out there alone?"

Luke shrugs his shoulders. "I don't know, he didn't specify. He was pissed that this happened to you."

"And you?" I say innocently.

"I was at first, but then I realized there's no point in arguing or staying mad." He smiles and it instantly brightens up the room. He presses the button to call in the nurse.

"They're going to release you soon." His tone of voice changes and becomes hesitant.

"What is it, Luke?"

"The doctor will want you to stay off your feet for a few days."

"No," I say shaking my head. "We were too close to Jack. I can't sit back and watch."

"You don't have to. You can work at your desk to try and find more information. Christopher is analyzing the knife to see if he can find anything unusual about it. You can work with him."

"I need to be out there with Fredrick."

Luke's face expression turns to anger. "No you don't. I think you can handle a few days sitting back. You're going to have to." Deep down I know he's right.

There is an awkward silence and I sigh. "Alright, fine. I'll stay at the desk till the end of the week."

"Thank you."

The nurse walks in smiling and bubbly. "How are you feeling, Mrs. Jackson?"

"Dandy," I say with sarcasm and I grin at Luke. She checks my blood pressure one more time and takes out my IV. She hands me some paperwork.

"Here's a prescription for pain medication just in case. If you have any severe pain, swelling, or puss that leaks through the stitches please come back right away. Clean with alcohol only and keep bandages on it until you come back to get the stitches taken out in two weeks."

I nod my head. "Thanks, but I'm sure Luke can take the stitches out for me at home, so there'll be no need for me to come back."

"I'm sorry, she can be a little stubborn," Luke says in my defense.

"A little?" the nurse says with a quiet laugh. "Oh and these are for you." I look at her as she hands me crutches.

"Crutches? Really? I won't be needing those."

"Oh really?" Luke says sarcastically. "Go ahead then. Try to walk."

I lift my legs and feel a sharp pain, but I ignore it, sit up, and move to the side of the bed. My legs are dangling. I slowly let my legs down to the ground and stand. "See, no problem!"

"Walk," Luke says as he motions his hands to let me by.

I step with my left leg first, the good leg. Then I begin to lift my right leg when I feel a sharp pain, but I move it anyway. I step down and try to put all the weight on my left leg but it doesn't work. I feel an instant sharp pain in my calf. I grab hold of the bed and Luke puts his hand on my back for support.

"Told-"

"Don't even say it," I interrupted. The nurse hands me the crutches. I take them quickly. After I get dressed I crutch out of the hospital.

Luke lifts me up and lays me out in the back seat of his Highlander. I see our bodyguard Mick get into his car and follow us home. "I guess it's a good thing we have bodyguards to drive me to work for the next few days," I say to break the ice.

"Yeah, I still think you should at least take one day to rest."

"Yeah, the rest of this day," I say and smile as Luke looks at me through his rearview mirror.

"Just don't push it please."

"I won't. I promise."

"Oh, and you need to call your Mom and May."

"What! You told them? They're going to give it to me."

"My thought exactly," Luke says proudly. I dial Mom's number first. I figured getting the Mom talk out of the way first would be better.

Protective Custody Cottage
5:00 p.m.

We pull into our home away from home and Ronald who is standing guard outside comes and assists us inside. As soon as I walk through the door, I see Michael sitting on the couch reading. His head perks up. "Mom!" He comes and gives me a big hug.

"Thanks Michael, I'm doing fine." He looks at me as if he doesn't believe me.

"Mom, you're allowed to hurt you know."

"Thanks Michael, I've had enough lectures today," I say as I hop over to the couch and prop my legs up. He follows closely behind. "What are you reading?"

"It's our reading story for the week."

"Oh, tell me about it." He jumps onto the couch beside me and opens the book.

"I'm going to get dinner ready," Luke says as he kisses me on the forehead.

My cell phone rings a few minutes later. "Linda, how are you doing?"

"Fredrick, thanks for calling. I'm doing fine. Were you able to find anything on Jack?"

"No, by the time I got to the shelter everything was gone. His knives that were in the tree were gone too."

"The knife he used on me didn't contain any poison."

"No, which is unusual. Christopher is working on the knife now."

"Okay, I can't believe he got away again."

"I know. We're getting closer and closer. You rest today and tomorrow and I'll get to work."

"I'll be in tomorrow."

"Linda."

"Fredrick, I'll see you tomorrow," I say as I hang up.

"I'm assuming Fredrick doesn't agree with you going into work tomorrow either?" Luke says as he swiftly moves across the living room to me.

I roll my eyes. "No. I'm just going to sit at my desk and try to map everything out. I want to see if I can piece any of my dreams together, maybe try to find bait for Jack or something. I don't know. All I know is that I need to be there tomorrow."

Luke sighs. "Alright, I'm not going to stop you."

"Thanks. Holly said he was going to hit Pavilion Bar for his next victim. I can try and dream tonight. I know that area like the back of my hand by now." I stare at the wall behind Luke remembering the herbs Maggie gave me. Not knowing what those things could do to me frightens me, but it would edify my dreams. The thought is amusing, but I feel like if I need to use the herbs, I'll know when the right time is and it's not the time yet.

"Linda, hello?" Luke says as I snap out of the thought.

I shake my head. "Yeah sorry."

He gives me a questioning look, "I think it's time for you to get some rest."

"I need to shower. I feel gross."

"You have to keep your bandaging on until tomorrow. I'll have to help you shower tomorrow morning before work. You'll probably have to use your crutches at work."

I laugh. "No I won't."

"I'm not starting this again. We don't want to wound to re-open. I'll carry you to bed." Luke gently puts one arm under my legs and the other arm around my back and lifts me off the couch like it's nothing."

I look back at Michael. "Goodnight sweetie."

"Good night, Mom. I'll try to help you tonight."

"Try to stay out of the dream, Michael."

He smiles, which is identical to Luke's bright smile. "Mom, telling me to stay out of the dream is like telling you not to work."

I laugh. "He's definitely our son," I say as I look at Luke then back at Michael. He holds his hands out and shrugs with an innocent smile.

"If you wake up in the middle of the night from a dream, wake me up," Luke says as he pulls the covers over me.

"I will. It'll be easy to put myself at the bar; I've done it a million times. I just want to be able to get a lead on where he'll be."

"I have no doubt that you will." He kisses my lips then turns out the light.

I glance down at my watch. It's 1:00 a.m — two nights from now, this is Jack's hunting hour. At least I know when and where he will attack next. If he walks in I will see him. I watch anxiously out of the car window. He picks a pretty high-class bar. It amazes me that he can get away with going in there. My eyes perk up when I see his tall body

151

walk up to the door. Even in the dim light I can see the outline of his nose. His long black hair is slicked back and he is in a black sports coat and jeans. If only those people knew what was walking into the bar. In order for this to work I have to play this out as long as I can so I can see his victim.

Now I know he is there, I have to stay alert. This is all too familiar. I can't believe it has gone on this long. How many more women will he kill before we can stop him? I glance at the top of the bar and I can see the colorful lights shining.

A few hours pass and I feel hopeless. Did I miss him walking out? I've been watching like a hawk. I don't understand. I look all around peeking through the windows of the car and I don't see anything. I glance at my rearview mirror and quickly double take. My heart starts to race when I see Jack standing behind my car with a woman in his arms and a knife to her neck. Shit!

I slowly get out of the car holding my gun at my side. I realize this is just a dream and the gun won't do shit, but maybe it will at least be a scare. I raise my arms up and glance over at Jack. I squint my eyes to adjust to the dim light we are standing under to see who he is holding.

"Holly! No!" I scream rushing forward.

Jack steps back and cuts her neck a little to make me stop. "I wouldn't do that if I were you," he says with his creepy high-pitched voice.

"Jack, please don't do this. Take me now, just leave her unharmed."

He tilts his head back and laughs. "This one got away. Linda. They never get away and they never will. I want you to remember those words."

"I will stop you Jack, before you do this."

He laughs again, this time the laugh is louder and his now-shaggy black hair rests in front of his eyes. "You won't have time to stop me, Linda. This is happening now."

I tilt my head to the side in confusion. "You can't kill her in a dream. You're good, but not that good. Plus, I can't even do that."

"No, but I can kill her at this moment in real life." I pause for a few seconds to grasp what the hell is going on. Then my eyes grow bigger because I realize I'm dreaming about this moment right now, not two days from now.

"How the hell are you doing this?"

"I have secrets too. By the way, have you heard from Maggie recently? Have you checked up on her?"

Tears start to form in my eyes, from hate. "What the fuck did you do Jack?"

"You think you're the only one who can get fancy dreaming medicine, think again. I'll always be a step ahead." Holly flinches as Jack digs the knife deeper against her throat. Her red hair is wet with sweat. Her eyeliner drips down her face. But there is a look of relief is in her eyes.

"It's okay Linda. I'm ready to die."

I shake my head. "No, no I was going to help you get back on your feet. This isn't right. I let you down."

She forms a small smile. "No Linda, you freed me. I'll be able to rest peacefully now."

"I'm so sorry," I say as tears fall from my eyes. I look at Jack and I can see his wide smile piercing through his hair. He slits her throat in one clean motion and she falls to her knees.

I run over to her and catch her and she falls back. "I'm so sorry. This is all my fault. You're dying because of me." I push her short red hair behind her ears.

"Stop saying you're sorry. Thank you for everything," she says slowly as she passes away into death.

I look up to see Jack missing but in his place is a vial of blood. It is labeled #6.

Chapter 13

I stare at the ceiling thinking about Holly and Maggie. I pray that he didn't kill Maggie. I should have never involved her. He must have stolen the herbs; that's the only way he could have made me think it was two days later in that dream. My phone begins to ring and I know it's Fredrick.

I answer the phone and listen. "Linda, we just got a phone call. I'm so sorry but Holly is dead. It was Jack. He left a vial of blood for us for victim six."

"I know. I was dreaming the whole thing as it was happening."

"What? How the hell did that happen?"

"Jack, he went to Maggie's. He has the dreaming herbs, Fredrick. He has power and control over his dreams and obviously mine. I think I know whose blood number six is." Tears form in my eyes and I swallow hard. "We need to get over to Maggie's now."

"Okay, I'll come and pick you up. Please be careful though and use your crutches." He hangs up without me protesting.

I put my phone down and look over at Luke who is sitting up in bed. "It's all my fault Luke. Holly, Maggie, all these women. I'm failing at my own special gift. I'm losing all control over my dreams. I don't know what to do. I don't know if I have the strength to fight harder." I begin to cry and he holds me in his arms.

"We'll figure something out."

"There's only one way I can be on the same level as Jack, or even be one step ahead of him."

"Linda, the herbs are gone."

I stretch out of his arms. "I didn't get rid of them. I had a feeling I'd need to use them."

"You're not doing it. It could possibly put you in a coma for life. It could kill you."

"Could is the key word there."

"You're risking your life."

"I'm risking to save you, Michael, Mom, Dad, May, and whoever else is in my life. Jack will kill you all and save me for last. I'm not letting that happen." I quickly get out of bed before he can respond. "Fredrick is coming to get me now. We need to get to Maggie's. I can't believe that if she's dead no one has called it in. Her body has been there for weeks, unless Jack did something with it." I shake my head with disgust. "I'm not letting anyone else die."

I walk downstairs to make a large pot of coffee. I call Maggie's house as I wait and I don't get an answer. I knew it was a long shot. I sit at the table and sulk in my emotions. I have to find a way.

***

"I can't believe he went to Maggie. How in the world did he find her?" Fredrick asks as he speeds on the interstate.

"He either followed us there, or Tom somehow communicated with him. Either way, if Maggie is dead, it's because of me. I know Maggie wouldn't have given Jack the herbs out of her own free will. He must have really persuaded her and then killed her so she wouldn't talk."

"Maggie is strong. I'm sure she held out as long as she could," Fredrick says as his voice chokes. I know Fredrick was always close with Arnold and Maggie. They were like a big family.

Maggie's House
8:00 a.m.

We pull into her driveway and the grass is so long and messy. No one has been here for a while. "What about her family? Wouldn't they check up on her?"

"From what Arnold used to tell me, her parents were dead and she had one brother who also died. She has a niece and nephew but she thought they would be better taken care of with an adoption home. She had no one."

"Fredrick, this is so sad. I don't know if I can handle this." He puts his hand on my shoulder.

"Linda, we have to do this, for Arnold and Maggie. Her body deserves a proper burial." *We don't know if she's dead yet, but I have a bad feeling.*

We slowly walk up her sidewalk that is covered with weeds. I

155

crutch up onto her patio and suddenly emerge into spider webs. I swat them away and off my clothes.

I lay my crutches against the house. Fredrick gives me a concerned look. "You didn't see that," I say as we pull our guns from our holsters and Fredrick kicks in the door. A rotten, dead smell takes over all my senses. I turn away from the living room and cover my face with my arm. It smells almost as bad as the time I went into the warehouse back in the deserted town where I found all the dead animals hanging. Fredrick grabs my arm and turns me around to show me what he sees.

Maggie's dead body lying in the middle of the floor covered with flies and maggots crawling over her skin. There is dried blood on the floor that surrounds her. Carved into her chest is the number six and lying in her hand is a vial. Fredrick picks up the vial and it is labeled with the number five.

"How did he do this? She has been here for weeks. He just killed number seven and now we're all the way down to five?" I ask as I hold back throwing up.

"He had this planned. He knew Holly would get out. She was tough and a fighter, and he doesn't usually go for those types of women. He must have known that Maggie didn't have family and he knew this would hurt us both." Fredrick shakes his head and then punches the wall with anger and frustration.

"I'll call forensics and get Christopher to run this blood ID as soon as possible. Who knows how long Jack has had this victim or if she's even still alive," I say as I try to storm out the front door but end up limping instead.

Fredrick and I sit outside in the car as they clean up the crime scene. We see them carry her body in the black bag. I look over at Fredrick and I see a tear fall from his eye. I never in a million years guessed anything could make him cry. I put my hand on his shoulder. "I'm going to do whatever it takes to stop him. I have a plan in mind."

He wipes his tear and looks at me. "Don't even think about it. I'm not losing another partner."

"Don't worry, you won't. I promise I'll come back. I'm going to spend some time over the next few weeks working on getting control back of my dreams. Once I feel confident I'm going to take those herbs and kill him. I think I'll be able to kill him in a dream. These herbs can do extraordinary things."

"If anything happens to you, I'm going to blame myself. Catching killers is the thing I do best. I shouldn't have to help. I got you involved with this FBI business."

"I wanted to do this. Even if you didn't get me involved I would have been involved anyway. This whole thing is happening because of Tom's obsession. Stop saying it's your fault when I got dragged into it because of some psycho."

"I'll still think it no matter what. But for the first time in my career I've never dealt with someone like this. I've never been not able to catch someone within a few days. I don't know what to do, Linda."

"I know how to stop him. There's only one way."

He puts his head down and shakes it. "You just got out of a six-year coma. You're willing to take a chance to go back or even worse?"

"Yes, because it's the only way. I won't go back to another coma. I'll fight harder than I've ever fought before. I promise you I'll come out alive and on time."

"I can't believe I'm saying it but okay." I feel a sense of relief; finally, someone is on the same page as me.

"He has number five now. I'll focus on my dreams tonight and start to get back to controlling them. I was able to do it with Tom and I can do it again. I don't care if he has the herbs because once I take the herbs I'll be in total control. I already have a special gift and Jack doesn't so it'll make my dreaming ability stronger."

"Alright. Let's head back to the station to see what Christopher finds out about the blood sample," Fredrick says as he backs out of Maggie's driveway.

CPD
Wednesday, November 3rd 11:30 a.m.

Christopher rushes out of his office. He pushes his big glasses up his nose before speaking. "The blood sample is back. The victim is a twenty-five year old waitress at the Pavilion Bar. Her name is Jasmine Brady."

I roll my eyes. "Of course. He probably got her last night somehow," I say with frustration. Just then a young man rushes through the door with dark short hair, a square jaw line, and worried brown eyes.

"Somebody please help me. My wife is missing." I look over at Fredrick and we both nod because we know that is Jasmine's husband.

Fredrick walks up to him. "Sir, my name is Detective Fredrick, how can we help you today?"

"It's my wife. She hasn't come home yet and it's not like her." He is talking so fast we can barely understand him.

Fredrick helps him to a seat. "Okay sir, calm down, we can help. Take a deep breath and tell us what you know." "Her name is Jasmine and she works at the Pavilion Bar as a waitress. They needed extra help last night so she stayed and worked a double. That's just the person she is. She'll put in the extra work whenever they need it. She's a wonderful person and a hard worker. She's always home right after work and she hasn't been home yet. I called the bar and they said she had left at four this morning after they finished cleaning. They didn't see where she went but they know she left. She'd never go anywhere but home. I have a bad feeling in my gut." He puts his hand over his stomach as if he is nauseous. His white gold and diamond wedding ring shines in the light.

"Okay, we'll help you find her. Do you have a recent picture of her?" He nods his head and pulls out his wallet and shows us a wedding picture of her in her wedding dress. I am stunned at her beauty. She has long red hair, bright green eyes, a few freckles on her checks, and a beautiful white smile. She has a face that shows kindness.

"She's beautiful," I say.

"Thank you. She's my world and we just found out last week that she's pregnant." His eyes tear up and my heart drops in my stomach. I have to do everything in my power to save this woman and her unborn child.

"We will find her, Mr. Brady. I promise."

He looks at me with sad eyes. "Thank you, and call me Chad."

"We'll go and interview the workers at Pavilion Bar and see if they know anything else." I fight the urge to tell him that we know she has been kidnapped and by who, but I can't do that to him. I want to find her alive and well.

"Chad, you should go to work and wait until you hear from us."

He looks at Fredrick in surprise. "I'm not going anywhere. Not until she's found."

"It might take us more than a day," Fredrick says with hesitation.

"What? No! You need to find her now!" he yells out as he stands up from his chair.

I put my hand on his shoulder. "Okay, we'll find her today. You stay here and wait."

Fredrick gives me a mean look. I grab my jacket and we head out the door. Fredrick pulls me aside. "What were you thinking telling him that? We haven't saved one of Jack's victims yet. Even if we do, he'll come back for her. You heard what he told you. He doesn't let anyone get away."

"Not this time. I don't care what time of day it is. I'm going home, taking those herbs, and dreaming now. I have to find them. I can control the dream and find exactly where they are at this exact moment. I can save her now and I will."

"This is nonsense. You haven't had any practice yet. Do you even know how much you're supposed to take at a time?'

"A pinch. I put it in water and gulp it down in one sip."

"Linda, I don't like this."

"Too bad, I'm doing it. The bodyguards are at the house. I'll have one of them watch me sleep and if they see struggle they can pour water on my face to wake me up. Don't tell Luke please."

He shakes his head in disappointment. His beard is slowly growing in. I can tell he is frustrated and tired because he always has the cleanest shave. I look him in the eyes and I can see bags underneath. He puts his aviators on as if he knows what I'm looking at. "What am I supposed to do while you're doing this?"

"Go question the workers at Pavilion Bar like we said. Take Detective Raymond with you. He seems bored in the office. He hasn't gotten in any of this Jack action." He runs his hand through his greased black hair.

"Fine. He's new and has a lot to learn. Throwing him into this case would scare him away from the job. What, you want me to get used to a new partner or something?"

"Well it'd be good for you to get to know him better and be familiar with the way he works." I sigh. "Again, please don't tell Luke. He'll stop me and it'll ruin everything. Once I get through this I can prove to him that I'm able to use the herbs a little at a time."

He nods in agreement. "It sounds like you're avoiding the

elephant in the room. Get in the car, I'm driving you to the safe house." I quickly get into his black sedan doing exactly what he said, avoiding the conversation of a new partner.

Protective Custody Cottage
1:30 p.m.

I walk into the house with determination. This is the last time he is going to kill; I'm going to make sure of that. I see Ryan sitting on the couch watching Fox News. Ronald must be with Luke and Mick is with Michael at school. As soon as Ryan sees me he stands tall as if I was going to tell him an order or something. Clean-cut, well dressed, and following the book by the rules is an understatement when it comes to Ryan. He puts Fredrick to shame. "Hi Ryan, I'm going to need your help with something."

He stands even taller. "Anything ma'am," he says as he stares straight ahead.

I move over to meet his stare. "It's going to sound a little strange, but I need you to trust me."

He raises one eyebrow slightly; his eyes are a coffee brown. "Okay, what is it?" he asks with hesitation.

"I'm going to sleep and try to find some answers from my dreams. I need you to watch me and if I look like I'm struggling in my sleep then I need you to do whatever it takes to wake me up." I lean in a little and stare harder. "Whatever it takes."

He turns his head slightly to the left. "Should I contact Mr. Jackson? I don't know if I feel comfortable doing this without his knowledge of what's going on."

"No!" I say sternly. "You can absolutely not call Luke. If you do, I'll have you fired." I'm serious about this. The herbs are my only chance, so I don't need someone stopping me.

He takes a step back. "Okay ma'am."

I nod my head. "Good. I'm going to the restroom then I'll be heading to bed." I never thought I'd say that at 1:30 in the afternoon. I swiftly move into my room to grab the herbs and my gun and head into the bathroom. The gun is what is going to kill Jack.

I fill a Dixie cup with water and I open the jar of herbs. An instant strong aroma of what smells like sage fills my nostrils. I gulp to calm my stomach down. I take a small pinch and put it in the water. The herbs separate as soon as they hit the water. I take a big breath. Here goes nothing. I throw my head back and down the herbs.

Dizziness.

Shortness of breath.

Light headed.

I feel as if I am going to wobble to the ground. My entire body feels like jello. "Shit, what did I do?" I mutter to myself. I grab onto the counter and the wall and force myself to make it to the bed. Lord knows I can't fall asleep on the floor as that would give Ryan a reason to call Luke. I hold onto the walls and the dresser as I make my way to the bed. I feel drunk times one hundred. I finally make it to the bed and I flop onto it. There is no need to get under the covers, I don't think I have the strength to even attempt that. My eyes close and I feel as if my entire body is spinning, so fast that the darkness is fading. Different colors are taking over my mind. Wait, they aren't colors. They look like images. I'm literally falling into the dream.

Spinning.

Spinning.

I open my eyes and I am standing outside of a log cabin. It is daylight so I can see everything clearly. I glance around and I see nothing but grass and trees. This looks like Jack territory. I see a black van parked on the sides. There is no license plate. Now how does he get away with that? How does he change cars and places so easily? Why is this son of a bitch still alive?

Stop and focus, Linda. This is the chance to end it. This dream feels different than my other ones. It feels more real than it has ever felt before. I feel as if I'm invincible. But the scary thing is, with these herbs I'm far from that. I believe if I die in my dream then I will die in real life, because that is what is going to happen to Jack. But I do feel stronger, more confident, and ready for revenge.

I carefully walk around the cabin to check out the premises. I pull my gun and hold it in front of me. I don't see any movement outside and the windows are covered with curtains. I can't see anything inside and I can't hear a thing. I quickly grab my phone and check the time of day and date. Well, this is right. I am right where I need to be today. It is so crazy that I can do this with my dreams now. Jack can't control my dreams like this.

I find a back door and I quietly open it. To my surprise it is unlocked.

I smell bleach as soon as I open the door. Shit, I hope I'm not too late. Last time I went to one of Jack's crime scenes he bleached everything clean. I carefully walk through the small kitchen when the floor creaks. I stop and listen. All I can hear is my fast heartbeat. Then I hear moaning.

I follow the moaning sound into the living room. That is when I see Jasmine's beautiful long red hair from behind. She is tied to a chair, no surprise there. I run around and take off the duct tape. "It's okay, I'm here to help you."

Tears are falling from her bright green eyes. "Oh thank you."

"Do you know where he is?"

She shakes her head. "No, he left not too long ago."

"Has he hurt you?" I ask as I glance at her body tied to the chair. I don't see any blood.

"No, not yet. But the things he said he was going to do to me." She starts to cry.

"Well, he won't be doing those things." I untie the rope around her and cut the duct tape that binds her legs with my knife. She stands slowly trying to regain her balance. Then I hear the door open.

She looks at me with panic and freezes with fear. Her eyes become watery again. I put my hand on her shoulder to comfort her.

"Well, well, well. Isn't this a nice surprise?" Jack says with his high-pitched voice.

I push Jasmine behind me to block her. "Why, yes it is. I believe we have something in common now."

He looks around the room. "This is a dream?" he asks with confusion. Then he smiles his awfully big clown smile. "You took the herbs? You risked your life just for me?" he says as he points at himself. "I feel honored. You brought the big prize right to me."

"Think again," I say as I hold out my gun and pull the trigger. I wasn't wasting any more time. I shoot him without hesitation.

His body falls heavily to the floor and blood begins to pour out of him. I stand over his body and glance at the bullet hole in his chest. "There's no coming back, Jack. This game is over."

I turn and see Jasmine crying. "Let's get you out of here," I say as I hold her and help her out of the door. I call Fredrick. I don't know if he will get the call or not, but it's worth a try.

"Fredrick, can you hear me?"

"Linda? I thought you were dream-" He pauses. "Wait, are you dreaming right now?"

"Yeah, at least I still think I am. This is the weirdest feeling. I hope I can get out of the dream. Anyway that's beside the point. I shot Jack and I have Jasmine right here unharmed."

"You what?" he yells into the phone.

"Jack is dead. I shot him."

"I can't believe it. Where are you right now?"

"I don't know. We're at some log cabin. There aren't any buildings around."

"Okay, I'm tracking your phone now. Stay there and be careful. We know Jack has nine lives."

"Got it." I hang up the phone.

I glance at Jasmine and then look back at the cabin. "I'll be right back."

I walk back into the cabin to make sure Jack really is dead, because Fredrick has a point. I open the door to see blood on the floor. Blood but no body. "Fuck! Not Again!"

I run out of the door and still see Jasmine standing in the exact same place I left her. "Is everything okay?"

"He's gone."

"What? How can that be? You shot him in the chest."

"I should have shot him in the fucking head. I don't know what I was thinking. I knew better than that!" I get so mad that my body begins to shake. The shaking won't stop.

Dizziness.

Weakness. I feel as if I'm losing control of my body. I fall to the ground and Jasmine comes running over. She shakes me. "Are you okay?" she asks with panic. But I can barely hear her voice. She is fading. I am fading.

Spinning.

Darkness.

Spinning.

I take a big breath as I wake up in my bed. Ryan removes his hands from me. He must have been shaking me to wake me up. "I'm sorry, ma'am. You were shaking uncontrollably. I was shaking you for a while trying to get you up. If you hadn't woken up I'd have called 9-1-1. Are you okay?"

I shake my head trying to grasp what just happened. "Yeah, I'm okay." I try getting out of bed but it feels like my muscles won't move. I need to relax for a minute. Ryan stares at me as if he doesn't know what to do. "You can leave for a moment. I'll be okay."

He nods and heads out the door shutting it behind him. After five minutes of lying there thinking about the dream and what happened I try moving again. This time I am able to. I sit at the side of the bed taking deep breaths. I feel as if I am going to puke. I feel a rumbling in my stomach. I feel the burning sensation coming up my esophagus. I rush into the bathroom and lift the toilet seat. Everything I ate comes up. I feel the burning in my stomach and in my throat. My eyes are watering. It feels like I'm puking my stomach up. I feel faint and dizzy.

I fall back from the toilet and my head begins to spin. I need water. I try to pull myself up to the sink. I turn the faucet on and stick my mouth under it, drinking the water. It tastes so good, as if life is filling back into me. I can't pass out. I won't be able to get away with using those herbs again if Luke finds out they affected me like this. I drink some more water and stand to my feet. I feel so much better. What I need now is something to eat. Once I get food in me then the dizziness will go away, I'm sure.

I begin to walk out of the room when my cell phone rings. "Linda, where are you? I tracked your phone and I found the cabin. I have Jasmine in the car with me now."

"I'm at the safe house," I say with hesitation.

"Holy shit, it worked?" Fredrick says with surprise.

"Yeah, it did. Is Jack's body there?"

"No, but I saw the pool of blood. I don't know how he survived that shot or how he got away."

Something dawned on me. "Wait, is there a black van sitting next to the cabin?"

"No, there's no van. Is there supposed to be?"

"Yeah, Jack must have gotten in it and drove away. But how the hell did I not see or hear it? How is he able to drive?"

"When you have willpower to survive, you'll be surprised at what the human body can withstand."

"I guess you're right. It was a black van and there were no plates."

"Okay, when I get back to the station I'll see if any traffic cams caught anything like that."

"Okay, I'll meet you at the station now. Are there any vials of blood anywhere?"

"No, I looked everywhere."

"I stopped him and he still got away."

"You stopped him for a while. There's no way he has the strength to kidnap or kill anyone right now. You bought us some time to try and catch him. That's amazing work, Linda. How do you feel after taking the herbs?"

"I was a little woozy when I woke up and I threw up. But I feel great. I can't believe it worked. Maggie is amazing."

"Yeah, she is. Just don't get too herb crazy. Who knows what that stuff could do to you if you use it daily?"

"Don't worry, I won't. I'll only take it for emergencies. Plus, there's only so much of the stuff; I have to save it."

"Good, have Ryan drive you to the station."

"Will do, see you soon."

CPD
3:00 Same Day

Fredrick pulls into the station at the exact same time Ryan does. I see Jasmine in the back seat. "Well, that's perfect timing," I say to Fredrick as he gets out of his car.

"That's what happens when you work with a perfect partner," he says as he winks at me. *Ouch, low blow, but a good one.*

Much to my surprise Jasmine rushes to me and gives me a hug. "Thank you for saving me. I don't know what the hell is going on or how you were there with me one minute and then gone the next, but I don't care. I'm alive because of you and I could never repay you."

I smile at her and hug her back. "You're welcome. There is one way you can repay me."

"Name it," she says with a perfect smile.

"You and Chad need to get out of town. Although Jack is seriously injured; neither of you are safe until he's dead or in jail. He never lets his victims live. You're the first one we've saved." Her smile quickly fades.

"Okay, we'll leave tonight," she says with panic.

We all walk into the station together. Chad is sitting at my desk with coffee. When he sees Jasmine walk into the room the biggest smile appears on his face. He sets his coffee down and rushes to her without taking his eyes off her.

They embrace each other with such love. Fredrick and I walk back to our desks to give them some privacy. "What's that on your face? Is that a smile?" Fredrick asks sarcastically.

"Hey, I'm allowed to smile every once and a while. I just saved this woman's life and brought the two of them together again. We don't see this often. It feels good to help."

"See, there are bright sides to this job," he says trying to change the subject.

"There are more dark moments than bright ones, Fredrick. This is too much for me to handle. I miss my harmless job at the coffee shop. I was in way over my head giving that up for this full time."

"No you weren't. You're perfect for this job."

Chad and Jasmine walk over and interrupt our conversation, thank god. "Excuse us, I just want to say thank you so much for saving my wife and bringing us together again. I wish I could do something to repay you. Jasmine told me we need to leave. We'll leave town for a little bit, but Charleston is our home. We'll come back to South Carolina when Jack is put away. Will you please call us when that's done so we can come home?"

I smile. "Absolutely. Do you know where you're going to go?"

They look at each other. "We're thinking of a second honeymoon and take some time to travel to all of our favorite places."

"That sounds like a great plan. Just be safe and watch your back. Contact us if there are any concerns."

"We will. Thank you again," Chad says as they walk hand in hand out of the station.

"Nothing better than a fairy tale ending," Fredrick says.

I look at him and start laughing. "What did you put in your coffee this morning?"

"Ha, ha funny. I think maybe that's something I'm ready for."

I raise my eyebrow and look at him, "Okay, where's my partner and what did you do with him?"

He looks at me and grins. "Partner? What do you mean partner?"

I roll my eyes and shove his shoulder. "Let's get back to work."

Some Doctor's Office
3:15 Same Day

I stumble into a Doctor's office. I don't even know who this is but if I don't get help now I am going to die. I remove my hand from my chest seeing the blood drip to the floor. The receptionist gets up from her seat and rushes over to me. I fall to the floor. "Please help me." Just as I am about to pass out I look at their bulletin board. I see a wanted poster hanging with my face on it. Fuck, this isn't good.

"Get Doctor Lambert out here now!" I hear the nurse yell. Well this didn't go as planned, but I will find a way out of it. Linda, don't you worry. I will finish this game.

Dizziness.

Darkness.

Cottage
6:30 p.m.

Fredrick interrupts dinner with Luke and Michael when he knocks on the door. He walks right in. "Well come on in," I say with a joking tone, motioning him to enter.

"Linda, I'm sorry to bother you during dinner but I have something important." His tone is bleak and his face long.

I swallow hard. "Okay Fredrick, what is it?"

"It's Jack. He's in the hospital."

My eyes become big and my heart starts to race. "What?! We have to go now."

"I guess the shot you gave him did do damage. He walked into Dr. Lambert's office asking for help. He bled out on the floor. They did what they could there then had an ambulance come get him. Good thing is, his Wanted poster was hanging up in that doctor's office so they called us."

"Oh my God, how could we get so lucky?"

Then he forms a small smile. "I don't know but this is our chance. He's having surgery on the bullet, getting it removed. It's deep inside his chest. They aren't sure if he'll survive the surgery. They won't let us inside the room or anywhere near him until the surgery is complete."

"Good, I hope he dies. I mean I'd rather be the one doing it, but this would make it be all over way easier than what we could ever have hoped for. But with our luck he'll survive and somehow come back stronger."

"This is the Linda I know," he says smiling. "Wanting revenge and won't stop until it's received in full. Getting justice is in your blood." I try to ignore his comment and insinuation. He is trying everything he can to get me to stay with the job.

"When it comes to my life and my family, of course I won't stop at nothing. But so would any sane person who cares about their family," I say with a small smile.

Luke comes walking out from the kitchen still chewing his food. "Is everything okay in here?"

"I'm so sorry for interrupting dinner," Fredrick says with true concern.

"It's okay. You came with good news. Want to sit down and grab a bite?"

"I'll sit down, but I just ate. Thank you."

Fredrick follows us into the kitchen and Michael smiles immediately. He loves Fredrick. Michael is the one person in the family who thinks I should stay with my job.

Michael's face lights up as if he saw fireworks, "Hey Fredrick! What bad guys are you hunting now?"

Fredrick looks at me and smiles then looks back at Michael and sits down next to him. "Well, the same one. We have a real lead and so we could catch him for good."

"Wow, that's cool. I want to be just like you and Mom someday." I look nervously over at Luke who is not thrilled about that comment.

"Really? I can't see it. I see you as a lawyer who puts the bad guys away for good," Fredrick says with enthusiasm.

Michael smiles and thinks. "Oh yeah, that would be fun!" We all laugh and get back on the topic of Jack.

"So when should we go to the hospital?" I ask impatiently.

"Well, they said not until the morning. He'll go through serious surgery and then he'll be sleeping the rest of the night."

"He doesn't need to sleep. I don't trust it. I want to go now."

"True, he'd be one to escape, but he won't have the strength to go. Plus, there'll be a nurse watching him around the clock. I also sent Detective Raymond down there to keep an eye out."

"Oh, so now you decide to involve him."

"It's an easy job for him. It's good practice to stay alert for hours because that's what he'll have to do."

"I agree," I say, nodding my head. "So, first thing in the morning then?" I ask.

"I'll pick you up and take you there at around 6:30 tomorrow."

"Okay, sounds good. Do we have enough to arrest him?"

"Well, we have fingerprints from his knives and luckily his blood at the log cabin putting him there at the same time as Jasmine. But he has kept his fingerprints and DNA off of all the other victims. But it still should be enough to arrest him."

"What about the notes he left me or the blood in the vials? That's all quality evidence?"

"It is, but again, he's kept his own personal DNA off of all of it."

"That bastard," I say under my breath.

"Tell me about it, but we've got him now. I'm going to call the DA now and meet with him."

"Okay, I'll see you tomorrow."

"See you tomorrow." Luke and I walk him out.

Michael comes running into the living room. "Bye Fredrick!" he says with excitement.

"See you later, Michael," he says with a smile.

After shutting the door, I turn around to face Luke. "Well, this is a good sign!" I say shrugging my shoulders.

"Yes it is. Hopefully this will be the end," he says with a grim tone. He turns and walks into the kitchen. Michael and I look at each other with concern. He walks closer to me and hugs me.

He whispers, "Is Daddy mad at me?" I instantly feel dismay.

I kneel down to meet his eyes. "No honey, Daddy isn't mad at you and never could be. He just worries about our safety, that's all. I promise, it's nothing to worry about." His beautiful tranquil eyes start to shine with tears. I hug him again. "It's okay, sweetie."

"Will you talk to him to make sure he really isn't mad at me?"

I wipe his tears and smile. "Of course I will. Now go get the bath started. You need to turn down for bed soon."

He smiles and his square nose and freckles pinch together and his dimples scarcely appear. I smile in return because when I see him happy it makes me warm inside. I never want him involved with this life and I'll make sure I keep it that way.

Luke, Michael, and I enjoy the evening watching TV and helping Michael with his homework. Luke and I don't talk about what happened because it is irrelevant. We both know how he feels. It will be over soon; I can feel it. But I also feel panic inside. I'm not sure why when Jack is currently getting surgery and will be arrested tomorrow morning, but something doesn't feel right. I swallow hard avoiding the nauseous feeling in my stomach.

MUSC Recovery Room
9:00 a.m. Thursday November 4th

I slowly start to open my heavy eyes. I feel numb inside but I also feel a slight pain. My head feels heavy and clouded. I see white robes around me but can't place where I am. "Mr. Bolder, can you hear me?" A faint beautiful voice is ringing in my head.

I shut my eyes and open them again. This time I am aware of where I am. I open my eyes even bigger when I fully come to. I see a beautiful blonde nurse in front of me. "How are you feeling?" she asks with such a sweet voice. *Oh, I'd love to cut her into small pieces.*

I smile. "I'm doing great, thank you. What happened?" She starts telling me the story and all the flashes come back. Me stumbling into a Doctor's office, me looking down at the blood on my hand, and seeing my Wanted picture right before I pass out.

I sit quickly when I realize what is going to happen, when a sharp pain interrupts and I fall back down to the pillow.

"Take it easy, Mr. Bolder, you were shot and had major surgery to get the bullet out. They were barely able to retract it because it was so deep." *That bitch,* I think when I picture Linda pointing that gun at me. *I thought it was all a dream. Wait, it was a dream? Well her dream and she was able to do this to me? Well then I can do so many things to her in my dream. Two can play this game.*

"There are detectives here to speak with you," the nurse says without a smile.

My eyes become big. *Shit…*

***

"Well, well would you look at this? Jack Bolder stuck in the hospital with nowhere to go. Guess you didn't see this coming, huh? Your game has now taken a turn for the worse on your part. Thank you for letting us reach the finish line," I say as I walk towards him with anger. I feel as if I am burning inside with vengeance. His shaggy black hair looks worse than it ever has. He is sweating. He is weak and vulnerable. It is taking everything in me not to kill him here and now.

He tries to smile to scare me, but it isn't working. "Well, well if it isn't my two favorite detectives. What can I do for you both?"

I can see the fear in his eyes and the adrenaline is pumping through my veins. "We're here to arrest you as soon as you're released," I say with a big smile on my face.

"Arrest me? For what exactly? And where's the arrest warrant?"

Fredrick pulls it out from inside his jacket pocket. "This one right here. We've got you now, you son of a bitch."

"Okay, I'll give you this one free time. It doesn't end here, I hope you know that," Jack says with a threatening tone. It's crazy that his high-pitched voice can be threatening but it is.

"You can say what you want, Jack. It isn't going to scare us. We finally got you," I say as I smile. Fredrick and I walk out of the room to speak with the doctor.

"When can we take him?" Fredrick asks bluntly.

"He needs to recover for a few more hours and then you can."

"Great, thanks," Fredrick responds. He looks at me. "Coffee?"

"Please!" I say desperately.

We wait in the waiting room. Luke comes up to us on his break. "How's he recovering?"

"He'll make a full recovery. The best thing is he'll be weak for a while so he can't possibly get away with anything," I say with pleasure.

"That's good. Is there anything I can get you all?"

I hold up my cup of coffee and Fredrick does the same. "This is all we need. Thanks honey," I say with a smile.

"Keep me posted please," he says as he kisses me on the forehead. He walks away, his white coat flowing behind him. I don't know why seeing him in his "doctor mode" is a turn on, but it is. He is one good-looking surgeon, that's for sure.

I feel as if I am a new person mentally and physically because Jack is in our custody. My leg is feeling much better. I am no longer crutching around thank goodness. I can't even feel the pain right now, and I am on cloud nine.

A few hours later the doctor tells us we can take him now. Fredrick and I look at each other and exchange a small ornery smile. We walk into his room to see him sitting there on the bed dressed in black pants and a white t-shirt that is stained with a mixture of dirt and blood. He looks up at us.

Fredrick looks at me and holds up his handcuffs. "Want to do the honor?"

I smile and take the handcuffs. "Oh please." I walk over, stand him on his feet, turn him around, cuff him tight, and read him his Miranda rights. I have been waiting for this moment for months.

The feeling is impeccable.

I shove his head as I put him in the back of Fredrick's car. He looks at me with anger. "You're going to regret this," he says as he blows me a kiss.

"The way I see it, you can't do shit right now. I've got you, Jack." I slam the door in his face and he smiles through the window.

When we get to the station I shove Jack into an interrogation room. The only way we can convict him to make it stick is if we get a confession. But I don't have high hopes of that. I shut the door behind me to find Fredrick, Sergeant Gordon, and Captain Sanders. It's unusual to see Captain Sanders, but this case is so big he has to be here.

I nod my head at Sanders. "Captain."

He nods back. "Detective Jackson, great work today. I'm as relieved as everyone else that he's finally behind this window."

"Oh, you have no idea," I say as I sigh with relief.

"You know we need a complete confession. We have enough to take him to court, but not enough to sentence him to life or the death penalty." My feeling of power burns out.

"Yeah, I know. I know Jack; he'll die before he confesses. So what the hell are we going to do?"

"You and Fredrick are going to try everything you can to get a confession. Then we'll take it from there. His lawyer and our DA are on their way."

"Great. District Attorney Ben Huffman I hope, right?" Fredrick asks.

"Yeah, we have to get the best to fight the best," says Sergeant Gordon.

"Good, that makes me a little more confident in this case," Fredrick says.

I have not met this DA yet, so I'll be excited to meet him and work with him to put this asshole away for good.

Minutes later Jack's lawyer walks into the station. He is about 250 pounds, short, and bald. I laugh at the sight of him. "This guy is going to help Jack? I feel better already."

Captain Sanders turns to me. "Don't underestimate this guy. He's here for a reason. He has let killers off before. He may not look the part, but he's a sneaky son of a bitch."

He walks up and shakes our hands. His brown suit is too long for him and he smells of smoke. He is a hot mess. I can't imagine him being too good. He shakes my hand first. "Let me guess, the infamous Linda Jackson who can catch killers in her dreams," he says sarcastically. "My name is John Whitney."

I give him a quick, short smile. "That's me. I haven't missed one yet," I respond to his comment with a confident tone.

"Yet, being the key word," he says walking into the interrogation room.

He turns around. "I'd like a few minutes alone with my client."

"Of course," Captain Sanders says nodding his head.

He shuts the door behind him. "Wow, he's a nutcase," I say.

"Yeah, a nutcase that wins cases," Fredrick responds. I look at the two of them in there talking and smiling. Looking at Jack smiling makes me sick.

"Well, it looks like the whole crew is here, so this must be a good case." A deep and masculine voice appears from behind us. I turn around to see a tall, confident, dark-haired man. He is dressed professionally in a dark grey suit with a white and navy stripped tie. His hair is short and groomed. His short beard has been cut clean. He is holding a black suitcase.

"District Attorney Ben Huffman, it's great to see you," Fredrick says shaking his hand.

"And it's great to see you all. So what are we dealing with here?" he asks in a playful tone. I can tell he's got an enthusiastic personality. He reminds me of Arnold in that way." Then he looks at me. "You're a new face? And a beautiful one at that."

I smile and blush a little. I hold out my hand. "My name is Detective Linda Jackson. It's nice to meet you," I say with professionalism.

"Wait, *the* Linda Jackson?"

"Yes, that's me."

"Well, it's an honor to meet you. I've enjoyed your work and your fascinating talent."

"Thank you. I've heard nothing but good things about you."

He playfully shoves Fredrick. "From these guys? Yeah, I bet they only tell you horror stories."

Everyone smiles. He is obviously a well-liked guy and good at what he does. "I think it's time to start our interrogation," Fredrick says.

"Here goes nothing," I say with a sigh.

When we enter the room, the two become quiet. Fredrick and I pull out our chairs, set our coffee on the table, and sit down. I glare at Jack who is smiling back at me. Jack moves his head in closer, not moving his glare from mine. "Go ahead, ask me anything you'd like."

His confidence scares me, but I don't show it. "What were you doing at that log cabin with Jasmine?"

He shrugs his shoulders. "Just visiting with an old friend."

I look at Fredrick and back at Jack. I raise my eyebrow. "An old friend? Really?" I say with a small laugh. "How did you know each other?"

"Well it just so happens we went to elementary school together, so technically we go way back." I am confused because Jasmine never mentioned that little detail.

"And how well did she remember that?"

"Well enough she wanted to grab coffee to catch up."

"And how did you end up back at the cabin?"

"Oh you know; I have a way with words."

"Mmm, and why did I find Jasmine tied to a chair against her own will?"

He is about to say something but his lawyer stops him and looks at me. "Detective Jackson, I don't mean to be frank but from what I hear you were there in a dream, and technically a dream isn't real."

I feel my face turn red with anger. He did not just use that against me! I am speechless. Fredrick interrupts. He laughs, "That is what you're going with? Saying it didn't really happen or it isn't real evidence because it was in her dream? You do know that everyone in Charleston knows who Detective Jackson is and they all know her talent is real?"

"Oh yeah, I know that, but there's nothing in any law book that says a dream can be used to prosecute anyone because a dream isn't real," the lawyer responds with a stern tone.

I glance at Jack who continues to smile. "We have evidence that can put him away for attempted murder," Fredrick responds.

"Attempted, being the key word. A knife with his fingerprints, but not the victim's blood; his blood at a crime scene but no blood from the victim, that will put him away."

"We will fight this with everything we have," I say as I get closer to Jack's face. I want to pull my gun and shoot that fucking smile off his head. We are interrupted by a knock on the window. Fredrick and I leave as I slam the door.

"I can't believe this! Can he really use the dream against me?" I ask the DA.

He nods. "Yeah, he can. Jack's blood was found at the log cabin, but Jack was not there when the cops arrived. The only real witness is Jasmine. We need her to go on the stands."

I throw my hands in the air. "They're MIA traveling around the world enjoying their freedom. How are we supposed to contact them?"

"Fredrick, get Christopher to run face recognition, we need Jasmine. Without her this case is down the drain," Captain Sanders says. I storm off and walk outside to get some air. I sit on the steps of the station looking out at the gloomy sky. It looks like it is going to storm. Well doesn't this fit the mood?

I pull out my phone with a few texts from Luke asking how it's going. I decide to text back letting him know it's not good. Out of the corner of my eye I see someone sit next to me. To my surprise it is Ben.

"I know the background with Jack and Tom," he says seriously.

I turn to meet his glance. "How?"

"Fredrick and I are good buddies. He told me everything."

"That's funny, Fredrick never told me about you."

"He doesn't say much about his life out of this station does he?"

I shake my head and lightly smile. "No, he likes to keep his personal life out of his work life. I wish I could say the same. Unfortunately, that will never happen."

"I'd kill to have the talent you have. It'd make my life as a DA a lot easier."

"Don't ever wish that upon yourself. It's living a true nightmare. I've come to terms with the fact that my life is different and I have to live with these dreams forever, but it doesn't make it any easier."

"I'm sorry. I want you to know that I'll do everything in my passion to put Jack away for good. I mean, I'm good at what I do, and I rarely lose," he says with a humorous tone. I know he is trying to make me feel better but it isn't helping.

"Even with as little evidence as we have?"

"It could be enough if I make the case believable enough. If we can get Jasmine on the stands, then it'll be a definite win. Either way, Linda you're going to have to take the sands."

I look at him with surprise. "Me? Why? I thought dreams aren't real and the court won't allow a "fake" testimony."

"Your testimony could impact a jury's mind. Remember, you're a hero around here. Take a look around you. The news is always following your life. We could really milk this, if we lay it on thick." I think for a minute. He's got a point.

"Alright, I'll do whatever it takes."

"Good, together we'll put him away," he says and walks back into the station. I sit thinking about what's to come.

Luke sends me a text back saying we will talk about everything when we get home. He is going to pick up Michael from school. Gosh, this day has been consumed with so many emotions I forgot what time it was. I head back into the station to see what is going on.

Fredrick approaches me first. His smooth, dark, slicked back hair shines as he walks. "We have enough to hold him here for a while. Christopher is trying to track down Jasmine and Chad as we speak. There isn't much else for us to do. You can go on home. I know it has been a tough day."

I glance over at Jack sitting behind the bars. He continues to smile at me. "Don't worry, there's no way of him getting out."

"Good," I say. I say my goodbyes to the Captain and Sergeant. I need a break. "I'll be back first thing tomorrow."

"Okay. Linda get some rest tonight, and I mean real rest," Sergeant Gordon says.

I nod my head in response. Real rest? Yeah right. I don't know what that is."

When I get home I am so tired that after dinner I head straight to bed. Luke lies in bed with me and rubs my head until I fall asleep. "Don't worry, I'll turn Michael in for bed," he says with his soft patient tone.

"Thank you so much. Today was just-" Luke stops me by putting his finger gently over my lips.

He kisses me softly. "Don't...get some rest." I nod my head and close my eyes.

***

CPD
Same Night 9:30 p.m.

I sit in this stupid jail cell, trying to figure out how I am going to get out of this. It is impossible for me to escape. Unless I had the herbs, then I could sleep and escape in my "dream." Damn, I knew I should have gotten someone to work with me on this. I picture Linda's confident smile as she interrogated me today. It makes me so mad! Just when I thought I had lost this game a ray of hope appears. I have a surprising visitor who has come to talk? Or maybe save me?

"You know what to do," he says holding out his hand in between the bars. I sit confused at what is going on. I stand to take what is in his hand.

The herbs! This can't be happening. "What? Why are you helping me? They'll know it was you."

"Trust me, they won't. Put an end to her, Jack." That is the last thing this man says as he walks away. I stare in shock as I watch him walk right out of the Charleston Police Department.

"Excuse me, could I get some water please?" They have to give me water. I sprinkle the small plastic bag of herbs into the water and chug it down. The feeling of the herbs soaking in my body is amazing. I lie down and close my eyes. It is time to escape and finish what I started.

Chapter 15

"ESCAPED!!?? How the fuck could that happen?" I scream into the phone at Fredrick.

"We don't know. The officers said the last thing they saw was him sleeping and then they looked again and he had somehow vanished."

"That motherfucker! He used the damn herbs! How the hell did he get those? We searched him and there was nothing on him!"

"Unless someone gave him the herbs?" he says with a questioning tone.

"Who would-?" I pause. "You don't think it was his idiot lawyer, do you?"

"I-I really don't know. He's a scumbag but I don't think he would stoop that low. But I can never tell anymore."

I shake my head. "I can't fucking believe this. What are we going to do?"

"I can't do anything. But you can," Fredrick says with hesitation.

"Alright, I'm going to have to. He's out there now finding his next victim, if he doesn't already have her. I'll see you in the morning." I hang up before he responds.

"You're going to use the herbs again? To beat him at his own game?" Luke asks as he sits up in bed.

"It's the only way. He's injured right now. I can finish the job."

He sighs. "If I see you struggle I'm waking you up."

"Okay, that's good. Thank you, Luke."

He nods and kisses me hard. "Please be careful."

"I will baby." I get out of bed and grab the herbs. I chug the herbs in bed this time. My head starts to feel dizzy and heavy immediately. This stuff hits me quick. Out of the corner of my eye I can see Luke watching me. It is nice having him here this time.

Doing this alone is scary. I lay my head down on the pillow.

Spinning.

Dizziness.

Darkness.

I hear screaming. Not just screaming but agonizing screaming. I follow the screaming and the closer I get to it, the worse I feel. I don't know if I want to see what she is going through. I find my way into the middle of a forest. There are no buildings. This is the usual for Jack. It is dark and I can't see much of what is going on, let alone where I am walking. I pull out my phone and turn its flashlight on. I see nothing but leaves underneath me. The scream is getting louder. I hold my phone up to see what is in front of me. I see two figures in front of me.

As I step closer, my stomach begins to turn. The moonlight shines through the trees right onto Jack and his victim. I'm too late. Jack is holding the woman in front of him. His hand is over her mouth. I can see the blood seeping through her tan tank top. I put my phone away. The moonlight is shining on them as if it were a spotlight. "Jack, I know you're hurting right now. Please put her down and let her go. You have me here now and this is what you want."

I can see the shadow of his ugly smile. "I knew you wouldn't be able to resist those herbs once you found out I'd escaped. I wanted to show you what I can do." Just then he slices the girl across the stomach just enough to make her quiver with pain and blood dripping. She's already been tortured enough.

"Stop! I see what you can do," I plead.

He shakes his head. He holds out her arm and cuts her from the wrist to her elbow. She screams bloody murder. I can't believe she is still standing. "What do you want me to do?"

"I want you to learn that you can't outplay me. You can't stop me. When you try to stop me there will be consequences." He stabs her in the back quickly and then slices her throat. Her limp body drops to the ground. I stand in shock at what I just saw.

"That's for saving Jasmine. Now I'm all caught up." He throws something at me that distracts me. I catch it. I hold it up in the moonlight to see it is a vial of blood with the number 4 on it. I look straight ahead and Jack is gone.

I stick the vial in my pocket and run to the woman. There is no helping her. I call Fredrick right away. "I'm in a dream right now. I'll explain the story tomorrow. I'm with his newest victim. I have no idea where we are. Can you track my phone to find us?"

"*Yeah, give me a second to get to my computer. Are you okay?*"

"*Far from okay. Jack tortured and killed this woman right in front of me to prove a point.*"

"*Oh Linda, I'm so sorry. Okay, I have your location. Calling an ambulance now.*"

"*Okay thanks. I can't promise I'll still be here when you get here.*"

"*It's okay, I'll see you in the morning.*"

"*Thanks Fredrick.*" *I put the phone in my pocket and stare at the dead woman in front of me. The moonlight makes the blood surrounding her shine bright. Her brown hair is spread around her. Another life gone too soon because of this bastard…because of me.*

I open my eyes and wake up calmly for once. I turn over and Luke is still awake reading a book. "What are you still doing up?"

He puts the book down on the end table. "Waiting for you. Do you really think I could sleep knowing you took the herbs?"

"I guess not," I say with a smile. Then the smile fades away when I think about the dream.

"Did you get anywhere with the dream?"

"Besides Jack slaughtering victim number five in front of me… no."

"I'm sorry."

"He has victim number four now and I have no leads on who it is." Then I pause for a second and remembered that I put the vial of blood in my pocket. *Is there a possibility? Could this really happen?* I think to myself as I reach into my pocket and pull out the vial of blood. My eyes become big and so do Luke's. "Holy shit, this can't be," I say as I examine the blood. It even has the same number 4 label on it.

"Linda, I don't think this is a good sign. With the herbs not only can you kill people in a dream but you can take stuff from a dream too? This is too insane and dangerous. We're playing with life's orders here. Dreams aren't supposed to be able to do things like this," Luke says with panic.

"My dreams have never followed the rules. Now I just have to be more careful, but think of the things I can now do. I have a huge advantage."

"Yeah but if you can do these things, can't Jack?"

I shrug my shoulders. "I don't think so. I mean, Maggie told me all these things could happen if I take the herbs because of my gift. Jack doesn't have a special dream gift. But he was able to control when and where his dream took place. I don't know. All I know is that I can use this new gift."

"You only have so many herbs left. You have to save it for the right moment," Luke says as if he is reading my mind.

"I know. I have a feeling it's coming up real soon." I look into his eyes and they have dark circles under them. "You need to get some sleep, Luke."

"Okay, and so do you." Yeah, I doubt I'll be getting much sleep after what just happened. I turn off the light and before I close my eyes my phone lights up. It's a text from Fredrick.

"Forensics took the body and set up the crime scene. There was no vial of blood. See you in the morning."

Yeah, there's no vial of blood because I took it from my dream. That's crazy. "See you in the am," I respond then shut my eyes hoping to get a few hours of restful sleep.

Charleston Harbor Marina
3:00 a.m.

"Shh, it'll all be okay, I promise," I whisper into the ear of Ms. Haley Kline as I wrap duct tape around her mouth. "Just take a look around at this beautiful boat. You're getting special treatment compared to my other victims. They are usually tied up in some abandoned house or shelter, but you get a nice arrangement here. I have to take her off track somehow."

I look into her wet and shiny eyes. Teardrops are falling over the duct tape. Sweat is pouring from her forehead. "Are you hot? Oh here let me help you. That long blonde hair of yours must be a hassle." I take her hair tie that is around her wrist and put her hair in a ponytail. Her short bangs hang down. I stare into her bright blue eyes. "There you go, is that better? Now back to our little arrangement here. You're probably wondering how I got you here in such a fancy place without people seeing? Well, I'm a professional at this, and you can thank my cousin for this boat. She's a great doctor in the area but she's currently on vacation and doesn't know that I've taken the boat. So we got lucky."

She can't respond to anything I'm saying but I don't care. Linda is going to have a hard time finding this one. I am getting so close to the end I have to play number four out the right way. I am going to take my time with this one. I gently rub my knife from her neck down to her legs and I stop right at where her short blue dress ends above her thighs without making a mark. Her entire body tenses. "Oh, don't worry sweetie. You have a while until you feel pain. I'm going to take my time with you." I take the knife and cut the thin straps on her dress leaving her shoulders bare. Her breathing becomes heavier. I love when they are scared.

"Oh Linda, where are you?" I ask. Let's see, what do I want to cut next? I dim the lights in the cabin of the boat and get to work.

CPD
Friday 7:00 a.m.

Ronald drops me off at work this morning. I thank him as I shut the door to his black Impala. I take a sip of my coffee and brace myself as I walk into the station. Fredrick is at his desk deep into work already. I pull out the vial of blood, walk over, and set it on his desk right under his nose. I brush the strands of hair left out from my ponytail behind my ears and sigh. "Is this what you were looking for?"

"How did you?" He looks at the vial and then back at me and stands up. "There's only one way you could have gotten this," he says holding the vial in front of me.

I nod my head. "You're right."

"Your dream? You really took this from your dream?" he says with shock. His dark eyes glare into mine.

"I literally took this from my dream. Yes, it really happened. No I'm not okay."

He pauses and then smiles. "This could mean a lot of good for us, Linda."

I walk over to my desk, which is only a few steps away from Fredrick's and set my coffee down. I sit on the edge of the table and cross my arms. "I know it can. I should be able to kill Jack in the dream and then it'll be all over. I just have to find the right timing and I can't let him escape or trick me. I only have a little bit of herbs left, enough for maybe two dreams."

Fredrick sits in his chair, crosses his legs, and rests his elbow on the desk. "Then we'll have to make these two dreams count. Now that we have the next victim's blood we can get to work."

"On it," I say as I take the vial to Christopher. I walk into his office and his glasses are on the top of his head. He is eyes deep into a microscope.

"Excuse me, Christopher?" He becomes startled and jumps back from the microscope and his glasses fall behind him on the floor. He shuffles to get them and puts them on.

"Oh, hey Detective," he says smiling trying to play off what just happened.

I ignore it. "Sorry to bother you but I have a blood sample for you to test."

"Victim number four?" he asks with almost excitement.

"Yeah, can you get that back ASAP please?"

"Sure thing. I'll have it right out."

I walk back out to my desk when I see Fredrick and Sergeant Gordon looking at some footage. "What is this?"

"This is from the footage of last night. We're trying to see who broke Jack out."

I stand behind the two watching between their heads. All I see is Jack lying in the jail cell. The few normal cops that work night shift, but nothing out of the ordinary. Then the screen turns black. All the camera views turn black at the same time. "What the hell?" I say.

"Yeah, who knows how to do something like that?" Fredrick asks.

Then the camera turns back on and Jack is gone. I rub my forehead. "It has to be his lawyer; he's the only person who could do this."

Sergeant Gordon turns around. "It could be him or it could be-" He stops as he looks forward. I turn to see what he sees. DA Ben Huffman strolls in like he is hot stuff. No, it can't be him. Why would he want to let Jack go?

"Hello boys and girls," he says as he nods at me. This time he is wearing a light brown suit. "Any more news on our perpetrator?"

"You haven't heard, I'm assuming," Fredrick says with caution. Fredrick stands tall in front of Ben.

"Heard what?" he asks, raising an eyebrow.

"Somehow Jack escaped during the middle of the night," Fredrick says.

"What? How is that possible?" Ben asks with surprise. I look into his eyes to try and read him. There is something off about it. He's too perfect and too good at his job.

"Someone knows what he can do, and slipped him the herbs.

There's only a handful of people who know that. Sergeant, Captain, Detective Jackson, his lawyer, myself, and *you*." Fredrick emphasizes the 'you.'

Ben takes a step back. "You think I'd give this psycho the herbs to escape? Why in the world would I do that? This is a case I could have won. It could have made me big. Why would I jeopardize that?"

Well he's got a point there.

"We're just following all leads," Fredrick says.

"Well, have you spoken to his lawyer?" Ben asks strongly.

Fredrick looks at Sergeant Gordon, and me. "We were just about to do that." Although I know he wasn't.

"Good, let me know what happens and if there's going to be a case. I'll be on my way now," Ben says without his charming humor.

Fredrick calls John and I slump into my chair. I sip more coffee. I am definitely going to need more of this. "I didn't get an answer," Fredrick says as he hangs up the phone.

"I'm sure he's probably busy."

"True, but don't you think he would have been here by now to speak with Jack?"

"Unless he knows Jack isn't here?" I say.

"Grab your jacket. We're going to pay him a little visit," Fredrick says. When I bend down to grab my jacket an instant pain shoots through my head.

Flash!

Flash!

Sharp pain!

Headache!

I stumble as I grab onto the chair. I rub my head in agony. Flashes from my dream run through my head. Every slash Jack gave that woman I am seeing over and over again.

Flash!

Pain!

I almost fall to the ground when Fredrick catches me and sets me in the chair. "Linda, are you okay?"

I shake my head a little and focus. I take a big deep breath and open my eyes. "I'm okay. I just had flashes from my dream last night."

"Do you want to stay here while I go question John?"

"No, no, I'm okay." I say as I stand up from the chair. "Just let me fill up my coffee mug first." Fredrick smiles and shakes his head.

"You never stop."

I shrug my shoulders and smile. "You know me!"

***

Defense Lawyer John's House
10:00 a.m.

We pull into John's house. His red Prius is in the driveway. "He would drive a Prius," I say as I laugh. Fredrick smiles at me and shakes his head.

Fredrick knocks on his door. We don't get an answer. "Mr. Whitney, it's Detectives Fredrick and Jackson. We'd like to speak with you for a moment about Jack." Fredrick yells. Still no answer. Fredrick motions for me to step back. Then he kicks in the door, holds his gun up, and walks inside.

I am startled when I see John's dead body lying on the floor in a pool of blood. "What?"

"Gunshot to the head," Fredrick says.

"Who would do this?"

"It has to be Jack. I don't know. He's really playing games," Fredrick says with a sigh.

I look closer when I see a piece of paper in John's jacket pocket. "Fredrick look," I say pointing to the picture. He puts on a latex glove and grabs it. He opens the note and shows it to me.

"Surprised yet?" is what the note says.

"That's Jack alright. But why would he do this to his lawyer? He had to be the one who let him escape?" I say with confusion.

"I don't know. Maybe he wasn't." Fredrick calls for a bus and forensics.

We start to head back to the car.

Flash!

Pain!

I stumble down the steps and grab onto Fredrick's arm. "Linda, you need to get some rest."

"I don't know why it's affecting me this much?"

"Maybe because you took the herbs so close together?"

"Maybe." The pain in my head is excruciating and I feel as if I'm going to pass out. I sit in Fredrick's car for a few minutes and drink some water. I feel much better now.

"I'm okay to get back to the station."

"No, you need to go home and get some rest first, then come back," Fredrick says with demand.

"Alright, fine. An hour nap then I'll be back." I send a text to Luke to let him know what is going on.

***

Cottage
11:00 a.m.

I shut the door behind me as I walk into the safe house. To my surprise there is no one in here. Where are the bodyguards? My heart begins to race and I worry about why I am alone. Did Jack find us? I grab my phone to call Luke and I open the front door. I jump back when I see Luke standing there. I look at my phone then back at Luke. I set my phone down on the table.

Luke still stands in the doorway. "Luke, what are you doing here? The bodyguards aren't here."

Luke steps through the doorway and shuts the door. He is different. He is serious. He is provocative. My insides are burning. His bright eyes pierce into mine. "I know the bodyguards aren't here."

"What?" I ask with confusion but still feel the passion burning inside.

"I told them to take a break and sit in the car. I said I wanted to be truly alone with you," he says slowly moving towards me.

I smile. "Oh, you want me alone huh?" In this moment of passion, I forget everything in the outside world, including how tired I was.

He nods his head and gives me his sexy grin. He takes off his white coat as he keeps moving me back. I don't even watch where I am going. I am caught in his deep gaze. He shoves me up against the wall. "I know you're going through a lot and so am I, but we need a break," he says as he kisses my neck softly.

"I agree a break is good." He takes off my black t-shirt and throws it to the side. He kisses my lips hard. I run my hand through his hair and kiss back. Then he kisses my neck again this time biting just a little bit. He kisses down my chest as he unhooks my bra.

187

He kisses my breasts then moves down leaving a trail of kisses. He gently takes off my black pants and shoes and throws them aside. He kisses down my thigh and pauses. He looks up at me and I meet his glare. He stares at me deeply and his glare makes me twist inside. Then he kisses his way back up to my lips. I slowly unbutton his blue dress shirt revealing his tight abs. I bend down and kiss his stomach letting his shirt fall off his strong arms. I unbuckle his belt taking it off him. Then he shoves me back against the wall and kisses me harder.

He picks me up and carries me into the bedroom. He sits on the edge of the bed and my legs wrap around him. He pulls my hair and kisses my neck. I let out a moan. "I want you now, Luke." He lays me back and takes off my underwear. Then I shove him over and take his pants off. I can see his erection through his boxes. I take them off to let it free. I look up at him and smile. He grabs me by the arms and pulls me up to him then flips me over. Then he is inside me so quickly. My head shoves back into the pillow with pleasure.

I don't know how much time has passed but it feels like we have made love for hours. I lie on top of Luke worn out. I am tired but I am so relieved it feels unbelievable. This is exactly what I needed. I stare into Luke's blue eyes. I run my hand through his short black hair. The sheets are completely off the bed, just our naked bodies covering each other. "How are you feeling?" he asks with a smile.

"So much better," I say as I kiss him.

"This is the first time we've had a house completely to ourselves," Luke says.

"I know. It's great. How did you get out of work?"

"I told them I had an emergency. Today was a light day. One surgery and I have another soon. I needed a nice break." He winks at me.

"Will you be able to pick up Michael from school?"

"Mick is going to pick him up. I should be out in time to meet him back here."

"Okay. I wish we could stay like this all day." We begin to kiss deeply again when my phone rings.

We smile at each other. I answer the phone. "Linda, did I wake you?"

"Fredrick, no not really," I say trying not to laugh. I continue to lie on top of Luke naked. He stares at me as I speak with Fredrick.

"Good, are you rested?"

"Yeah, I'm rested alright," I say as I wink at Luke. He kisses my neck distracting me from my phone call.

"Good, we need you to come in. We got the blood sample back on the vial. Also we got fingerprints on the note. You'll never believe whose prints we found. Going to arrest him now." Fredrick hangs up before he tells me whose prints they are.

I set the phone down. "I have to go in, babe. We have some new leads."

Luke looks at his watch. "I've got to get back too. I have a rotator that needs fixing."

We kiss each other again and then get dressed.

CPD
1:30 p.m.

I feel like a million bucks when I walk into the station. "Wow, you're glowing. I'm glad you got some rest," Fredrick says.

I smile shyly. "Thanks, me too. So what's the news?"

"The blood belongs to a Haley Kline. She's twenty-five and sells insurance. She was living by herself but we have a parent's address. We'll go and check it out."

"Okay. What about the fingerprints on the note?"

"They belonged to Ben Huffman."

"What? I knew there was something about him. He was too perfect."

"I can't believe it," Fredrick says as he looks down at his watch. "He was a great DA. I can't believe he would let Jack out and kill John. Detective Raymond is heading to his place now to arrest him."

"What if Ben didn't kill John? What if Jack did and made it look like John? Jack is capable of doing that."

"Oh, he's very much capable of that," Fredrick says as he drinks his coffee. His phone rings on his desk.

"Detective Raymond is everything okay?" Fredrick listens intently. His eyes squint together. "What? You're kidding? Alright, yeah call the team please." Fredrick slams his phone on his desk. "Dammit!"

I gulp before I speak. "What's wrong?"

"Ben is dead. Gunshot to the head."

I sit down in my chair confused about what is going on. "Why? What the hell is going on here?"

Fredrick shakes his head and his gelled black hair stays right in place. "Jack is killing anyone that gets in his way. Now we really don't know who let him escape. I guess that doesn't matter now. He is sending a warning to us. Anything we do to stop him, there will be consequences."

I sit at my desk staring into my computer screen. I can see my reflection in the screen. I notice my long black ponytail is messy. My black eye liner is still intact, which is good. I run to the restroom to fix my hair. I fix my ponytail so it isn't as messy. I tuck my black shirt into my black pants to make it look more professional. Then I look myself in the eyes thinking about what we are going to do next. Then a vision of a body appears behind me. I jump with fright and turn around and nothing is there. *What the fuck?*

I look back in the mirror and there is a woman there, but not any woman. It's Maggie. "Maggie? How are you-? Are you a ghost?"

She smiles her joyful smile. Her curly hair is still out of control. She still has on her oversized earrings. "I'm here to help you."

"No, no this can't be. I'm seeing ghosts now? This has to be some sort of hallucination or side effects from the herbs. I've never seen ghosts before."

"You've never taken anything like that before. The herbs dig deep into your spiritual world. Linda, you're able to kill in your dreams. You don't think there are side effects from that? I don't consider it a side effect; I mean you've always been a spiritual person. Now you can use this to your advantage even more than you thought."

I can't take my eyes off of her in the mirror. "I'm so sorry for what happened to you."

She shakes her head. "No honey, don't be sorry. I'm here with Arnold and we're happy."

I put my head down for a second and smile. I look back up and she is gone. I turn around quickly to find nothing. "Maggie? Wait? I need help." No response.

I take some deep breaths. I don't know if that was a hallucination or what but I'm crazier than I thought. I wet a paper towel and dab my forehead and neck. "Okay, focus Linda. Pull your shit together."

I walk out of the bathroom and see Fredrick standing by the door waiting. I grab my gun and jacket and walk towards him. He looks at me with confusion, "Are you okay? You look pale."

"I'm fine. Let's go talk to Haley's parents." I walk past him and I can feel his glare on my back.

Kline Residence
3:00 p.m.

We are greeted at the door by a happy looking couple. The mom and dad are both tall with blonde hair. They must not know their daughter is kidnapped. Great, this is going to make for an excellent visit. "Mr. and Mrs. Kline, I am Detective Fredrick and this is Detective Jackson. We would like a few minutes of your time to discuss Haley." Their smile turns to blank confusion.

"Please have a seat," the mom says as she motions us towards the black leather couch. "Would you like some coffee?"

"Yes please, that would be great," I say. A few minutes later she hands us our coffees. Her and her husband sit across from us in a matching couch. They are smiling at us waiting for us to speak. I quickly glance around and see so many pictures of them and Haley. She is their only child from what it looks like. The silence in the room is broken by the crackle from the fire in their fireplace.

"So what can we help you with today?" the dad chimes in. I don't even know where to start. I'm at a loss of words. This family seems perfect.

"When is the last time you heard from Haley?" Fredrick asks.

The mom responds. "She was over for dinner two nights ago. I did try to call her this morning to see if she wanted to go shopping but it went straight to her voicemail." Then the look on her face turns to fear. Her eyes become big and her mouth drops. "Is everything okay? Did something happen to my baby girl?" The dad puts his hand on her lap.

"This is going to be hard to hear, but we believe that Haley has been kidnapped." Fredrick drops the bomb.

The dad stands up quickly. "Kidnapped? By who? Why?" The mom begins to cry.

"We know who took her. We don't' know why. We're working as hard as we can to find her."

"Wait, please tell me it's not the guy who's all over the news? News reporters say he leaves a vial of blood at every crime scene of the next victim." I hate the damn press. Fredrick and I don't respond. "No, no he kills all of his victims!"

"Mr. Kline, we won't let him kill her. You could possible help us find her." The dad sits back down. The mom is crying in her hands.

"We'll do anything we can. Just please get her home safely."

I nod my head. "Do you know if she goes anywhere after work?"

"She attends a Zumba class and then she usually goes home. How could he take her?"

"Is her apartment secure?"

"You have to have a key to enter the building, it's always locked. But people are in and out of the building pretty often," the dad responds. A phone call interrupts Fredrick and he gets up to take it in the kitchen.

I am sitting here with two parents that are devastated. I try to make conversation but it is difficult to find anything to say. Fredrick comes back in seconds later. That wasn't long. "Detective Raymond is at Haley's apartment now. He said he found something. We need to go."

The dad gets up from the couch again. "Found what? We're going with you," he demands.

"I'm sorry sir, but you can't be at a crime scene. Signs show she was taken from her apartment. We need to check it out. We'll call you when we have something."

"But our baby girl is out there," the mom says as she sniffles.

"I know ma'am and we're doing everything we can," I reply. "We'll be in touch."

They walk us to the door and the happy couple is now a sad and depressed couple, no thanks to us. They stand in the doorway as we get into our car. They are both so skinny they fit next to each other in the doorframe. Talk about good genes. This poor girl has a happy life and a great family. I have to save her.

Haley's Apartment #76
3:30 p.m.

When we walk into the spacious apartment I am shocked at what a mess it is. The furniture is thrown all around. Vases and picture frames are broken on the floor. She put up a fight. There is a bloodstain on the floor. Let's hope it's Jacks but I highly doubt that. Detective Raymond walks up to us. "This is what I found," he says handing us a note.

"Classic Jack, always leaving brags," Fredrick says. I take the note from him.

"Linda, I am closer to the end. You won't see what's coming. I can't wait to see you plead for your life. As for this poor girl, I've decided to take my time on this one, cutting every inch of her body. By the time you find her, there won't be anything left. Get ready for the finale."

I scrunch the note in my hand and throw it to the floor. I look at Fredrick deep in the eyes. "I'm going to kill this son of a bitch."

Chapter 16

Cottage
6:00 p.m. Same Day

"I'm using the herbs again tonight." I break the silence at dinner with Luke and Michael.

"Do you think it's the right time?" Luke asks. "You only have a little left. You want to save it for the perfect moment."

"There's no better moment than to save a girl's life and to kill Jack once and for all. I could end it tonight."

"Or he could get away again. Then move on with the next victim."

I shrug my shoulders. "I'll take my chances."

"Mom, I want to help you," Michael tunes in. The good thing is when I use the herbs Michael can't dream the same or follow me.

"No, Michael. The only way you could do that is use the herbs too, and I'm definitely not letting that happen. I need to do this on my own, sweetie." He drops his head in disappointment.

I take my last bite of Luke's amazing baked chicken and mushrooms and begin cleaning the plates. I watch Michael walk quietly into the living room and listen as he turns on the TV. I remind myself that I am doing this for him, Luke, and my family. Once this is over I can go back to my normal life. Well as normal as it can get.

As Luke and I lie in bed I tell him about what happened earlier with Maggie. "Luke, I swear I'm being honest. I saw her and spoke with her."

"First the dreams, the herbs, and now ghosts? I can hardly grip the idea of controlling your own dreams." He turns to his side and props himself on his elbow resting his head in his hand.

I turn over and do the same. "I know, I can't either. It was like she was trying to help me. But I didn't get much out of her. I might be able to use her help to catch Jack. Maybe I need an outside force."

He closes his eyes and shakes his head. "Are you sure we aren't just crazy? What if this was all just a bad dream and we could wake up from it."

The thought pops into my head. "Now that would be crazy," I say with a smile.

He smiles back. "Yeah I know, I'm just ready for the end."

"Me too," I say as I kiss him. I grab the herbs from my bedside table. "Well it's action time."

"One last kiss first." I give Luke a deep kiss and then take the herbs.

Dizziness.

Heaviness.

Darkness.

I glance at my watch and it is 2:30 a.m. I am walking down Rainbow Row when my attention turns toward a woman who is walking by herself. She is dressed in skinny jeans with a gold, shiny tank top. Her long blonde hair falls down to her waist. That looks like Jack's type but that isn't Haley. It looks like her but it's not. Maybe that is his number three? She is turning down the cobblestone road S. Adgers D Wharf. She is walking herself into a kidnapping. This place isn't well lit and it is away from a crowd. What is she doing? "Excuse me Miss?" I say to get her attention but she continues to walk forward.

I pick up my pace. I catch up with her and tap her shoulder. "Ma'am, is everything okay?"

She turns around and she is crying. It looks like she has been crying for a while. Under the dim light from the street I can see her swollen red eyes. "Ma'am, do you need help?"

She shakes her head, "No, I'm doing what I'm supposed to do. It's what he told me to do."

My heartbeat begins to pick up speed. "Who told you?"

"A creepy man." She talks as if she is in a daze. When I look at her in the eyes she is looking past me not at me.

"What does this creepy man look like?"

"Shaggy hair and a big nose. He laughs like a clown."

"Shit. Why did he send you here?"

She slightly turns her head so her eyes are on mine. "He sent me here for you."

I take a step back. "Me? Why?"

She shrugs her shoulders. "I don't know. He said I'd catch your attention and would try to help me. He wanted you far away from him." She isn't making any sense. What the hell is going on?

"Did he say anything else?"

She digs into her purse that is on her hip. I back off thinking it is a gun. She hands me a vial of blood with the number 3 on it. "He wanted me to give you this. I'm sorry. If I didn't do what he said, he told me he'd kill my son."

I take the blood. "It's okay. He's a malicious man. Let me call you a cab so you can get home safely."

"Thank you Miss." I call her a cab and I wait by her side. She doesn't move much. She is scared stiff and in shock. I don't blame her. I would be the same way if he were to mess with Michael.

The cab comes a few minutes later and I help her in and pay the cab driver. I walk to the end of the road, which leads to the bay. I glare at the water. Why would he lead me here? How did he do that when it's my dream? I look at the vial of blood. This blood must be of importance. So he has Haley still; if she is even alive. Now he has victim number three. He is getting way too close to number one. I am not liking this one bit. I stare at the water again and close my eyes. I hold onto the vial tightly and concentrate on waking up.

When I open my eyes, I move my hand to see if I brought it back with me. I pull it our form under the sheets. "Holy fucking shit, it worked again," I say as I turn on the light and look at the vial of blood. Luke rolls over when he sees the light.

"What happened?" Then he looks at what I am holding in my hand and gets up quickly.

"What the hell?"

"He tricked me. I followed a woman that fit his style and looked just like Haley except it wasn't her. He sent her there with the vial."

"So you didn't even see Jack?"

I shake my head. "No, that bastard did it again." I glance at my clock. I still have two hours until the alarm goes off. There is no way I'm sleeping now. "I'm going into the station."

"At 3:00 in the morning? I don't think so."

"What else am I supposed to do? I can't go back to sleep knowing I have blood that needs to be tested."

"No one is at the station right now to help anyway. Just try to relax for a little bit." I put the vial on the table by the bed. Then I lie in Luke's arms.

"Luke, I have a sick feeling that Jack is going to do something really bad. What if he tries to hurt you or Michael?"

"We're always safe. That's why we're at the safe house. That's why Fredrick hired the best bodyguards. He won't get near us."

"I hope not," I say as I rub my face into his chest. My eyes feel heavy. I guess I do need a little bit more rest. I snuggle closer to Luke and close my eyes.

The alarm goes off as I wake up with a jolt. It feels like I just closed my eyes ten minutes ago. I hate when that happens. I kiss Luke and roll out of bed. I send Fredrick a quick text warning him that I got something from my dream. He texts back immediately with a "thumbs up" emoji. I chuckle. Got to love his sense of humor.

Luke and I make a quick breakfast for the three of us. Michael wants Lucky Charms. He says he feels like it brings him luck when he eats them. I smile as I watch Michael enjoying his cereal. He smiles at me. Those dimples get me every time. I soak in the moment. I feel as if I have been so busy I haven't spent much time with Michael. Come to think of it, I haven't.

"How's school going?"

He nods his head. "It's good. Yesterday was test day but I felt like I did well. Ryan has been helping me study the spelling words. I glance at Ryan sitting in the corner of the kitchen drinking coffee and reading the newspaper. He sneaks behind the newspaper and looks at me. I mouth, "thank you" to him. I'm so busy I haven't helped Michael with his homework. What kind of mother am I?

Michael must be able to read minds as well. "Mom, it's okay you know."

"What?"

"I know you feel bad because you haven't spent that much time with me."

I smile at him. "How did you know I was thinking that?"

"You're my mom and we do share a special gift. I know you better than you think."

"You're such an amazing boy. I do feel guilty."

"Don't. I want you to catch this guy. I know it'll be better once he's gone."

"It will be, I promise." I smile at him. He tilts the bowl up to his mouth to drink his milk.

I finish my oatmeal and pack my bag for work. I place the vial of blood in the front pocket of my black backpack. I can't lose that. "I'm off. I hope you two have something planned for this beautiful Saturday while I'm working," I say with a smile.

Luke responds quickly. "He has a full day planned with Dad," he says with a wink.

"Good, just make sure Ryan takes you wherever you go." I glance over at Ryan and he gives me a thumbs up. I kiss both of my boys and head out to work. There are no days off when I'm this close.

CPD
7:00 a.m. Saturday November 6th

"So what did you retrieve from your dream last night?" Fredrick asks as soon as I put my bag down on my desk. He makes something that sounds so crazy come out to be so professional. He has his clean face, slicked back black hair, and tucked in shirt professionalism ready. He means business.

I pull out the vial from my bag and hold it up for him to see. His eyes become big. "No way? You really pulled that from your dream?"

"Yeah. Actually Jack sent it to me." He gives me a questioning look and raises his one eyebrow. I explained the whole story to him.

"I can't believe there's still no word about Haley. I've been checking street cameras and put up fliers around the stores, restaurants, and gas stations. No one has seen her."

"He must be keeping her somewhere we wouldn't think to check. Now he has another victim," I say as I hold up the vial. I catch Christopher coming in and he sees me holding the vial. A smile forms on his face. He is a weird character.

"Another victim? Let me test the blood," he says excitedly. He pushes up his big glasses and walks into his office. I glance through the glass at Sergeant Gordon hard at work.

"Has he said anything to you yet about Haley?"

"No. He's quiet this morning."

"I'm going to let him know that I got another vial." Fredrick nods his head as I walk into Gordon's office.

"Excuse me Sergeant Gordon, I have some news." He slowly

moves his eyes away from his computer and up at me.

"Please, tell me, it's good?"

I shake my head in disagreement. "I found another vial. He has victim number three now."

He puts his face in his head and sighs heavily. "I want to catch this son of a bitch!" he yells out.

"We will Sir, eventually."

"Thank you," he says. I know that is my cue to leave.

Fredrick and I spend the next hour or so making phone calls around the area to see if anyone has seen Haley. We haven't had any luck. Just then Christopher walks out of his office looking different. His face is blank. There is no weird smile and his glasses are on top of his head. Something is wrong and my heart drops into my stomach. Fredrick looks up and notices the same thing because he looks at me and mouths "uh oh."

"Christopher, is everything okay?"

He keeps his head down and shakes it. "No, it's not okay. I can't believe this."

"Believe what?" I ask with a little less patience.

"The blood sample came back."

"Whose blood is it?" Fredrick asks. My hands become sweaty. Nerves fill my senses as I wait to hear who he has to say.

"The blood in the vial belongs to," he clears his throat. "It belongs to May."

Frozen.

Fear.

Panic

I can't seem to move.

I stare in shock at nothing.

I feel numb.

I feel pain.

I feel sick.

Not May, not again. This can't be happening again. My body begins to tremble. People seem to be talking to me but I'm not hearing anything. I see Fredrick's mouth moving but I can't hear what is coming out. Christopher is standing in front of me waving his arms. I picture May tied up to the chair in the basement when Tom captured her. Now she is trapped with Jack and all of his knives. What have I done? Again? This has to be a dream. I close my eyes.

Wake up.

Wake up.

Wake up.

I open my eyes and I am still in the station. Fredrick is kneeling in front of me. He shakes me. "Linda, Linda. Snap out of it."

I shake my head and I can hear all the sounds of the busy station, including Fredrick's voice. "I'm here, I-" I can't finish the statement because I don't know what to say.

"Linda, listen to me. We're going to do everything in our power to find May. I won't go home until I do." I stare into his dark brown eyes. His eyes are truthful and trusting. I know he is going to do what he says. But he can't be the one to do it.

"It has to be me, Fredrick. He took May to get to me. And I'm going to give in. I'm going to him. I'll save May at all costs, and I don't care what that cost is." Tears fall from my eyes.

"No, we're going to do this together."

"How? The only way Jack can be stopped is in my dreams. I can contact you through my dreams, remember? As soon as I find him I'll call for backup." But I'm not going to do that this time. I am going by myself just like Jack wants. I can't believe this is happening all over again. "I'm going home now. I'm taking the rest of the herbs and I'm going to fight."

"Linda, I don't know how safe that's going to be. Taking all those herbs could put you-"

"Put me what? In another coma? Like I haven't been there before. Fredrick, this is May we're talking about here. I'm not going to let him hurt her or anyone else in my family. I'm doing this and you can't stop me."

"Alright, alright," he says defensively raising up his hands. He puts his hand on my shoulder. "But please make sure to call me as soon as you get something."

I nod my head and walk away, emotionless. I can't feel anything right now. Ronald is outside waiting. "To the safe house please," I say bluntly.

Is everything okay, Mrs.?"

"No, it's far from okay," I say and end the conversation.

I send Luke one quick text. "The vial of blood is May's. Jack has her. This is happening all over again and I'm going to stop it for good. I'm taking all the herbs. I'm doing whatever it takes to save May. I love you, Luke." And I turn off my phone. I don't need any distractions.

Cottage
10:15 a.m.

Luckily Luke and Michael are not home when I get there. They must be out having fun. When I get walk through the door I tell Mick that I am taking a nap and I go in and lock the bedroom door. Jack has gone too far. I pour the rest of the herbs into the water. This is my last chance and I'm not failing. I chug down the herbs. I feel as if my insides are burning.

Spinning.
Spinning faster.
Numbness.
Spinning.
Darkness.

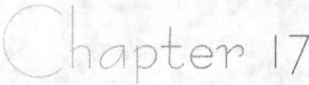

Chapter 17

I find myself on a dock at the Charleston Marina. What the hell? This isn't like Jack at all. What is he playing at here? I stand looking out into the water. The sun is almost fully set. The sky is not quite black yet. The sky is a mixture of red, blue, and purple colors. It is peaceful yet horrifying at the same time. It is calm before the storm. I look all around at all the boats. I don't know how to find them here.

I walk around the different boats to see if I can find anything but I am coming up short. I know May doesn't have that much time. Unless he wants to wait and harm her until I can watch. Sounds like something Jack would do; just like his brother. I walk down at the end of one of the docks clueless. Then I see a figure out in the water. The figure is walking on water. I squint my eyes. What in the world? The figure moves closer and I realize its Maggie.

"Maggie. Man, am I glad to see you. You have to help me." I look closer at her face expression and for once she is not smiling. Her look is serious and grim.

"Linda, none of this is real. You have to wake up," she says with a short tone.

I shake my head in confusion, "What are you talking about? Jack has May. I have to stop him."

"I understand that but listen to me. You could save yourself some trouble if you'd just wake up for good this time."

"Maggie, I'm not waking up from this dream. I need to be here. It's my last chance. I'm out of herbs."

"You took all of them?"

"Yeah, I had to. It's my only chance."

She shakes her head in disappointment. "This isn't good, Linda. I don't know if you'll ever **truly** wake up now."

"I don't know what you mean. Is there anything you can do to help me?" Truly wake up? What is going on?

She pauses then turns her head out towards the ocean and points. "He's out there in a boat where no one can see them or hear them."

I gulp and panic at the thought. Kill them and dump their bodies. I bet that is what he has planned. "How big of a boat does he have?"

"Big enough. It has a cabin underneath it. It's his cousin's. You need to get out there fast. He isn't wasting much more time. All I can say is be careful and I pray that you wake up in time."

"In time for what?" She disappears like steam before she can answer. What does she mean wake up for good? She is a ghost, so what does she really know? But then again it is Maggie. I redirect my thinking. How am I going to get a boat?

I walk around again to see if I can find something. I hate to steal but at this point I'll do anything. I find a small wooden boat with an ore attached to it. It is tied off with a rope. I look around and I don't see anyone. Here goes nothing. I untie the rope and hop into the boat. Now I just have to find where Jack is.

I start to paddle when I see Maggie again. She is pointing. She is leading me into the right direction. Thank you, Maggie. I continue to follow her directions. I row about ten minutes when I see a boat resting in the water. I look around. There are no other boats and I can barely see the land from here.

As I pull in closer to the boat I can see a dim light on in the cabin. There is no one on top. My heart races rapidly the closer I get to the boat. It is a huge boat, more like a mini yacht. I take big deep breaths. "Okay Linda, you can do this," I say to myself as I touch the gun in my holster. Don't give him any time to talk. Just point and shoot in the head this time. I paddle close enough to the boat where I can grab onto it and I hop onto his boat quietly. I tie the small wooden boat to this one for a getaway. I slowly creep through the boat. I see the door to the cabin is shut. I open it and brace myself for what I'm about to encounter. The blood inside my head is boiling. My breathing becomes heavy.

Stay calm.

I open the door to the cabin and walk in. I see two chairs in front of me with people in them. They are covered with a sheet. I can't see who they are. I have no idea if May is even under there. I hope this isn't a trap. A door to my right begins to open and I quickly grab my gun. "Oh Linda, Linda, Linda. I'm so happy to find you here," Jack says as he shuts the door and walks towards me. He easily knocks the gun out *of my hand so I am left with nothing.*

I step backwards toward the chairs. "Jack, what game are you playing here? Where's May?" He continues to walk towards me and I continue to walk back. He doesn't stop smiling. He is holding a long knife in his hand. I step around the chairs. Now the chairs are in between Jack and me.

"Go ahead. Take off the sheet to see who we're playing with." I glance down and on the sheet written in marker is the number three, and on the other person is the number two.

"Let me guess. I'm number one?"

He begins to clap.

"You figured it out, Linda. This is my grand finale. Go ahead, take a look at who I have under here. You will watch me kill them slowly and then I'll kill you slowly."

I nervously take off the sheet labeled with the number three. It is May. She has duct tape around her mouth. Her hair is messy but she is asleep. I quickly fall to my knees and shake her shoulders. "May, May wake up. It's me." She slowly raises her head and opens her eyes. Her eyes become big as she sees me. She starts to moan under her tape and motions her head as if she is pointing to the person next to her. Her eyes are filled with fear.

I look up at Jack. His shaggy hair is pulled back into a slick ponytail as if he cleaned up for the occasion. He smiles, "Go ahead, and see what's under door number two." He laughs.

I cautiously raise the sheet.

My heart drops into my stomach.

"NO!" I scream.

Jack's laugh becomes louder and higher.

"Michael!!" His poor head is bent down. His clothes are wet with sweat. My poor boy. I shake him gently. He begins to wake up. His eyes are locked on mine. I hug him tightly. I take off his duct tape. "Oh Michael, I'm so sorry. Are you okay? Are you hurt?"

"I'm okay, Mom." I hug him again. Then I quickly take off May's duct tape.

"Kill that son of a bitch," May says to me. I look up at Jack who continues to smile. He holds his long, skinny, sharp knife. I have nothing. I glance at my gun that is lying on the floor of the cabin near the door. I have so much anger building up in me that I don't care if I die trying. I will kill him in one way or another.

"So this is how you wanted to end it, huh? What killing my sister

and my son in front of me? And then finally putting an end to me? All for what? Your dumb ass brother Tom who no longer lives?" I can tell I hit a sore spot. His smile turned into a frown.

"Yes, all for Tom. He's my brother and I made him a promise. Plus, I kind of like making you suffer. It's appealing."

I shake my head. "You're just a sick as him. You do know that I got away, right?"

He smiles forms again. "Really? Cause it seems like you're stuck right now. If you even walk an inch towards me I'll kill May and then kill Michael without any hesitation."

I hold my hands up in defense. I give in. "Okay, okay. Let's talk about this."

"Talk about what? I finally got what I've been waiting for. Plus, look around you," he says as he waves his arms around. "You're out in the water with no one to hear you scream."

I'm starting to feel hopeless. I have no idea what to do. "Kill me, Jack. Let them go and kill me. Please. I'm the only you truly want. So let them go. Let me free them and get on the boat I tied out there. Then you can kill me."

He brings the tip of the knife up as he taps his tooth. "Hmm, that's a generous offer. But my orders were to hurt you deeply and then kill you when you feel you have nothing left to give. So I think I'll pass," he says. He holds his knife out and points it towards May.

"No, no please, I'm begging you." I look down into May's eyes. Tears are falling.

"I love you, Linda." Then I watch as Jack pierces the knife right through her chest. She stares at me and grunts with pain. Blood begins pouring out of her mouth.

"No!" I scream at the top of my lungs. I fall to my knees in pain, fear, and agony. My insides are becoming numb. "May, no! I love you May," I say as I watch the life in her eyes burn out. I begin to cry harder.

"Please Jack. Don't hurt Michael. You've hurt me enough already. Just take my life and save his. Please, I'll do anything," I say looking into Jack's cold eyes.

He wipes May's blood off the knife with a towel. He shakes his head from side to side. "I told you what I've had planned. I'm sorry but it has to end this way."

Before I can get onto my feet quick enough he stabs Michael through the chest. Everything inside me is dead. I crawl over to Michael and I grab his head and look him in the eyes. "I love you, Michael." I hear him choking. I can feel his blood soaking into my shirt as I hold him tight. Not my baby boy. I can't let him go. I have nothing left in me. I have no strength left. I give up. My body feels completely numb. I don't let go of Michael. I sit here holding his body. I can't even think anymore.

Shock.

Terror.

Guilt.

Emptiness.

Jack walks over to me. He pulls my arm and yanks me off Michael. He makes me stand to my feet. He is holding onto my arm. I can barely stand. He stands me tall and looks me in the eye. "How much pain are you feeling, Linda? I know Tom is happy."

I don't respond. I just stare into his eyes. I didn't realize how much his eyes look like Tom's. He's won. He raises the knife and the blood from Michael still drips. "Are you ready for death, Linda?"

At that moment in time I was ready. I could be with my boy and my sister again. The thought of Luke all alone runs through me. I ache with pain knowing what he is going to feel, but there is nothing left that I can do. I say nothing.

Jack moves closer to me and whispers in my ear, "Say hello to my brother for me." Then a sharp pain fills my insides. I glance down at the knife sticking out of my stomach. The pain is unbearable. I begin choking on my own blood. Jack steps back as he watches me suffer. I fall to my knees. I look at Michael and May. I touch the blood that is dripping from the knife. I can feel the life fading away inside me. I fall to my side feeling nothing but dizziness. I look up into the light of the cabin.

Death is peaceful.

My entire body feels numb.

I'm fading away.

I feel as if I'm floating in the air.

The light begins to fade away.

Everything is fading.

Slowly fading.

Gone.

Chapter 18

I slowly open my heavy eyes. My vision is blurry but I see nothing but white. I sit up. My body feels heavy. I squint my eyes to soak in the bright light. My gut starts to turn because I know I have been here before. I look all around me. I am surrounded by white walls. What the hell am I doing back here? Maybe this really is Heaven? I look down and I see an image. I see my body in a pool of blood. I see Luke hovering over my body on the hospital bed. Wait a second, I've done all this before! This is right after I gave birth to Michael. Luke looks the same as he did when I was here almost seven years ago. So what am I doing back here?

I touch my stomach where Jack had stabbed me and there is nothing there. No wound, no blood. I must be dead. I have to be. But why here and why now? I look back down and it looks like Luke is whispering in my ear.

"Come back to me, Linda." I hear it echo through the white walls. I quickly turn my head around; it's as if Luke is right next to me. I am so confused at what is going on. I don't know what to think. I begin to panic. I try to stand up but I am wobbly. Then I fall straight back to the ground. My breathing becomes slower and my eyes become heavy.

Dizziness.

Darkness.

I hear a beeping noise in the distance. My eyelids are heavy but I can slowly lift them. "Oh my God, I think she's waking up!" I hear a deep, familiar voice. I slowly begin to move my fingers and toes. My entire body feels heavy, including my mind. I have no idea what is going on. "Linda baby?" I hear the soothing voice that only belongs to my Luke.

"Yes," I say as I try to catch my breath.

"Are you okay? How are you feeling?" He asks both questions quickly with worry.

I open my eyes fully and see Luke's gentle, kind face. His bright blue eyes are glaring into mine. He hasn't shaved in a few days but his scruff looks amazing. I feel as if I just saw him a moment ago, but he looks younger. This is so strange.

"Luke. Where am I? What day is it? What year is it?" I say with panic now that I realize what has happened. Somehow I either traveled through time or spent years in a dream.

He lightly squints his eyes and looks at me with concern. "Linda, what are you talking about? It's July 2, 2015. You gave birth to our son Michael two days ago. You lost a lot of blood during the birth and you were in a coma. But you're awake now and I couldn't be happier."

I sit up quickly in panic. *This can't be happening. I dreamt that far into the future and saw my fate along with my son? How can this happen?* I am in shock. "Linda, what's going on?"

I shake my head. "You're never going to believe this. Was I really in a coma for only two days?"

"Yeah. Why? Did something happen?"

"Oh something happened alright. I dreamt six years into the future. I know what happens to us, to Michael. I have to stop it."

He shakes his head. "What the hell? You what?"

I begin to speak when I pause. "Where's Michael?"

"The nurse is bringing him in now. We can talk about this later. I'm just glad you're back and safe."

"Okay, but I have a lot of work to do. What about Tom? What happened to him?"

"He's on trial to go to jail, which he will."

"Yeah, I know he will." He raises an eyebrow at me. *How the hell am I supposed to explain all this? I don't know if I can even grasp what has just happened?*

"Here he is. He has been waiting for you," the nurse says with a sweet voice.

My mind shuts down when I see my baby boy for the first time…again. This is so weird. I've already done this. No mom has ever gotten the chance to see their baby born twice. I am going to cherish this moment. I missed six years of his life before and I don't intend to do that again. She gently places him in my arms. His smooth tan skin and blue eyes makes my heart melt. He is a dead ringer of Luke. "He looks just like you."

Luke smiles. "He's a good mixture." I smile at his comment and kiss Michael on the forehead.

"I promise I'll do it right this time. You won't have to worry about a thing," I whisper into Michael's ear.

Doctor Hue comes in a few minutes later. "Mrs. Jackson, how are you feeling?"

"I feel great. I'm ready to go!"

"I'm glad you're doing well, but you need to stay another night. We need to run a few more tests to make sure you're okay after the coma."

I roll my eye. "Trust me, I'm fine. I'm more than okay to go home now."

Dr. Hue smiles. "I'm sure you are. But this is procedure. You'll be able to go home tomorrow as long as everything is okay tonight."

I sigh. "Okay, fine." I hold Michael tight. My pride and joy. My second chance to see him grow up. I guess the first chance since that was all a dream before. I can't believe I know what he is going to look like six years down the road. This is all so crazy. I have to protect him. We need to stop Tom and Jack soon. How do I go about meeting Fredrick for real and telling him this story? He is going to think I'm crazy. There are so many things to do and talk about. I have to get this done right away so I can enjoy my life with Michael and not constantly look over my shoulders for the next six years.

The nurse comes and gets Michael. I don't want to hand him over. She looks at me with a kind smile. "You need to get some rest. Doctor's orders."

"Rest, I've been resting the past two days. I'm not even tired."

"Okay, I'll let you spend a little more time with him. Just don't tell the doc," she says in a whisper, smiles, then leaves the room.

Luke is sitting in the chair gazing at Michael and me. I smile. "What are you looking at?"

"My two favorite people." He smiles his bright amazing smile.

Jackson Household
Friday July 3

When we walk into the house I feel overwhelmed with emotions. I am home in present time. I hope that this is real and not a dream. I don't even know anymore. I have to treat this like it is real life. I need to get to work. "Luke," I say as I hold onto Michael. "I need to get to work immediately."

"The coffee shop will be fine without you for a while." *Oh yeah, I still work there.*

"No, I mean with the CPD."

"What are you talking about? Who would you work with?"

I sigh and lay Michael down in his crib. I grab Luke and sit him on the couch. "This is going to be hard to understand and believe, but you have to trust me."

He puts his hand on my lap. "Of course I'll believe you, Linda. We've been through so much, how can I not?" he says with a small smile.

"Well, while I was in that two-day coma, I dreamt and saw the future six years down the road. Michael was a young boy. But the crazy thing is, I saw these next few months as well. Then there was an accident and I was in a six-year coma. Then I woke up to see Michael. I missed six years of his life." I explained in detail everything that has happened from now until I just woke up… again.

"Wait you, May, and Michael were murdered by Tom's brother Jack to get revenge? Well, we have to stop it."

"Exactly. If everything happens the way it did in my dream then Tom has people on the inside of prison who help him get into his coma and then they capture me. So we need to put an end to Tom before he gets the chance to do that. If he finds out that I know what's going to happen then he'll speed up the process. Then we need to find Jack and end him as well before he even gets started."

Luke takes a deep breath. "Okay, how do we do it?"

I softly shrug my shoulders. "Well, first things first, I need to visit CPD and talk with detective Fredrick. He's the detective I'll work with in this case. I need to convince him that I've seen the future. In my dream he already knew who I was because of what happened with Tom, so I think I have a good chance."

"Okay, well I'm off today. I'll stay with Michael."

"But I'll need to breastfeed him. I can't leave his side yet. I bet if I call Detective Fredrick and have him come over then he will. Actually, that's what happened before." I shake my head. "It's so strange to know what's going to happen. I mean all the details."

"I can't imagine." I pick up the phone to call CPD but it already started to ring.

I look at Luke. "Mom."

"Hey Mom."

"Linda, why didn't you tell me you were home from the hospital? Are you okay? How's Michael?"

I shake my head and smile. "Mom, I'm fine and so is Michael."

"Okay, well your Dad and me are coming over there."

"Mom, not yet. I need to take care of some business. I'll explain the story later, but it's very important. I promise, I'll explain. And before you even ask, yes I'll be okay."

She pauses for a few seconds. "Okay honey, please call as soon as you can."

"I will, I promise. Will you and Dad do me a favor please?"

"Anything."

"Please be careful wherever you go. Watch your back. I don't want you and Dad going anywhere alone. There might be a cop car sitting outside your house. Don't be alarmed, as they're for protection."

"Um, okay."

"Good. I love you. Say the same to Dad."

"Love you too honey," she says with confusion.

I hang up the phone. "I have to call May as well and warn her. She'll be the first to be taken...again." Luke nods in agreement.

"Linda! How are you doing? Wait a second. Are you home and you didn't tell me?" I roll my eyes. My family loves to worry. I guess they have good reasons.

"I'm fine. I need you to listen to me very carefully."

"Linda, what's going on?" She sounds worried and not her usual bubbly self.

"I have a very long story to tell you, but I need to take care of some business first. It's very important that you and Charlie are careful when you go out. If you see a cop car in front of your apartment, don't worry, it's for your protection. Don't go anywhere alone. If you need to take the cop with you to run an errand, then do so. Please promise me." I feel so redundant right now.

"Linda, you're scaring me."

"I know and I'm sorry but I have to tell you how it is. Promise me, May?"

"Okay, I promise."

"Thank you. As soon as this is all over I'll have you and Mom and Dad over for dinner and I'll explain the whole story."

"Okay. And Linda…"

"Yes, I'll be okay, I promise."

I hear a small laugh. "Okay good. I love you, sis."

"I love you too."

I hang up the phone and sigh. "Phew, it takes a lot out of me trying to protect my family without telling them the whole story. In my dream Sarah and Bobby set up the coffee shop with a crib for Michael. I need to let them know I'm okay and that I'll be back to work as soon as possible. And tell them thank you for the crib."

I sigh again and smile. Luke shakes his head and smiles back. As I dial Sarah's number I glance at Michael sound asleep in his crib. He is so precious.

"Sarah, it's Linda!" I give her the whole speech I gave May and Mom and thanked her about the crib.

"Okay." She emphasizes the O. "Wait, how did you know about the crib?"

Shit, I didn't think about that. "Well, it's part of the long story. How is the shop doing?"

"It's doing great but it misses you."

"I'll be back as soon as possible."

"Good. Stay safe out there."

"Will do. Thank you for everything, Sarah."

"Of course, Linda." I hang up the phone.

"Okay, now CPD. This should be interesting." Luke is sitting on the couch watching me. I can tell he is happy to have me back and safe. I rush over and give him a soft kiss on the lips as I hold the phone up to my ear.

"This is The Charleston Police Department, Sergeant Gordon speaking." I smile. It feels good to hear his voice.

"Hello, this is Linda Jackson. I'm calling for Detective Fredrick."

"Wait, *the* Linda Jackson? The one who worked with Tom Walker?"

"Yes, that's me." *I knew this was coming.*

"How are you feeling? All of us over here have heard of you. We're sorry for what happened with Tom. I always thought he was one of the best. I still can't believe it."

Okay, enough with the talking.

"I'm good. Thank you. Is Detective Fredrick there?"

"Oh yes, here sorry."

"Detective Fredrick speaking."

"Hi, it's Linda-" I couldn't finish my statement.

"Linda Jackson, am I right?"

"Yeah."

"Yes, you're well known around here."

"I've heard."

"What can I help you with today?"

"This is going to sound crazy but I really need your help."

"Trust me, it can't sound that crazy. I know what you can do."

"Okay, well I hope so. I can't come into the station to talk because of my newborn. Is there any way you could come to my house so we can talk? It is an emergency. Can you bring Detective Arnold as well?" *I am so happy that he is alive. We are going to keep it that way.*

"Yes, of course. I haven't mentioned Arnold before. How did you know about him?"

"Part of the story and what I need to tell you."

"Oh boy. This is going to be good. We'll be there in fifteen minutes."

"Thank you. See you soon." He hangs up the phone.

I sigh. "Okay, they're on their way."

"They?" Luke asks.

"Oh yeah, I forgot to tell you. I work with two detectives this time around. Fredrick and Arnold. You'll like Arnold's personality," I say with a smile.

"Alright, whatever you say."

I decide to put on a pot of coffee for everyone. I feel as if we are going to need it. I fed Michael before we left the hospital and he is still out. He should be okay for another hour or so. I pace around the house. I am nervous for some reason. I hope they believe me.

"Linda, relax. From what you've told me about them in you dream, they'll be okay about everything. They'll believe you. They'll stop Tom and Jack."

I crack my knuckles and sit down on the kitchen chair. "Okay, you're right."

A few minutes later there is a knock on the door. "Here they are." I wonder if they will look the same as they did in my dream. I open the door and smile because they are exactly the same. Fredrick is the tough, play by the book detective. He is clean cut and tall. They are both wearing the same black t-shirt and black pants. Arnold still has his shaggy brown hair and beard. Arnold is smiling his big goofy smile. It takes everything not to give him a hug because the last time I saw him, he was dead. I shiver inside at that thought.

"Detective Fredrick and Arnold," I say as I shake their hands. "Please come in." I open the door wider and step aside. This is so weird. I know these two like they are family and they've never met me before. It gives a sick feeling in my stomach. "Please come have a seat in the kitchen. Coffee?" *I already know the answer.*

"Yes please," they both say at the same time. They look at each other and Arnold smiles widely and Fredrick rolls his eyes. Oh, it is good to have the two of them back together.

I bring over their coffee and Luke brings ours over. They both look at me with wide eyes as if I'm a ghost or something. This is weird. "Okay, I have no idea where to start. But I can say that this is very important and life threatening to not only myself and my family but yours. I look to Arnold. His smile turns to a frown and he slightly tilts his head to the side."

"We're all ears," Arnold says with a serious tone.

"Okay. First thing, I need a protective detail on my parents and my sister May."

"You've got it. Let me make a quick phone call. What are their addresses?" asks Fredrick. I tell him and he gets cops out there.

"Thank you. Okay anyway. You all know about my ability. I can dream about events before they happen, but what I'm about to tell you is far more than serious." They nod their heads in response. Luke sits aside and listens. I tell them everything in detail. From meeting them in my dream like we just did, to working together in killing Tom. I tell them how he is in jail and has people on the inside working for him. I explain that he caught me in a dream and I was in a coma for six years. I explain how I met Maggie, Arnold's aunt, and how he and she both die. I tell them about Tom's brother, Jack. I explain how Maggie helps me find Jack and how he killed May, Michael, and myself. I explain everything step by step, when it occurred, and how it all happened. It took about thirty minutes to tell the whole story. The entire time they listened and didn't take their eyes off me. At points their eyes got wider and their mouths dropped a little.

I take a deep breath and wait for their responses. Luke fills up our coffee. Fredrick is the first to speak. "Wow. That's a lot to take in. I don't know where to start."

I look at Arnold and he looks like he is going to get sick. His face is green. "Detective Arnold, are you okay?"

"Not really. It's scary to think that I could die in six years and my Aunt Maggie is such a sweet lady."

"Yeah, she is."

"It's got to be weird being here right now? Knowing everything. And knowing us even though we don't know you?" Fredrick asks.

"Oh, it's so weird; beyond words."

"Well, we need to take care of Tom first. Once he's taken care of for good then we'll get Jack. Do you know anything about Jack that could help us out?"

"I don't know. I mean he's going to be six years younger now so I don't know what he even looks like or if he's even the same person. He could have been sane until Tom's death. I don't know. I do know he has a cousin. I'm not sure of her name or where she lives. I do know at one point in my dream Jack was injured and magically fixed. I'm thinking she has something to do with it. She could be a doctor."

"Okay, well it's a start. It looks like we have a lot of work to do. Maybe we can beat it out of Tom," Fredrick says.

I shake my head. "You won't get anything out of Tom, I promise. He'll die before he says anything."

"Okay, well that's good to know. Looks like we'll just end him and do work on Jack. We should track down Jack before he finds out Tom is dead. Maybe we can get to him before and hit him when he least expects it."

"That's a good idea. But we need to move fast. Tom certainly will."

Arnold chimes in. He has been unusually quiet. I don't blame him. "I know who can help find Jack." My mind immediately goes to Maggie.

"Maggie, she could find Jack for us using some kind of a spell I bet," I say.

Arnold nods his head. "Yeah, she's our best bet for a quick find."

"Alright let's start there," Fredrick says.

"I want to go."

"Do you want us to put you on speaker phone throughout the process?" asks Arnold.

"Yes please." I wonder if Maggie will remember me. I mean, she is a psychic and can connect with the other side, I wonder if she remembers me from the dream?

"Okay, we will. Talk to you soon," Fredrick says. They both get up from their chairs and politely push them in.

"I told you it'd be okay," Luke says. He hasn't spoken the whole time.

"Yeah, I'm glad. I just wish I could go with them and be a part of it."

"You were already a part of it. That's enough. Sit back and let them do their job."

"Yeah, I guess. But it's hard. In my dream after I woke up from the six-year coma the doctor did a bunch a tests on me and figured out how I could dream the way I do. It has something to do with gamma and theta waves in my brain. I guess it's unhuman."

"Interesting, well at least you have an explanation," Luke says trying to comfort me the best he can.

"Yeah, it's still weird though. I mean how come my brainwaves are messed up and no one else's are? Although Tom has something weird going on too. It's all too confusing to try and come up with an explanation. I just know that when this is all over I'm done with police work. I want to go back to my normal life at the coffee shop. I miss it and the people."

"I am glad to hear that. But you can't help your dreams."

"That's true. Maybe after killing Tom and Jack the dreams will stop?"

"I don't know, Linda. But you have to realize that you might have to live with this forever."

"Michael has the same problem. I hope he grows up to be normal. I hope he doesn't get this nightmare of an ability, but if he does I'm prepared and you need to be too. We were able to dream together. It was the craziest thing and he saw things no boy should ever see."

"Maybe there's a cure?" Luke asks.

"A cure? I don't think so, other than shock treatment, which I don't want to go through."

"No, absolutely not."

"I'm going to have fight through them and try and control them. If I can't then I'll just call the CPD with the details and let them handle it. I'm done going out on cases. It's too dangerous for myself and you all. I don't want to put you all in danger ever again."

"Sounds like a good idea, baby." He smiles and kisses my forehead. Michael begins to cry. It is time to feed him.

Chapter 19

Jackson Household
Friday July 3ʳᵈ 1:00 p.m.

I receive a phone call from Fredrick. I answer it and put it on speaker. "Hello Linda, are you there?"

"Yeah, and I'm all ears."

"We're here with Maggie."

"Hello Linda dear. How are you doing, sweetie?" *She does remember me.*

"Maggie? You remember?"

"I saw everything. I'm here to help like I did before. Nothing bad will happen." It sounds so good to hear her soft sweet voice. I picture her crazy curly hair, big earrings, and bizarre colorful clothing.

"Oh, thank god. It has been hard to explain to everyone what happened."

"The other side is a scary place and very complicated. No one will truly understand unless you've been there."

"You're right about that." I sit at the kitchen table, feeding Michael, and listening in.

"Alright, let's get started," Maggie says. I swear I can smell the incense from her house. It's as if everything happened yesterday.

"We're trying to track down Jack, correct?" Maggie asks.

"Yes," I reply quickly.

"Okay, this will be hard without an item or object that belongs to him but since I've been through the dream with Linda, there's a special connection."

"Good," replies Fredrick.

"Okay, everyone connect hands," Maggie says. I can picture myself connecting hands with everyone. I can see all the candles lit and the lights off. "I'm calling someone from the other side for help. We need to find a person of interest. A killer," Maggie says with a soft, deep voice.

It is silent for about two minutes. "Someone is here and willing to help." I get goose bumps even though I'm listening through the phone.

"I need to find Jack Bolder." There is some humming noise. This is probably when Maggie sways back and forth and is being taken over by an entity.

No one is talking but I still hear the humming noises. This goes on for about five minutes. I stand and gently bounce Michael. Then I can hear the table shaking through the phone. It's almost over. Maggie takes a loud gasp. "Maggie? You okay?" I ask.

"Yes, I'm fine. I know where he is."

"That's great news," says Fredrick in the background.

"He's in North Charleston working as a Fed EX driver."

"What? Are you sure you have the right Jack? That doesn't sound like him at all?"

"It doesn't sound like the Jack we know six years from now, but it is the Jack now."

"Great, so he could be a normal person right now?"

"Well, I don't think he was ever normal. He might not have begun his killing spree yet, but we both know he does, Linda. He doesn't just kill one person, he kills many."

"I know."

"I pulled up the FedEx location on my phone. I've got it," says Fredrick.

"Okay, we need to make sure it's him before we do anything," I say.

"Arnold and I will go check it out for ourselves and send you a picture."

"Okay, sounds good."

About an hour or so later I receive the picture from Fredrick. It is Jack alright except he is different. He is smiling kindly, his hair is short and slicked back, his nose gave him away otherwise I wouldn't think it was him. I show Luke. "This is him." I explain what he looks like six years from now. "What if he's an innocent man right now? How can Fredrick get away with killing an innocent man? What if he doesn't end up changing in the next six years?"

"You saw him kill Michael and your sister Linda. He's a murderer deep down inside. The dark side might not be showing yet, but it'll rise at some point. He's always going to have a vendetta against you. Whether it's six years or ten years down the road. He needs to be taken out," Luke says with force.

"Okay you're right, but I feel guilty for some reason."

"Don't."

Michael is sleeping in my arms and I look down at him. I have to protect him no matter what. Even if it means killing a man who doesn't deserve it yet.

I call Fredrick. "That's him. Different from what I've seen but it is. What are you going to do?"

"Well now that we know it's Jack, we need to stop Tom first. Jack has no idea about Tom's plans as far as we know."

"Okay, how are you going to get to Tom?"

"I'm going to pay him a little visit."

"You've done this before and nothing worked," I say with a little frustration.

"Alright then we need to catch him off guard."

"And how do you suppose we go about that?"

"He's going to need a prison transport. I can find out when that is and create a diversion. Then I can shoot him when he least expects it."

"And what about the guards that surround him? They'll all see that it's you who shoots him," I say with worry.

"Not if I do it from a distance."

"That could work, but it's going to be tough to pull off."

"No, it won't. It'll just take a little planning and a few people to help. I'm going to make some phone calls. I'll get back to you."

"Okay." He hangs up the phone quickly.

"I hate being on the other side of this!"

"You've got to relax, Linda."

I sit on the couch when a flash hits me hard.

BANG!

My head starts to hurt immediately. I see flashes of Tom in his baseball cap and blue jeans. Then I hear a whisper, "I'm still with you, Linda. I'll be your nightmare forever."

Another flash!

I grab my head and whimper in pain.

"Linda, honey are you okay?"

"It's Tom. He's already started. This is exactly what happened in my dream. This is how he starts getting in my head with these flashes. It only gets worse from here on."

"Call Fredrick now. Whatever he has planned he needs to move faster." I nod my head in agreement.

"Fredrick, Tom has started contacting me. He starts with flashes. I think he dreams and then comes to me somehow. This is how is started before. We need to move fast."

"Okay, I'm almost done with my plans. He's getting transported to prison today. Arnold is going to create a diversion with a few of my officers. Tom will die tonight."

"Fredrick, I've heard this way too many times."

"This time it's real."

"Okay. Call me as soon as you know something."

I look at Luke and pout on the couch. "The good thing is, if Fredrick can really take care of Tom now, then there's no chance of him leaking information to the press about me. I was kind of famous in my dream. The Today Show wanted an interview with me. That will help me to keep leading a somewhat normal life."

"I think Fredrick will take care of it, Linda."

"Then the real threat will begin…Jack."

"They already have a lead on him, so that will get taken care of as well. This will be over in no time."

I shake my head. "I sure hope so."

We sit watching TV while we wait in agony. "You know, Sarah and Bobby are going to Vegas to get married!" I try to lighten the mood as much as I can.

"What! No way," says Luke with surprise.

I shake my head. "Yeah and Charlie proposes to May! They'll end up getting married as well."

"Wow, what about us? Are we-?"

He doesn't finish his sentence. "Babe, you waited six years for me when I was in my so-called coma/dream. Nothing can separate us."

He smiles, "I'd wait a lifetime if I had to."

I smile. "You said that exact same thing to me in my dream."

"I'm not going to lie, we had some pretty amazing 'haven't seen each other in a while sex'," I say with a cheesy grin.

"Oh yeah? Well we'll have to replay that won't we?"

"Oh yes!"

Prison Transport
Leeds Ave. 4:30 p.m.

"Well, it looks like your fate is about to start," says the dumb ass guard sitting across from me acting like he owns me. Does he know who he is talking to? I look up at him with a grin.

"Oh, Mr. Tom Walker, let me guess, nothing scares you? Oh just wait until you get there. You're in for one wild ride."

I continue to smile without saying a word. Silence is the best medicine. All of a sudden there are sirens sounding in the distance. The two guards look at each other. "What the hell?" I'm thinking the same thing.

Three cop cars pull up behind us and make us stop. I have a feeling that bitch has something to do with this. I was just getting started with her. The cops get out of their cars and walk towards the van then they start banging on the back doors. "Everyone needs to get out now!" they yell.

"What the hell, man?" the guard who commented at me says. He gets up and opens the door. "What's going on?"

"Everyone needs to get out, including the prisoner. There has been word that one of you guards is smuggling drugs into the prison. The guards look at each other. I am stunned at what is going on. I could make a run for it right now. Are these policemen stupid? Then I think. Wait a second. This is too good to be true.

I glance around and see nothing but open land. I see a few trees and I look up. I can't believe my eyes. I see someone with a sniper. "Shit, everyone down!" I yell. Then I hear a loud BANG!

And I feel immediate pain.

I've been shot. How in the world has this happened?"

I fall to my knees and I feel my body and mind getting heavy. Death has come too soon. Linda was supposed to join me. I hit my head on the pavement as darkness takes over.

Jackson Household
4:45

I fall on top of Luke out of breath. "Wow, that was something else," I say trying to catch my breath. My phone rings.

I answer it trying to slow my breathing. "It's done." I hear Fredrick's deep voice.

"He's dead? Like really dead?"

"Yeah, I watched him bleed out. Everything went as planned, like I said it would."

"Fredrick, that's wonderful news. Thank you so much."

"I have some stuff to finish up today. I'll stop by tomorrow to talk about the next step, Jack."

"Okay." I hang up the phone and smile at Luke.

"Tom's dead," I say with relief.

Luke sits his sweaty body up against the back board of the bed. "Wow, that's the best news we've had in a while." I smile at him. It's like a whole new me is forming. Tom is dead and Jack will be next.

Michael begins to cry. I quickly get dressed and pick up my baby boy from his crib in our room.

I am walking down a small dirt road. I look around me and above me and the road is surrounding by beautiful trees. When I look up, the limbs look like they are reaching for each other. It forms a nice tunnel. But what am I doing here? I continue walking until I find what I am looking for. I look at the date on my phone. Two days from now. So I'm here for a reason. The sun is about to set creating a pink and orange glaze through the tree leaves. It almost looks like the road leading to the bed and breakfast Luke took me to when he proposed. I continue walking for a few minutes when I see a small house up ahead.

It veers off to the left of the road, hidden behind some trees. It is a log cabin. It is very cute but it doesn't look like anyone has been there for a while. The right window is broken. I notice a small white car parked in front of the house. There are no lights on in the house though. I slowly walk up to the house. I hear a faint voice coming from the broken window. I slowly creep up next to the window. I hide on the side of the house. I can hear from here. I listen intently. I recognize this voice.

"I'm going to get revenge for you, Tom. Whatever it takes, I will do." Jack speaks to himself. I didn't realize he started his revenge this early. It took him six years to come up with a plan to attack me? Maybe since I'm not in a coma he is planning on attacking sooner? He waited six years to start killing people. He waited until I woke up, but now that I'm not comatose what does that mean?

My heart starts to race. He might come up with a completely different plan. "I'll find out who did this to you and kill them with my bare hands myself. Please brother, is there anything you can tell me? Point me in the right direction please."

It sounds like he is trying to speak with Tom. Tom was able to communicate with him from the other side before. I used to be able to contact Fredrick in my dreams to where he could track my phone. I know I had Maggie's herbs to do so, but maybe I can get it to work. My dreams are powerful when I use them to their full ability. I pull out my phone from my back pocket of my jeans. I close my eyes and take a deep breath. "Okay Linda, concentrate," I say to myself.

I dial Fredrick's number and it rings. Bingo! "Hello, Linda?"

His voice sounds as if he is sleeping. That is a good sign that he is in real time and not dream time. "Fredrick! What time is it?"

"Linda, what's going on? It's three in the morning. Are you all okay?"

"This is going to sound crazy. I'm calling you from a dream."

"What!" His voice turns sleepy to loud and awake. "How is this even possible?"

"Long story. I was able to do it before. Well when I was dreaming in my coma so I figured I'd give it a try. Anyway, we're in trouble." I try to keep my voice down so Jack doesn't hear me. I walk away from the cabin. "Two days from now, Jack will be at this location I'm at, beginning his plan for his revenge. I want you to try and track my phone. If we can meet him here at this time two days from now, we can put an end to it before it even begins."

"Linda, I don't know. I mean this is all so strange. How do I know I'm even awake? What if I'm dreaming?"

"Look at the calendar on your phone and check the date." I hear a pause for a few seconds.

"Holy shit. This is really happening. You're talking to me from the future. This is so strange and so against everything I've ever believed in. I mean, are there vampires and werewolves too? Because this is on the same level as insane."

I smile into the phone because this is Fredrick's way of freaking out but trying to stay cool. "No, there are no vampires or werewolves that I know of. Anyway, can you track my phone from home? You have a computer at home that can do it, right?"

"How do you…wait don't answer that. Yes, I have a computer that can do it and I'm tracking you as we speak."

"Great, so on Monday we'll come here and Jack should be in this cabin scheming his plan. He's out in the middle of nowhere. No one would see you kill him."

"I'll go there with Arnold and you'll stay home safe. You're already *risking yourself by being there now even if it is in a dream."*

"True, but I can't help when or where I dream. I didn't even force this one. So this is really good. I've never come this close to ending such a big case this fast. But for me it seems like it's been going on six years."

"That's so weird. Okay, I've got your location. He's off some ways from the scenic highway near Folly Road. Now that I've got your location you need to get out of there before he sees you."

"Okay, thank you so much, Fredrick, and thank you for believing me. I'll talk with you tomorrow."

"Be safe." I hang up the phone and now it has become dark out. I can barely see anything around me. Shit. I can't ruin this. This is our one chance of catching Jack before he can harm anyone around me. I look around and listen carefully. Jack can't know that I am here.

I close my eyes. "Wake up Linda, wake up." I hear footsteps ruffling in the leaves behind me. I gasp and open my eyes.

I wake up in a panic. "Shit!" I hope Jack didn't see me. Luke wakes up immediately.

"What happened?" I tell him. "Well let's hope he didn't see you, and if he did, maybe he doesn't know who you are yet."

"That's true. God, I hope so. This could be it, Luke. Forever. Tom dead and Jack dead. I can finally move on. We can start our new chapter with Michael."

He kisses my forehead. "It will be, babe. You've been through too much now for it all not to end."

He is right about that. If I could write a book about everything I've been through I would. No one would ever believe it, but it would be a good fiction story to tell. A girl who sees the future in her dreams. Who gets kidnapped by a crazed murderer in her dreams. Who goes through two comas and sees six years into the future but feels like she lived through it all? I think that would be one hell of a story. Now we just have to find a perfect ending.

Chapter 20

Jackson Household
Monday July 6th

These next two days couldn't have gone by any slower. I sit at home with Michael while Luke is at work. I am going crazy cooped up in the house and I can't relax! I receive a text from May checking in on me. I respond by telling her that it is almost over and once it is we are all celebrating. I check my watch. It is only two in the afternoon on Monday. We still have six hours to go until Jack's death.

Michael is sleeping in his crib. It is a gloomy, rainy day. Maybe I will lie on the couch and take a nap. I haven't gotten much sleep with all the worry and Michael waking up every few hours. I lie on the couch and close my eyes.

All of a sudden flashes start coming back from when I was in my coma. One after the other.

Bang!

Bang!

Bang!

I see flames on a big boat. I see oxygen masks falling from the ceiling. I hear people screaming. My head is pounding. I scream out in agony when more and more flashes hit me.

Fire.

People screaming.

Water.

Dark skies.

My body is trembling. It's all coming back to me. I couldn't save people from a cruise ship bombing. But I saved people from a plane. How can I do it all over again? Wait, the plane crashes on July 6. That's today! Shit! I have to try and stop it. Fredrick is dealing with Jack and he can't lose focus.

I need to do this on my own. I stop for a minute because my head feels like it is spinning at a million miles per hour. I drink some water, sit at the kitchen table, and write out everything I saw so I won't forget. I have to relax and take one thing at a time.

I call Denver Airport. I remember exactly what flight it was and what time. The shaggy man had a knife. I have to try and convince security to check the man and stop the flight like I did before. "Hello, I need to speak with someone from security right away. I believe there's a threat in your airport and they're targeting flight number DL1428 to Washington National."

"Um, is this a prank? Because if it is that's a serious felony." Some woman speaks to me as if I'm stupid. She is making me mad.

"Listen, this isn't a prank. I'm telling you, this man needs to be stopped."

There is silence.

A man's voice comes on the phone. "Miss, can you tell me how you know about this threat?"

"It doesn't matter right now! Just be at the terminal. The flight is at 5:00 p.m. Look for a man in a long black overcoat with a Kelly green shirt and black boots. He has shaggy long hair and a beard. He'll be holding a knife under his coat."

I hang up the phone before the man can speak. Police might be knocking on my door but I don't care. The flight needs to be stopped again.

I wait for the time to pass, hoping to hear from Fredrick. If the plane gets stopped I need to try and stop the cruise ship as well. Last time my dream was too late and everyone died. I had the coordinates to the ship's exact location, but I don't remember what they were! Maybe if I think hard it will come to me in flashes. Yeah, the flashes hurt but it does give me the information I need.

I close my eyes and concentrate on the ship. *Think about the shuddering of the boat when it explodes. Think about the fire and the people screaming. Think about all the details.*

Bang!

Immediate pain strikes my head. I cry out.

I see the ship go up in flames. I push past those images to the name of the ship. I find the name of the ship. *Think of the details before going on the ship*. I push past all the horrible images to see if I can find which port the ship takes off from.

Bang!

The screams get louder, which makes my head pound harder. I scream in pain and fall to my knees. I can hear Michael screaming in the background. I shake my head and force myself to stop the flashes.

I can control it.

I fight the pain.

I fight the images.

I take big deep breaths.

I come back to reality and hear Michael screaming even louder.

I walk over to his crib in the living room. I gently pick him up and hold him close. "Shh. It's okay baby," I whisper to him as I gently sway around. I turn on the news just in case I see anything pop up. Once Michael calms down I sit on the couch and begin to feed him.

I couldn't find enough information except that I know the name of the ship. There are only so many places that ship ports from. I need to google ships leaving within the next few days and then call each one. I know that's a lot of work but they need to get the bomb squad and check each ship. It may be a lot of work for the departments but it will save thousands of lives.

Luke calls me as I'm feeding Michael. "Hey honey," I say.

"Hey, how are you doing?" *Do I tell him what just happened? He will worry. No, not yet.*

"I'm doing good. I just woke up from a nap and now I'm feeding Michael." I try to sound convincing but I am a horrible liar.

"Linda, what is it?" He can detect my insecure tone. Dammit!

"It's nothing. I just had some flashes and visions of dreams I had when I was in my dream."

"That sounds dangerous. A dream within a dream. Are you okay?"

"Yeah, just a little headache. But I found out information about some big events that I stopped in the future that need to be done again."

"This sounds like a job for Fredrick and the CPD, not you."

"Luke, Fredrick is busy dealing with Jack. I have to do it. I'm the only one who knows what's going to happen and it'll take too much effort to convince someone else that I'm telling the truth. I need to do it. I already took care of one problem, so now the other."

"I'm coming home."

"No Luke. I'm fine, I promise. You have surgeries to do today and patients to see. I promise, I'm truly fine."

He sighs into the phone. "Okay, okay. If anything goes even slightly wrong, then call me."

"I will, baby. I love you."

"I love you too." Phew, that went better than I thought. Michael finishes up and I gently bounce him around. Once I get him back to sleep I need to google the ship information and get to work. At least this is keeping me busy.

I lie Michael back down in his crib, grab my Mac Book, and start researching. There are three places this ship is leaving by tomorrow. Okay, here goes nothing.

I call each port and tell them how they need to get the bomb squad out there to check the ship. There was a threat about a bomb being on board. I try not to sound too crazy like I know it is going to blow up. I try to avoid as many questions as I can but I get through to them. The cruise ship lines are having enough problems with people getting sick and things going wrong they will take the threat seriously. So I hope this helps. Now it's the waiting game again.

About two hours has passed and I haven't heard from anyone! The wait seems to be getting more intense as time goes on. I turn on the news to see if anything is on there. That is when I see a breaking news story. The words are scrolling on the bottom of the screen as the newscaster is reporting the story.

"We have breaking news. What could have been two horrible terrorist attacks have been stopped. The FBI is in shock at what they have found and how they found it. Denver airport received a phone call from a mystery woman who explained what was going to happen and that these men (their pictures show up on TV as she continues to speak,) were going to attack this plane and it was going to go down. Well, the Denver police found the men and stopped them. They had knives as weapons and admitted they were going to take down the plane. But it isn't over yet. There was another case out of Florida. A cruise ship has been stopped and canceled because of what we believe was the same mystery woman calling in to say there was a bomb on the ship. The bomb squad came out and found the explosive on the ship. Whoever this mystery woman is, please show yourself because you are a hero. You have saved many lives. The FBI doesn't know who the caller is, but they did track the caller and it is someone from Charleston, South Carolina. We hope to find this hero and congratulate her. More about this story later."

A huge smile appears on my face with a sense of relief. "They're safe." I say out loud. But now everyone knows it's someone in this area, they won't stop asking around until they find me. I don't want this to get out. I like my personal life and I don't want to become known publically. My phone starts buzzing, and it's Luke. "Hey babe," I say as if I don't know anything.

"Linda," he says as if he's waiting for me to explain.

"Yes?"

"I just saw the news. Let me guess…it's you?"

"Ugh," I sigh into the phone. "Yeah. I've been sitting at home doing nothing! I remember some events from the dreams in my coma and I had to stop it. Now that I know what's really going to happen so far in advance, I can stop it all."

"I understand. Thank you for what you did. I'm just making sure you're okay. They know it's someone in Charleston."

"I know; I saw that too. I'll speak with Sergeant Gordon to see if he can help me out. I know they'll be calling CPD to see if they know anything. Actually, I should probably call him now so he won't give my name."

"Okay, stay safe, and don't go anywhere." He raises his voice.

"I won't I won't. I have precious cargo in here, Luke. I won't do anything stupid."

"Okay, I love you."

"Love you too," I say as I hang up the phone. I know Fredrick is tied down right now hunting Jack, so he probably has no idea what is going on.

I call Sergeant Gordon. "Hi Sergeant, this is Linda Jackson."

He stops me before I say anything else. "Ah, the woman who just saved many lives."

"How did you know it was me?"

"Come on Linda, we all know what you can do. The FBI from Washington has been calling asking if we know anything."

"Oh no, what did you say?"

"I told them we don't know anything, but when we find out we'll call."

"Oh, thank you so much. I was afraid you'd tell them it was me."

"We wouldn't do that unless we had your consent. We know how hard it must be to have such a wonderful yet scary ability. If you're ever ready to tell your secret and become a hero to many, call me and we'll set up a press release."

"Thank you for your kind words, but I don't think that will ever happen. I saw what happens when my secret is let loose. I don't want to let that happen again. I like my somewhat quiet life, and I can't handle it getting louder."

"I understand. Just know everyone here at CPD has your back and won't say anything."

"Thank you, Sergeant."

"Anytime, rest up and have a good day." I hang up the phone and sigh with relief. Okay, it looks like I'm good there.

It shouldn't be too much longer until Fredrick does the job and kills Jack. Let's hope it all goes well.

Abandoned Cabin
8:30 p.m.

Ah, just look at the beautiful sunset. This is a perfect time to start planning Tom's Revenge. I have to figure out who did this. I need to speak with Tom somehow. I've seen on movies how people can talk to spirits, so maybe I can call Tom. I sit on the floor. I take deep breaths and concentrate on nothing but Tom. I focus all my energy on him. "Tom, brother please help me revenge your death. Who did this to you?"

I sit around waiting for some kind of response. I get nothing. Hmm, maybe I should light some candles and use something of his. I look down at my wrist and see his watch. I take it off and put it on the floor. I light some candles that circle the watch and a picture of the two of us. I take a deep breath and try again.

"Tom, brother, can you hear me?" I pause and slow my breathing to see if I can hear anything.

"My brother. Why are you contacting me?" I hear his voice but it is distant.

"Tom, I can't believe it's you. I'm calling because I want to get revenge on whoever did this to you." He laughs in response.

"You? My brother who's as gentle as a mouse wants to get revenge on my death? Now this is good. And how are you going to do this? You wouldn't harm a fly."

"I'm angry that someone murdered you in cold blood. I want revenge for my family. I know I'm not like you, but I've always looked up to you. I can do this, brother."

"Alright, but you have to change your look, your way of thinking, and you have to become strong. Strong enough to kill someone. I can help you with that, just listen to me."

I take a deep breath. "Okay brother. I'm ready. Tell me what to do."

"You're going against someone who can see the future in her dreams. She will see you coming. She has probably already seen you before. So that means we need to act fast."

"Wait, you're saying I have to kill a woman? A woman did this to you?"

"Well a man, but it was the woman who helped him. This woman can't live. She has a talent that is too strong for any of us killers. She has to die. I can train you to become a fierce killer."

"After you dying, I have nothing left. You're my brother, my blood. So let's get started." I hear ruffling outside the window that causes me to jump.

"You have company. I told you Linda has already seen you. Someone is here to kill you, Jack. Don't let them."

I get up from the floor and blow out the candles. I grab the knife I left sitting on the counter and make my way to the window. It is now dark out and I can't see a thing. I sneak out the back door to find my first victim. I creep around the side of the wooden cabin carefully listening for sounds. I look around the corner when I see a man about to open the front door of the cabin. I smile at his stupidity. The adrenaline is running through my veins. My first kill is about to happen. I guess this is how Tom feels.

I wait for him to step inside the house and I follow behind him quietly. I have my knife in hand, ready for action. I take deep breaths. "I can do this. This is for Tom," I whisper to myself. I sneak across the front of the house and peak my head through the front door. I see a tall man wearing a black t-shirt and black pants. He has detective written all over him. I don't know if I should kill a detective?

"Do it Jack," I hear Tom whisper into my ear. The man is standing with his back towards me. I move quickly before he can turn around and I stab him right through the back! The feeling of the blade going through the body gives me a fever. I want to

do it again. I hear him choking on his own blood and watch him stumble to the ground.

"Good job, brother. Your first kill. Many more to come." I can hear Tom's voice in the distance. I look at the dead body on the floor, smile, and then laugh at the top of my lungs. I check his badge.

"Detective Fredrick. Not so good of a detective now, are we?" I can hear his phone ringing. I look at the name: Linda Jackson. Wait, *the* Linda? Oh, this should be good. I decide to answer the phone.

"Linda Jackson, the one and only," I say into the phone.

"Jack? Where the hell is Fredrick?"

"Oh, he's a little um dead at the moment." I can hear her sniffling through the phone.

"Did I hit a soft spot? You shouldn't have sent one man after me. You obviously know me better than that. Tom spoke to me and told me what I have to do. Are you ready, Linda?"

"If you killed Fredrick, I swear to God I'm going to kill you slowly, Jack, so slowly you'll be crying for your brother's help, but guess what, he's dead. You want to know why, Jack? Because I fucking killed him." Linda hangs up on me.

I throw Fredrick's phone across the wall and is breaks into pieces. "That bitch!" I yell out with anger. "She's going to get what's coming to her."

Chapter 21

CPD
9:30 p.m. Same Night

"Arnold, I need you now. I'm over at CPD. It's Fredrick. I think he's-" I couldn't finish the statement. "Just hurry please."

"On my way," Arnold says with his serious tone.

Until Arnold gets here, I speak with Sergeant Gordon. "As soon as I heard it was Jack on the phone, I started recording the conversation. Take a listen," I say to him. We both listen intently to each word Jack says. I look at Sergeant's cold, yet scared look. His dark eyes are glistening with water. He shuts off the recording when it's over, sits back in his chair, and rubs his hands over his bald head.

"If this bastard really killed Fredrick, I'm going to personally put a bullet through his head."

I shake my head. "No Sergeant, he deserves far worse than a bullet. How can he kill one of the best detectives in town?" I ask softly.

He looks down and shakes his head. "I don't know. I truly don't." He slams his fists onto his desk. "We're going to need back up going there. Why didn't Fredrick take back up?"

"He wanted to kill Jack with no witnesses," I say, quick to respond.

"Wait a second. You knew he was going there alone? You didn't think to call back up on standby just in case?" he says with anger.

Oh shit. "I'm sorry. I know I should have. You know how Fredrick is. He likes to do things on his own."

"Did Arnold know about this?"

"Did Arnold know about what?" We both turn around and see Arnold standing in the doorway to Sergeant's office. His hair and beard is shaggier than normal. He has dark circles under his eyes. His shirt is halfway sticking out from his pants.

"Arnold, what's gotten into you?" I ask.

"I was in a hurry, you caught me off guard," he says pushing his hair back. He tucks in his shirt in his pants. "So, what's such a big deal that I had to rush down here? What's wrong with Fredrick?"

"He was trying to kill Jack. I led him to a cabin where I knew he'd be because of a dream I had. When I tried to call Fredrick, Jack answered the phone." I stop and swallow hard. I glance at Sergeant Gordon and he nods to continue.

"What?" Arnold asks with impatience.

I clear my throat. "On the phone Jack said that he killed Fredrick."

His eyes become bigger than I've ever seen them and his mouth drops open. He is in shock. "Is he?" he asks, trembling.

"We don't' know. I called you down here so we can go check it out with backup."

He doesn't say anything else except, "Let's go." He turns around and rushes out of the station. Sergeant follows his lead. Then I follow them. A few officers join us. My stomach is in knots. It wasn't supposed to happen like this. Now the timeline I know will be completely screwed up. I have no idea what Jack is planning now or where he is. It's a nightmare all over again.

***

Log Cabin
Same Night 10:30 p.m.

We pull into the wooded driveway. It is dark but the car lights make it easy to see. "There is the cabin," I say pointing my finger. I look at my hand and it is shaking. I am so nervous. My stomach feels sick. I can see candle light flickering through the windows. "The front door is open," I say. We stop the car and all rush out.

Sergeant Gordon motions for the officers to check the surrounding of the cabin while we check inside. Arnold leads the way but clearly he his blinded. Sergeant Gordon stops him. "Stay behind me. You're upset right now. I don't need another detective hurt."

The car lights give only enough light to see the hurt in Arnold's eyes. He nods his head and steps back. I follow behind Gordon and

I pat Arnold on the shoulder. He follows behind me. Gordon points his gun first and moves in through the front door. I follow but fall to his right side and check the surroundings. There is nothing. I shine my flashlight on the floor and that is when I begin to panic. "Oh my God, Fredrick!" I yell out.

I rush towards his body and fall to my knees and check his pulse. I begin to cry when I realize Fredrick really is dead, and all because of me. "Oh no, no no," I cry out.

Arnold rushes over. "Partner, no please," he says putting his hand on his chest. I can see tears fall from Arnold's face.

Officers come in the front door. "Sergeant, everything is clear out here." Gordon nods his head and motions for them to leave. It's just the three of us and our dead partner, one of the best detectives to ever come through CPD.

We sit there in silence for a few minutes. "I don't understand how Fredrick was caught off guard. If Jack can kill Fredrick, then we're in for something bigger than what I thought," Gordon says with a disappointing tone.

"I know how I can stop him. I can be smarter than I was in my dream. I can handle this, Sergeant."

Arnold and I both stand up and face Gordon. "And how do you suppose you're going to do this on your own? Look what happened with our best detective."

"I can kill Jack in my dream when he doesn't see me coming."

"That's impossible," Gordon says.

"Really? After everything I've told you about my ability?"

"Is there anything we can do to help?" Arnold chimes in.

"The CPD can't do anything. This is solely between Jack and me. But Arnold, I need to visit the one person who can help me."

He slants his head to the right a little. "Who?"

"Maggie."

He nods his head. "Of course you do. Alright, when do you want to do this?"

I glance down at Fredrick's dead body. "We need to move now. Jack is on the loose and he needs to be stopped before he murders dozens of innocent people."

"Alright, let's go."

"Wait," Gordon stops us before we move. "Please be careful, and if there's anything we can do, please let me know."

"I will, Sergeant. Thank you."

"Oh and Linda," he says and I glance back. "Kill that son of a bitch."

I smile confidently. "Oh believe me, I will. It's way overdue."

He nods and smiles in return. Arnold and I head out.

"I need to stop by my house first," I say as I close the door to Arnold's car. "I need to feed Michael once more before, and explain to Luke what is going on."

"Okay, no problem." He pauses. "Linda."

I look over at him. "Yeah?"

"What happens if this doesn't work? What if Jack gets away? What if we can never stop him?"

I swallow hard. "Arnold, I'm not going to let that happen. Not again."

"How is Maggie going to help?"

"It's hard to explain. She'll do all the explaining when we get there." He nods in response. The rest of the drive is quiet to my house.

Jackson Household
11:45 p.m.

We pull into our driveway and I feel nervous. I know Luke isn't going to take this well, but this is literally the last chance. Maggie is our last hope of helping us catch Jack. Luke opens the front door before I even get out of the car. He must have seen the car lights. He is holding Michael in his arms.

I rush towards them because I can hear Michael crying. "Linda, where have you been? It's late and Michael has been crying nonstop. He's hungry," Luke says with anger.

"I'm sorry," I say as I take Michael. He immediately stops crying when I hold him. "Fredrick was murdered."

Luke's anger turns to sympathy. "Oh no, I'm so sorry. Who did it?"

We all walk into the house. I sit on the couch as Luke shuts the door. "It was Jack," I say coldly. I begin feeding Michael. Arnold doesn't seem to care. He is in his own little world right now. He is still in shock about Fredrick.

Luke shakes his head as he sits next to me. "Are you okay?" Then he looks at Arnold who is staring at the floor. "Is he okay?"

I nod. "He's in shock. Not only was he his partner but best

friend. Jack is only just getting started. He's going to kill dozens of women if I don't stop him. I know what I need to do. I've seen it before. Now I know what I **have** to do."

Luke grunts. "And what exactly is that?"

"I'm going to dream and then kill him in my dream."

He laughs a short laugh as if I'm joking. "Is that even possible?"

"There's one way to make it possible. Arnold and I are going to see Maggie. She has these special herbs." When I say that both Luke and Arnold look at me as if I'm crazy. "They're specially made to intensify and control dreams. They're made for a normal person to find information from a dream, but with my ability they enhance my dreams in ways you couldn't even imagine. Killing people in my dream is one of those enhancements. He will die in real life. I did this exact thing in my dream while I was in my coma and I wasn't quick enough. He ended up murdering me. But I know now that I can't hesitate. One shot and he'll die."

Luke stands up with his hands out. "What? And what happens if he kills you again?"

"Luke, I won't let that happen. I know now what I need to do. He isn't as powerful right now because he hasn't murdered many people. The longer I wait, the stronger he becomes, and the further away we get from ending him. I need to do this."

Arnold is silent the whole time. Michael finishes and I stand with him gently tapping his back. "Linda, I can't lose you again."

"Luke, babe, you never lost me. To you I was only gone a few days. But for me it was six years I missed. All these crazy dreams, comas, and killers that want my family need to end once and for all. I learned how to control my dreams in my coma and I learned what I need to do. I'm finally ready to end this once and for all."

Luke stares at me intensely. "Okay, I want this to end too. But Michael and I are going with you. I don't want to be away from you. I want to be there for you."

"Okay, but keep Michael safe."

"Arnold, can you call Maggie and tell her we're coming over and that we need help asap?"

He returns to earth. "Yeah, of course."

We all pile into Arnold's car and take off.

Maggie's House
12:30 a.m.

When we pull up Maggie is already standing outside her A-framed house. She knew we were coming. She's got true psychic talent and she is our key in killing Jack. We get out of the car and walk towards Maggie. She walks up to me immediately. "Linda, sweetie," she says grabbing my face. "How are you doing? Everything you've been through. I don't know how you do it."

I smile at her. Her curly hair is falling over her shoulders.
Warmth.

"I'll be better when Jack is ended for good and I can go back to a normal life." She brings me in for a hug and my nose hits one of her dangly earrings.

I walk into her incense and candle lit house. "This must be Michael," she says as she gently touches his head. Luke holds Michael out and she takes him in her arms. "He's beautiful Linda and I can feel he has a strong spiritual aura."

"My smile fades. Please don't say that. I don't want him to have any special gifts like me.

She gives Arnold a big hug and says how sorry she was about Fredrick. Of course she already knew about that as well. Michael is in his car seat carrier right next to the couch and we all sit around the circle table.

"Well, shall we get started?" Maggie asks with a soft voice. "I know what you want Linda, but we need to find out where Jack is located first. Once we have his location and you take the herbs, it'll be easier to find him and it'll make this process quick. You do have a newborn over there, so let's get this over with."

"I couldn't agree with you more," I say smiling at Michael then at Luke, who looks nervous.

"Okay, do you have anything of Jack's?" Maggie asks.

"I found this on Fredrick's body." I take out a picture of Jack and Tom. Arnold looks shocked.

"I didn't want to say anything. I quickly grabbed it and put it in my pocket."

"Perfect, this will do. Obviously this picture means a lot to Jack. It should be easy to track him," Maggie says with excitement. She lives for this kind of stuff.

She places the picture in the middle of the table and the candles.

"Alright, everyone join hands." We all join hands like she says.

Maggie closes her eyes and starts humming. "I need to find the location of Jack Bolder."

We all close our eyes and focus our energy on Jack and where he could be. Maggie continues to hum and the candles begin to flicker. "I'm getting something here. Linda, be ready."

I shake my head with confusion. "Be ready for what?" I ask and then I see flashes. My eyes are closed and I am seeing what Maggie is seeing. How is she doing this? *I can see Jack. He is walking through Waterfront Park. He sits down on one of the benches under all the trees. There is no one else around. It is like he is waiting for something. The dim light from the lamps that surround the park light his face. I can see that ugly smile shining. He is waiting for me.*

The candles go out and we all break loose from the grip. I take a deep breath. "Holy shit, how did you do that, Maggie?"

"You're powerful Linda, in many ways than just your dreams. Now you know where he is right at this moment. There's no one around him. He's waiting for you. He wants a fight just with you."

"Well he's going to get one. Maggie, you know what to do." She nods and goes to her dresser and opens the door with the herbs.

"You're going to have to take the whole thing," she says with fear.

"I never did that in my dreams before. Is it safe?"

"It's going to give you the power over Jack. To kill him both in the dream world and in waking life, you'll need to take all of the herbs."

Luke stands up right away. "Linda, what if-" I stop him before he continues.

"No what if's. I'll be fine." I pull my pistol from its holster and I check to see if the bullets are in it. We are good to go. "It'll only take one shot. I won't hold back this time. He doesn't have any of my family to distract me. I put my gun in my holster and a knife in the back of my pants and I nod my head. "Okay, this is it. It is finally time to end this once and for all."

Luke comes over and grabs my face. He kisses me hard then gives me a hug. "Please be careful, baby. I wish I could go with you and help," he whispers into my ear.

"I know, baby. I do too, but this has always been just about me. I pull away and look into his deep, bright blue eyes. The eyes I fell in love with at first sight. "I love you so much, Luke."

"I love you so much more, Linda." We both smile at each other. Then I walk over and gently give Michael a kiss on his forehead.

"I love you baby boy," I say as he soundly sleeps.

Arnold shakes my hand. "Thank you, Linda."

"Don't thank me until he's dead."

I walk over to Maggie who is holding the glass of water filled with the herbs. She laid out blankets and pillows on the floor for me. "Are you ready, my dear?"

I smile with confidence. "Oh, I'm more than ready." She hands me the glass and I down it.

Dizziness.

Weakness.

Maggie and Luke hold onto me as I fall to the floor.

Darkness.

I stand in front of the beautiful Pineapple Fountain in Waterfront Park. The lights that surround the fountain make for an exquisite view. It's kind of ironic because what is about to happen is not exquisite in any way. I walk onto the cobble walkways in the park. The trees are hovering in the starlight sky. There are a few people on the pier but that is too far away for them to notice anything. There is no one else in the park. I look to my right and I see Jack sitting on the same bench. He turns his head, looks at me, and smiles.

I pull my gun out and put the silencer on. I walk slowly towards him hiding the gun for now. The last thing I need is someone to see the gun then blow the whole thing out of the water. He stands up and walks towards me as well. "Well, well Linda Jackson. Is this the place you imagined dying? I have to say, it's a beautiful sight," he says as he waves his long knife around.

I laugh in return. "Oh, I won't be the one dying here," I say as I point the gun at him.

"Oh, a gun. I'm so scared," he says with sarcasm.

Okay, Linda stop stalling and shoot him, I say to myself.

"You won't shoot me because I know something that you don't." I shake my head. I can't listen to him.

"Stop stalling me Jack."

He steps closer to me holding his knife. "Don't you want to know what I know?"

Shoot him, Linda.

I steady my hand holding the gun. He smiles as me confidently. He doesn't think I'll shoot. He walks into the gun and looks me in the eyes. "Do it," he says. He holds his knife up in the air.

I get ready to pull the trigger when I drop the gun and quickly pull out a knife from the back of my pants and stab him right in the chest. "Shooting you would be too easy, Jack."

I look into his shocked eyes as he drops his knife and stumbles to the ground. I twist the knife one way and then another making him scream out. I cover his mouth. "How do you like this, Jack?"

I take the knife out and stab him again right in the heart. I look deep into his fading eyes. "That was for Fredrick. You'll never hurt anyone I care about ever again." I twist the knife one more time bringing him completely to the ground. I watch his blood drain from his body. I watch the life seep out of him. I feel relief beyond words. I quickly take the knife out of him and he doesn't move.

Jack is finally dead. I look at his lifeless body for a moment longer. I have been through so much and my family has been hurt many times, even if half of it was just a dream. They still went through the pain in my eyes. Tom and Jack are now dead and I can finally move on.

I call Sergeant Gordon and tell him to rush over here. Before he asks any other questions I hang up the phone keeping the knife in my hand. I close my eyes and feel the warm breeze run through my hair. I take in this moment of clarity, relief, and accomplishment.

"Maggie," I whisper. "Wake me up."

Suddenly I start to feel my body shaking. I get one last glance of Jack's dead body.

I wake up to Luke shaking me. I gently sit up realizing what I pulled from my dream. I hold up the bloody knife I used to kill Jack. Everyone looks in shock. Their eyes are so big they could pop out of the sockets. I drop the knife. "It's done. I killed Jack," I say with relief.

Luke looks with confusion down at the knife. "A gun was too easy. He deserved worse."

"I couldn't agree with you more," Arnold says. "Thank you, Linda. Fredrick would be proud." I smile in return.

Luke and Maggie help me up. I leave the knife on the ground. "I'm sorry for bringing that back into your house, Maggie."

She laughs and gives me a hug. "Oh, stop it. I'm so glad you're okay and it's finally over." I hug her tight.

"Thank you for everything. I could have never done this without you."

"Anything for you," she responds.

I look at Luke and he is smiling. I rush into his arms and we hug each other as if we haven't seen each other in months. "I'm so happy it's over, Luke. It's finally over." I begin to cry with happiness and relief.

"I'm so proud of you, Linda. I love you so much. I didn't realize how strong of a woman I married." We continue to hug tightly.

"I couldn't do it without you, Luke. You've been by my side through all this craziness from the beginning. I hope things can go back to normal."

"Just promise me you won't ever get involved with another case like this! I did have a few heart attacks along the way." He smiles.

"I promise. I don't want to go back to CPD. I want to go back to my coffee shop where I belong." We hug again.

My phone beeps from a text message. I look at it. "It's Sergeant Gordon. They found Jack's body and he's taking care of the rest," I say out loud for everyone to hear.

"Now it's time to rest," Luke says as he rubs my back.

"I couldn't agree with you more," I sigh in relief.

I say my last goodbyes to Maggie. Luke gets Michael and we head out of the door. "Now don't be a stranger, Linda. You may not need my spiritual powers but you're family. You and me have been through a lot."

"I know and I'll never be a stranger. Talk to you soon!" Arnold gives her one last hug and we head towards the car.

I sit in the back seat with Luke and Michael. Luke puts his hand on my leg. I lay my head on his shoulder and let out a sigh of relief. Luke kisses me on the top of the head. "It's all over babe. Finally." His soft tone is soothing.

I smile at the thought I have and laugh out loud. "How in the hell are we going to tell this story to everyone?"

Luke laughs too. "Oh, this should be fun." I grab Luke's hand. For the first time in a long time I feel relaxed.

Chapter 22

Two Weeks Later
Sweet N' Spice
Saturday 5:00 p.m.

"Congratulations!" everyone says as the champagne pops open and fizzes everywhere. Sarah, Bobby, and my family decided to throw me a welcome back to work and congratulations on ending Tom and Jack party. I couldn't be happier right now. The coffee shop is decorated with balloons, streamers, and glitter. There is a ton of alcohol. It has been so long since I've enjoyed a drink.

Everyone is here. May, Charlie, my parents, Luke, Michael, Maggie, and Arnold. The music is playing in the background "A toast to Linda, one of the bravest people I know. A woman who has been to hell and back. A woman who never stopped fighting. A woman so strong she was willing to risk her life to stop those killers. A woman I am proud to call my wife, my soul-mate, and the mother of my son!" Luke says. Tears fall from my smiling face.

"Cheers!" everyone says as we clank the glasses together and take a sip of the sweet champagne. I hug him and give him a kiss on the lips. He gives me a seductive look. I know what I'm in for tonight and I can't wait.

"Alright, alright, enough with the girly champagne," says May strutting her stuff to the front counter. "It is time to bring out the real stuff." She pulls out a bottle of tequila.

"Oh no. I don't think I can do that! You know how long it's been since I've been able to drink!"

May walks towards me. "Are you scared?" she says jokingly. She knows I can't turn down a challenge.

"Alright, fine. Let's do it." My mom and dad sit out of this one. Mom currently can't let Michael go. She is in seventh heaven with him right now.

I look at the bottle that is all glass and oddly shaped. It looks like a smaller version of patron but I look at the name. "Cruz Tequila. Where did you find this?"

May smiles. "You know that liquor store on Easy Bay St. near Rainbow Row? That's the oldest liquor store in America!"

"Oh yeah, I know that place. It's a cute hole in the wall shop. It has its own old feeling and aura to it. There's a lot of history there. So that's where you got it?"

"Yup! I even brought limes." I shake my head. I know this isn't going to be good. May pours us each a shot. Sarah and Bobby join us.

Luke walks up behind me and whispers in my ear, "This can make for a fun night," he says seductively.

I feel my body shiver at the thought. It feels like it's been forever since I've felt his soft touch. I smile at him and he winks. We raise our shot glasses. "To a normal life and no more pain," I say out loud. We down the shot and bite into the lime for a sour taste.

"Wow, that was so smooth," I say.

"Good choice May," Sarah says. May nods in response.

"Well Linda, Monday is your first day back to work and Bobby and I have a surprise for you. We're so happy that you've decided to come back to the shop after everything that happened." I smile and follow Sarah as she walks towards the break room. I know what's behind the door.

She opens the door and I am still in shock at what I see. A beautiful and clean break room. There is a new couch, table, and chairs. Right off to the right of the table is a crib for Michael. His name is painted on the beautiful wooden bars. It is different from what I remember, but it is beautiful. Tears form in my eyes. There is a small changing table right next to the crib. "Oh my goodness Sarah and Bobby, this is amazing. I can't believe you did all this. I can't ever thank you enough. I'm speechless."

I smile and give them both a hug then I walk towards the crib. I gently touch the smooth wood. There are baby blue blankets and pillows inside. There is a new package of diapers and wipes on the changing table. "Guys, this is too much; you didn't have to do this."

Sarah walks towards me. "Yes we did, Linda. You deserve it. We couldn't imagine this shop without you. So we want to do everything it takes to keep you here. This is our shop and now it's ours and Michael's." She smiles sweetly. I give her another hug and wipe the tears away from my cheeks.

"Thank you so much again. I can't wait to get back to work on Monday!" We walk back out and continue the party. They catered food from Mellow Mushroom. They have the best pizza in town. I walk behind the front counter and watch my family and my friends grabbing pizza, laughing, talking, and truly enjoying life without fear and pain.

I prop up on my forearms and look out the floor to ceiling windows at the beautiful sunset sky. I watch people walking around downtown. I look at the couches and the different colored walls. I look out at the back patio towards the harbor. I close my eyes and take it all in. I am finally free. I haven't had any dreams, flashes, or headaches. I don't know if they will ever return, but if they do I will make one phone call to Gordon and then I'm done. I will never get back into the detective job. I love my job at my coffee shop. This is where I belong. For once in my life I am free, and for once in my life I am normal.

Luke carries Michael and walks towards me to join me behind the counter. I turn my back towards everyone so it's only Luke, Michael, and me. Luke hands me Michael and kisses me on the lips. "Everything okay over here?" he asks.

I smile and nod. "I'm more than okay. This is everything I've ever wanted. Thank you for being my rock Luke, and thank you for being my inspiration my baby boy," I say as I kiss Michael on the forehead. He looks at me with his big blue eyes. "Wow, his eyes are just like his daddy's," I say then look at Luke.

Luke hugs us both. We turn to face the party. Michael is in my arms, Luke has us both in his arms, and we watch our family and friends enjoying themselves. This is the perfect ending. This is **my life.**

Epilogue

Jackson Household
Six Years Later

I sit on the patio furniture smiling as I watch Luke and Michael kick the soccer ball around. These past six years have been wonderful and so different than what I saw in my dream. My coffee shop has been doing so well that we got an offer to expand the shop to another location in North Charleston. I never thought my coffee shop would be a chain but Sarah and I are more than excited.

Unfortunately, two weeks after my welcome back party at Sweet N Spice my dreams started coming back. I was seeing murders and robberies before they happened. I didn't want to live my life like that so I met with Maggie. She worked hard on a formula of herbs to help stop my dreams. It works! It is a day by day cure. I have to take the herbs each night before I go to sleep and it keeps me from dreaming completely. I sleep great through the nights and feel restful when I wake up. It is a miracle. I do have to take them each night or else I will have the dreams. So if the police department desperately needs help, and I am their last resort, then I will help, but otherwise my life of dreams is over.

My genes did pass on to Michael, but we caught it early enough to have him start taking the herbs as well. Maggie thinks since he has been taking the herbs at such a young age, it will cure his dreams. I went beyond the dream world in my coma and experienced dreams on a whole new level that mine will never be cured for good. But at least I have a daily cure. Maggie taught me exactly how to make the herbs, so we should never run out.

So overall, my life has turned out to be normal. May and Charlie did get married. A beautiful wedding on the beach! May is currently pregnant with a girl. I am so happy that everything has worked out for the best. I pray each day that my life continues on this path of happiness.

The thing about the dream world is that it is very spiritual and it can change at any moment of time. Although I take the herbs each night and haven't had any problems, if there is something that needs to break through that barrier it will. But I have been through enough that I am always ready for a fight if it comes to me.

But right now, my life is perfect. Michael is a healthy six-year-old boy who is very active. Luke is working hard and is known as one of the best surgeons in the area. My parents are retired and spend as much time with Michael as they can. My coffee shop is doing better than I've ever imagined.

I am thankful for everything God has given me. A second chance is very rare and I intend to live my life to the fullest and give Michael everything he deserves.

Michael comes running over and grabs my arm. "Mom, come play with us." I smile and look into his bright blue eyes and at his big smile.

"Well, how can I resist that smile?"

"Come on, Mom. You and me versus Dad!"

Luke shakes his head. "Are you sure you two want to lose?"

"Oh, I don't think so," I say and I give Luke a playful kiss on the cheek.

Then I look at Michael and pass him the ball. "Let's do this, Michael!"

About the Author

Megan Johnson was born in Cincinnati, Ohio but she currently lives in Charleston, WV, working as an elementary school teacher. This is her third published book, part of a trilogy series. *The Dreams Trilogy* is very special to Megan because she believes that dreams mean more than what people think. She has always been intrigued by dreams; why we have them, what they mean for our waking life, and how they can help us in life. These thoughts gave her the idea to write this series. She couldn't do this without the support from her family and from her fans. Megan will never stop writing as it is her passion. She is now working on a completely new book!

Other Books
By Megan Johnson:

Dreams Become Reality
(part 1 of the Dream Triology)

Dreams become a Nightmare
(part 2 of the Dream Trilogy)

www.ingramcontent.com/pod-product-compliance
Lightning Source LLC
Chambersburg PA
CBHW071234250626
47163CB00001B/180